SHAKE

IN REAL TIME, BOOK 2

CHRIS MANDEVILLE

*Elizabeth,
You can never so fack . . .
or can you?*

PARKER
HAYDEN
MEDIA

for my parents: Judy, Bill, and Nan

ISBN: 978-1950349-14-2

Parker Hayden Media
5740 N. Carefree Circle, Ste 120-1
Colorado Springs, CO 80917

Art credits:
Cover design: LB Hayden
Cover graphic: © Rashed AlAkroka

CHAPTER ONE

My sister's arms are wrapped tightly around me as we fly through the wormhole toward the future—her real time. It's not a loving embrace, to say the least. I struggle to break free, but Bel's stronger than I am, her strength probably fueled by the fact we just found out we're half sisters, which she doesn't like one bit.

The panels of the wormhole show image after image of San Francisco in ruins. Buildings blackened by age or fire or both. Where—I mean *when*—is she taking me? And what the heck's happened to my city in the future?

"We have to go back," I plead. "We can save them. I know we can." *We have to.* My mom, our dad, the crew—they're all dead because of me. I have to go back. I have to fix this.

"Get ready," Bel says.

"For what?"

"The end."

What?

The panels encircling us darken. I wrench my head around to look forward—it's pitch-black.

"Bel...?"

There's a jolt and we jerk to a stop. Bel's arms fall open, freeing me, and I tumble to the floor, my legs tangling in my Victorian skirt. Light floods my vision and I blink against the brightness, focusing on Bel. She's standing, hands raised. I roll to my back and see what she's looking at—two armed men pointing guns at us.

I gulp and raise my hands, my heart pummeling my chest.

One of the men is huge with tribal tattoos covering his face and bald head. The other is skinny with freckles and a blue afro. Both look equally terrifying behind their guns.

"Null it, you guys, it's me," Bel says, lowering her hands.

Null it?

"I don't cog you," the bigger one replies. "Hands high."

"Spires, it's me, Bel."

Spires, the tribal hulk, shakes his head and gestures upward with the muzzle of the large handgun.

"*Bel*," I say. "Put your hands up." I can't fathom why she's not as scared as I am—she's the one who told me people are killing time travelers.

She rolls her eyes and returns her hands to shoulder height.

"Daum?" she says to the skinny guy. "Don't play with me. Come on."

I stare at the freckles under his eyes. They're lighter than his brown skin. Light *blue*—so weird.

"Sorry, I don't cog you either," he tells Bel in a gentle voice, and he does seem sorry.

"Seriously?" Bel says. "How do you think I know your names? This is my real time. I can prove it—tag my mom."

"Shut it!" Spires barks.

Daum turns to me. "Can you stand?"

"Not with my hands raised," I say.

He nods. "Go ahead, do it graddie."

"Graddie?" I look at Bel, no idea what that means.

Bel rolls her eyes again. "*Go slow*." I think she called me a nafe under her breath.

I roll to my knees and push myself to standing, but the room spins and I lose my balance. Daum grabs my elbow. I wonder if the time-travel woozy feeling ever goes away. Bel looks fine, so maybe I'll eventually get used to it.

I steady myself. "Thanks, I'm okay," I tell Daum. I'm far from okay, but I don't think I'm going to fall over.

Daum's mouth quirks in an almost-smile as he lets go of my arm. He doesn't seem scary anymore, especially now that I see he's my height and age. Plus it doesn't hurt that his gun's pointed at the floor.

I glance around the room to get my bearings, but there's nothing to see—we're in a cement box with one lone, gray door.

"Move on," Spires, says, motioning toward the door with his gun. He's just as scary, if not scarier, now. He's a foot taller than Daum, built to carry boulders. He probably eats boulders for breakfast. His eyebrows are inked in a permanent scowl, along with his black mouth. The dark-and-scary look is completed by a skin-tight black bodysuit, black combat boots, black utility belt with holster, and the black gun in his meaty hand.

Daum's dressed in the same get-up, but it doesn't look quite as sinister on him. Maybe it's the blue hair and freckles.

"Don't get carried," Bel says. "It would save trouble if you'd just tag my mom."

"We'll see after you're in lock-up," Spires says. "Now bust it."

"Sluff this," Bel growls, stomping through the door with Spires on her heels.

She doesn't seem scared at all, so I try to convince myself I'm not either as Daum ushers me though the doorway.

The next room is bigger and less cement-y. There are a couple of easy chairs, an overflowing bookcase, and a card table with a chessboard mid-game. At the end of the room— where we're headed—is a jail cell, complete with iron bars. I look back and spot a cluttered desk below a window with a view of the cement room. How is that possible? There were no windows in there.

Spires stops in front of the cell, holsters his gun, and takes a stick off the wall. "Arms out," he tells Bel.

"Good." Bel extends her arms. "Now you'll see I have a tat and I'm telling the truth—I'm from this time."

A tat? Like a tattoo? How would that prove anything?

Spires waves the stick down each of Bel's arms, spending a long time on her wrists.

"You're wasting your time. I'm not wearing one," Bel says.

One *what*?

Spires snorts and continues scanning, moving to her neck and head. The wand makes a beep when it reaches her left ear.

"Told you I had a tat," Bel says.

I *know* she doesn't have a tattoo behind her ear. And why would a tattoo make the wand beep anyway?

"Proves nothing," Spires says, moving the wand down the bodice of Bel's Victorian dress, and all around the full skirt. When it gets to her ankle, it beeps again.

"What've you got?" he asks.

"Standard issue detector," Bel says. "I'll get it."

"Negative," Spires says. "Keep static. I'll get it." He looks to Daum. "Got her covered?"

Daum nods, raising his gun to point it at Bel. "Don't try anything."

"I'm not a nafe," Bel says.

Spires lifts Bel's dress to her knees. There's something strapped to her ankle that looks an awful lot like a smart phone. I bet it's the detector she used to pinpoint where the wormhole appears.

Spires removes it, then opens the door to the cell.

Bel looks like she's about to say something, but then seems to think better of it and stomps through the doorway.

"Now you." Spires sweeps the wand over my arms, back, bodice, and legs. It doesn't beep even once. "Clear. Go on."

I step inside and before I can turn around I hear the door clang shut.

"Okay," Bel says. "You said you'd contact my mom now."

"I said we'd see. Not the same thing." Spires walks to the desk and lowers himself into the chair with his back to us.

"*Come on*, Spires. Don't make this worse for yourself." Bel says. "You're already flicked for locking me up. Once my mom finds out you made her wait?" She laughs, and it's not nice. "Pal, you're vanked."

"Who's your mom?" Daum asks.

"Piers Dietrich."

"*Rake me*," Spires says, looking at us over his shoulder.

"Uh, Dr. Dietrich has a daughter," Daum tells Bel. "But it's not you."

"What are you talking about? Of course it's me." Bel's agitated, face flushed.

"What's your name?" Spires barks.

"Raskin. Bel Raskin," Bel says.

"Running it." Spires keys something into a laptop. "Not in the sys."

"That can't be," Bel says. "Try my dad. Steinbeck Raskin. Or Beck. Beck Raskin."

Spires types some more. "Neg. Not here."

"You must be doing it wrong. Try again." Bel's voice has climbed an octave. She's afraid now, which makes me very, very afraid.

Spires swivels to face us. "There are no Raskins."

"Oh my gods, I don't exist," Bel says, turning to me. "What have you done?"

CHAPTER TWO

W hat have *I* done? She's blaming *me*?

Bel's sitting on a bench attached to the back wall of the cell, leaning over with her hands cradling her head. Her fingers are twined in her long red hair so tight I'm afraid she might pull out clumps.

I guess now's not the time to point out it's *her* fault she doesn't exist in this time. That she's the one who killed her own father. Technically, I killed him, too, but she doesn't know that. Plus I killed the older one, the one who raised Bel—that wouldn't have affected her existence. She's the one who killed Maxen, the younger version of Beck, I'm betting before she was conceived.

She's the reason no one knows who she is, not me.

Wait—oh God, I'm in the same boat! In this timeline, my parents died when my mom was pregnant with me. My life's been erased, too.

No one on the planet—at any time in history—knows Bel or me.

Wait, that's not entirely true—we have each other.

So now is definitely not the time for me to cast blame

and make Bel feel worse. Plus, even if her life's been erased, she's got to know more about this place and time than I do. I'm going to need her.

The idea of making nice with Bel is hard to stomach. But I've done harder things. I can do this.

I crouch beside her, touching her shoulder. "It'll be okay. We'll figure it out."

"Don't!" She shrugs off my hand. "We're only in this mess because you vanked my past. I don't want you anywhere near my future. It's bad enough being a time orphan without you effing up the life I've got left." She turns her back on me.

So much for trying to bond. I go to the other end of the cell.

I'm on my own. So what. I've been on my own the past five years since my mom disappeared.

Tears rush to my eyes as I think of my mom. I can't believe I found her, only to lose her again. Twice.

I clench my fists. I'm not going to cry. My mom may be dead, but she's not gone forever. I need to focus on getting out of here so I can go back and change things. So I can save her. So I can save all of them—Maxen, the crew, my younger mom, and my older mom, too. If I travel back to before they died, I can change everything.

I can even change that I killed Beck.

But the truth is heavy in the pit of my stomach—even if I erase my crime from history, I'll still know what I did, what I'm capable of. What I am.

Somehow I'll have to learn to live with the fact that I'm a killer. But first I need to get out of here.

I lean against the wall and scope the situation. Daum is definitely a better mark than Spires. What angle do I go for?

He seemed genuinely sorry for Bel. If I play it right, I can leverage that empathy and get him to help me.

Spires is still at the desk with his back to us, doing something on the computer. Daum's sitting at the card table, leaning back, legs splayed. His gun is holstered and his hands are on his thighs, fingers tapping away against his black pants like he's playing a piano.

Okay, here goes.

I cross the cell and peek my face between the bars across from Daum.

"Do you play?" I ask, my voice quiet so hopefully only he can hear.

He looks at me, fingers motionless now. "What?" His voice is low, too.

"I thought you might play piano, the way you were thrumming your fingers."

"Oh." He looks at his hands as if he doesn't know who they belong to.

"So...do you play?"

His brow furrows. "Used to."

"Why'd you stop?"

He shrugs.

This may be harder than I thought.

I search for another way to get him to engage. I can't push too hard, or he'll clam up even more.

I spot the chessboard, the pieces spread in what looks to me like a random pattern. "We interrupted your game."

He glances at the board. "Affirm."

I pause, hoping he'll continue. But he doesn't. "I've always wanted to learn to play." Not true. It looks boring as heck. "Maybe you could show me? I mean, if we're going to be here awhile."

He squints and presses his lips together. I think maybe I

crossed the line and he's going to tell me to shut it. But before he can say anything, a woman enters.

She's tall and beautiful with flowing red hair, dark eyes, and full lips. She's wearing black pants and boots, and a white blouse.

"Dr. Dietrich," Daum says, jerking to his feet.

"Mom!" Bel rushes to the bars. "Thank gods."

"Hello," Dr. Dietrich replies, looking at Bel, then at me.

"Mom, get me out of here," Bel pleads, her tone bordering on demand.

I don't like being petty, but I did notice she said "get *me* out of here" not "us."

"I'm sorry, but I don't know you," Dietrich replies, her voice kind.

Bel looks like she's in shock.

Dietrich looks at me. She doesn't *seem* like someone who kills time travelers, as much as you can tell that from a first impression.

"I'm Allie," I say, crossing to where Bel is standing at the bars. "Allison Bennett."

"Am I supposed to know you, too?" Dietrich asks.

"No, we've never met."

"When are you from?" She looks me over. "1906? 1911?"

"We came from 1906," I say, indicating my dress. "But I'm actually from 2018."

"And you?" she asks Bel.

"I'm from *this* time," Bel says. "I'm your daughter. You sent me back on an auth mission."

"You're mistaken," Dietrich says. "I stopped authorized missions when I took command."

"You're wrong," Bel says. "In 2152, you sent me on an

auth mission to the past—multiple foci—with my father, Steinbeck Raskin."

"I don't know any Steinbeck Raskin, I've never seen you before, and there have been no missions, authorized or otherwise, in the past six years." Dietrich looks from Bel to me, then back to Bel. "So what exactly are you trying to pull?"

"Do a DNA test," Bel says, practically shouting. "Check my tat. You'll see."

"That would prove nothing," Dietrich says, so calm in contrast to Bel. "You could have faked—"

"The hist-reports!" Bel blurts. "They're in a time-vault so they can't change. Check—they'll tell you all about me. In the reports, *you* tell you that I'm your daughter. There's no way we could fake that."

"I have no such report. And I have no time for this." Dietrich turns and walks away from the cell.

"*Mom*," Bel shouts. "Please, you have to check!"

At the door, Dietrich turns to Spires. "I'm locking you down. No shift changes, no one in or out, zero information exchange. Security Priority One until further notice. Understood?"

"Yes, ma'am," Spires says.

"Affirm," Daum says.

Then she exits.

"I'm so sorry," I say to Bel.

"Go to hell."

I go back to my end of the cage. Sister or not, I'd rather be stuck in here with Spires, or a posse of rabid raccoons. Pretty much anyone who's not Bel.

I lean against the wall and cross my arms, facing away from her. What's her damage, anyway? You'd think she'd welcome an ally, given that both our lives have vanished, making us...what did she call it? *Time orphans.*

She's being such a witch, I don't want to feel bad for her. But I can't help it. I don't doubt Dietrich's her mom. Sure, they look related, but mostly it's Bel's reaction. Bel *believes* that's her mom.

Mom or not, it's clear Dietrich's not going to be of any help. And neither is Bel. I'm on my own. It's up to me to get back to 1906.

Okay, time to assess. Neither of the guards is a good mark, but they don't have beds, so they don't live here. Eventually, we'll have to get different guards. Plus they can't expect to keep *us* here for long—we don't have beds either. There's also no toilet, and no water. That puts a natural limit on the amount of time we'll be here. They'll have to take us out of this cell to somewhere else. Out is good.

Unless they move us somewhere worse. Somewhere the guards don't keep their hands to themselves, or somewhere we won't need a bed or water *ever*. Or somewhere far from that cement room where the wormhole appears, which is where I need to be.

No, I can't risk a move. I'll have to work with what I've got. I cross to the bars and lower myself to the ground, cross-legged. I stare out at Daum—the lesser of two bad choices—and try to formulate my con. He's at the desk now with his back to me. Spires is asleep in one of the easy chairs.

"Daum?" I say quietly.

I see his back stiffen but he doesn't turn or reply. I need to ask a question he can't ignore.

"I'm not feeling well. Can I have some water?"

His shoulders drop. He rises and crosses to the right side of the room. There's nothing there but a blank wall, painted industrial beige. Then he puts his palm to the wall and a panel—that wasn't there before—lights up. He presses some buttons, then a section of the wall slides away. Inside looks like something from a spaceship—a cubby lined with sleek white paneling, a white countertop, and several insets.

He taps a white panel and it lifts, revealing dishes. He selects a glass and places it in an inset. Water streams from above, filling the glass. Then he holds his hand to the wall panel again. The wall closes, hiding the kitchenette, and he brings me the water like all that was normal.

"What the heck was that?" I ask.

Daum's eyebrows raise. "You've never seen a hologram?"

"The kitchen-thing's a hologram?"

"No, the wall hiding it. You've really never seen that before?"

There are a ton more questions swirling in my mind, but I can't risk spooking him now that he's talking. "Thanks for the water," is all I say.

I focus on the glass in my hand. Though it looks like glass, it feels like plastic. I bet it's some special material that won't break so I can't use it as a weapon. I take a tentative sip. Tastes like water. Maybe slightly chemical, but not terrible. I take another drink.

"Sorry you're not feeling well," Daum says, meeting my gaze for a split second. "They should have taken you direct to Med. It's a serious deeve from proto."

I realize what he *almost* said. "They deviated from protocol?"

"Affirm."

That's interesting. "Any idea why?"

He shrugs. "Not really."

It's good he's talking. But there's talking and there's *talking*.

I try a different angle, keeping my voice low so I don't wake Spires. "How long before Dr. Dietrich comes back?"

"Could be an hour, could be tomorrow morning."

"Tomorrow?" It was a little before dawn when we left 1906, but I have no clue what time it is here. There are no windows to the outside, no clocks I can see. "What time is it?"

"Ten-thirty-seven."

"In the morning?"

"What else?"

"And Dietrich might not come back until *tomorrow*? But there's no bathroom in here—that doesn't seem very humane."

"You want to take a bath?"

I start to roll my eyes, but I catch myself. I won't be like Bel. Besides, Daum seems to be legit asking.

"Not a bath. It's the room where you...use the toilet. You know. To pee." My cheeks sting and I hope they're not visibly red.

"We call that the lav. Do you need to use one?"

"Maybe." I kinda have to pee but not bad enough that I'd go in a bucket in front of him.

"Let me know and I'll auth-open it."

"You'll *what*?"

"Open. The door to the lav."

There are no doors in the cell, so that means getting out. Definitely worth pursuing. "Yes, please, I'd like to go—to use the...lav."

He holds his hand to the wall a few feet from the cell. There's a faint whooshing sound.

I glance over my shoulder. Inside the cell there's now an

open door in what was a blank wall before. So much for getting out.

I might as well check it out anyway. I set my glass of water on the floor and get to my feet, trying not to groan. My joints are complaining like I'm an old woman. Must be some residual wormhole-lag or something.

I poke my head in the lav. It doesn't look like any bathroom I've ever seen. It's shallow like a closet. The back wall is spanned by a shelf, waist-high on the left with a sink and faucet, swooping down on the right, becoming a toilet.

I wonder if the door will close when I step inside. I hope so for privacy, though I don't love the idea of being locked in a closet. Tentatively I step across the threshold. As I do, it gets brighter inside—must be some sort of sensor. The door is still open so I turn to close it and it *whooshes* shut past my face. It's good I don't have big boobs—they'd have gotten lopped off.

I lift the lid on the toilet and do my business, grateful I don't have to pee in a bucket. I wash my hands, availing myself of the automatic soap dispenser, all the while scoping the walls, floor, and ceiling for anything useful. I don't see any doors or seams, but I run my hands along the surfaces anyway. I'm not expecting to find anything—I'm in a jail cell—and I don't.

I go to the door and reach for the knob, but there isn't one. For half a second, I panic. I'm not usually claustrophobic, but this weird, ultra-modern cubbyhole feels like it's closing in. I put my hands on the door and it slides open. Crisis averted.

I step back into the cell. "Bel? Do you need to use the bath—toilet?"

She doesn't move. Maybe she's asleep, but I think it's

more likely she's just being Bel. I regret my momentary lapse into caring.

"Pillow?" Daum asks, holding one through the bars. "I could get in trouble for giving it to you. Don't use it to suffocate your cellmate."

A short "ha" escapes my mouth as I take the pillow. No matter how I feel about Bel, my killing days are over. I'm hit by a wave of nausea as I remember what I did to Beck. I hope I never, ever have to do something like that again.

I glance at the bench, but that's clearly Bel's territory, so I set the pillow on the ground near the bars and sit on it, facing out. I've got to keep the conversation going with Daum.

"Thanks for being so cool. For a guard."

He shrugs.

"Have you had a lot of prisoners here?"

"No."

"The ones you had, were they all travelers from other times?"

He shrugs again.

"When were they from?" I persist.

Daum glances at Spires, who's still asleep. "I'm not supposed to talk to you."

Still, it seems like he wants to. "I don't want to get you in trouble—I need to take my mind off being locked in here. Can we play chess? We don't have to talk. Except for you to teach me."

He looks like he's considering it, then shakes his head. "I better not. You should try to sleep. While you can."

While I can?

Just when I was starting to think maybe they *weren't* going to kill us.

CHAPTER THREE

FLYX

I found her. My odd-clothed girl. She's here. She's here *now*.

I lean back in my chair, my hands falling free of the CTAR's keys. How can it be that this girl, this magined love, is in this time—*my* time? I rub my eyes to make sure I'm not dozing. I look back at the screen and see the words again, words that say she's here, now, in Detention.

I need to cog if it's her, actual. I reach to tag Daum, but my fingers touch bare wrist. It's such habit, I forget I don't have my personal in here

The clock-read shows more than an hour on shift before I can find out what Daum cogs. That's eternity. I've never felt so desp about being info-segregated before.

This girl, my odd-clothed past-beauty—somehow she's my destiny, my future. Ever since the first mention of her in the news-reps, I can't think else. I rationed it my own runwild maginations. But now that she's *here*...this goes beyond maginings and coince.

I need to doc this in my Liferep. I'm supposed to be

immune to mem-change, but the high-ups create hist-reports as a caution, and I decided long ago it would be dim not to do samewise. My fingers find the keyboard again.

Flyx Hansson
Liferep 17.02.18.1349 (PRIVLOCK)

The odd-clothed nat-beauty from 1906, in all proba-bility one Allison Bennett of 2018, is in 2153. Broke all rules and scanned, found her in Detention. Can't expl why put self in jeopardy for this girl, nomatter how swelt a looker. Can only desc as destiny, like we are meant together.

My plan: erase search hist best-can. Get out of TIC and locate Daum immed. Thank gods he's on shift now. He'll know if she's here intrue, and, if so, can take me to her.

I'd been careless in order to learn what became of my odd-clothed girl. But now that she's here, I have to eye her. I can't risk consequence that would prevent that. I hope-pray I can erase my path entire so the high-ups don't cog what I've done.

I push back my chair and slide to the floor. Using my fingernail, I unscrew the panel under the desk and expose the electronics. I slide out the coding keyboard with mini-monitor that I eyed months past but was too chary to try.

The first part is hardest. If it blanks an access code, I'm vanked. There's no faking that.

I key in a request for access. The cursor blinks, processing.

The microseconds pass like hours. My mouth is dry, hands sweating. I'm holding my resps, expecting an alarm or shut-off. Or worse, the whole TIC could power down and someone storm in, gun pointed.

But the cursor turns solid. I'm in.

CHAPTER FOUR

"What do you mean, I should sleep *while I can?*" I ask Daum, unable to keep the alarm from my voice.

He shrugs. "There will be lots of testing and stuff. Unless...there's not." He looks away and now I know there's something really bad he's not telling me.

"What are you talking about?" I demand, my voice low.

"I'm not supposed to say."

"Please, I need to know what to expect, what I'm up against. *Please.*"

I see him swallow. He glances at Spires—still sleeping—then looks back at me and squats near the bars so his face is opposite mine. "Dietrich will decide if you can be salvaged. If you're lucky, you'll just be recycled."

That doesn't sound good. "And if I'm *not* lucky?"

He cocks his head, then runs his finger across his throat.

I suck in a breath, but it feels like there's no oxygen.

"So try to rest, okay?" Daum gives a tense smile, then stands and walks away.

Did he seriously say they might kill me, then tell me to rest? As if.

"Psst, hey," I whisper, but he doesn't turn around. I grab the bars and lean forward. *"Daum."*

Spires snorts and sits up in the easy chair. "What? What's going on?"

"Nothing," Daum says. "Everything's norm."

"You talking to her?" Spires asks. "You gave her a pillow? What's wrong with you?"

"I'm not talking to her," Daum says, showing Spires a pair of headphones and then clamping them over his ears. "Go back to sleep." He sits at the desk, his back to me.

"You," Spires says, pointing at me. "Shut your hole and make use of that pillow. Or I will. You cog?"

I gulp and scoot down until my head is on the pillow. I stare at the ceiling, my heart throbbing in my ears, tears spilling from the corners of my eyes.

SOMEONE SHAKES ME AWAKE.

Bel.

She puts her finger to her lips, then motions for me to follow.

I can't believe I fell asleep. I guess the last few days finally caught up with me.

Bel motions again furiously.

Nothing's changed, so I don't know where she expects to go, but I get up and join her in "her" corner of the cell, sitting beside her on the bench. Spires is asleep again in the easy chair, and Daum is slumped over the desk, clearly sleeping, too.

It's too much to hope that Bel has a plan. Whatever she's up to, it's not about helping me. More likely she wants something.

She leans close. "Have you figured a way out of here yet?" she says in her ridiculously loud whisper.

Sometimes I hate being right. "No, have *you*?"

"I thought you were supposed to be some sort of expert escape artist.'"

"I thought you were from this time and knew what to do."

We both go quiet, glaring at each other.

Then I realize—I finally have a sister and this is how we act. That makes me feel bad enough to try for a truce.

"Look," I say. "We both want the same thing. Let's work together, okay?"

She blinks slowly, but does not roll her eyes. I consider that progress.

"Fine," she says. "Can you get the cell open?"

Now is not the time to confess I've never *actually* picked a lock, only studied it on the Internet. "I'll check out the lock. If I can open it—big if—do you know what to do next?"

"Maybe. I mean, I know how things used to be."

"Let's say I can get us out of here and into that cement room where the wormhole appears—we still need a quake. When's the next one going to hit?"

"I have no idea. We're in the *present*—that means no record of what's going to happen."

"Crap."

"Don't be so drama. We don't need a quake. There's a machine that triggers the wormhole."

Finally some good news. "Where's the machine? There was nothing in that room."

"Duh," she says with a hint of an eyeroll. "You saw how the walls are holograms. I assume the controls are still there but hidden."

"I hope you're right. I'll get to work on the cell door."

"Hold on. Even if the controls *are* in that room, we won't be able to do anything because I don't exist in this time. I won't have authorization."

Great. No solution, only more problems. "Then what do you suggest?"

"They're supposed to take us to Med. At least that was the protocol in my time."

"It still is—Daum told me."

"Good. In Med, I should be able to get to a computer. I know a backdoor into the system. Assuming it still works, I'll confirm the location of the wormhole machine and grant myself access."

"Daum didn't say why they hadn't taken us to Med yet. What if they don't?" I start pacing like a lion in a cage. "What if they skip Med and go straight to recycling us?"

"*Shhh.*" Bel glances at the guards. "That's exactly what will happen if you don't ease out."

I return to Bel and lower my voice. "How do you recycle *people*? What does that even mean?"

"A large dose of the memory loss drug."

But the drug doesn't cause memory loss. It *kills*.

I open my mouth, then snap it shut. If I tell her, it will destroy the small amount of progress we've made.

"We can't get recycled," I say, leaving out the rest. "We need to be ready for any opportunity, so I'm going to scope out the lock on the cell door. I won't try to pick it yet."

I tiptoe to the front of the cell and press my face to the bars, trying to see the locking mechanism. My head doesn't fit between the bars, and I can't get a good angle on it, so I slip my hand through to scope it by feel. As soon as my hand touches the lock, an alarm blares.

I jump back, covering my ears, heart pounding out of

my chest.

Daum and Spires leap to their feet. I stand there, guilty, plugging my ears. I glance over at Bel and she rolls her eyes. Great, we're back to that.

Spires comes to the bars. And I thought he looked scary *before*. I step back, out of reach.

"Sorry," I say, though I'm sure he can't hear me over the alarm.

He puts his hand to the lock and the alarm stops. He glares at me.

"Sorry," I say again. I don't even try to explain. It's not like they're going to believe I wasn't trying to get out. And it's not like the truth makes me look any better.

"Go sit on the bench," Spires says.

I sit by Bel and try to look contrite.

Spires turns on Daum. "What the hell? Were you sleeping?"

"I only turned my back for a minute to check something on the computer," Daum lies.

"Uh, excuse me?" I say.

Daum looks at me, eyes wide. I cock my head, letting it sink in that I could rat him out. Daum stares, silently pleading.

Spires narrows his eyes at me. "You got something to say?"

I watch Daum, dragging out the moment. From the look on his face, it won't be a minor thing if I spill that he was sleeping. Finally I look back at Spires. "He wasn't asleep. He had his back turned so I sneaked over to check out the lock."

I glance at Daum, making sure he reads me loud and clear—he owes me. He's not happy about it, but he nods. So the lock fiasco wasn't a total bust.

A woman in a burgundy jumpsuit storms into the room. "What's going on?" Her scowling face has more ink than a comic book cover.

"Everything's norm," Daum says.

"It didn't *sound* norm. What in the eff happened?"

"Novalie," Bel calls.

The woman turns to Bel. "Who the eff are you?"

"Bel Raskin, Piers Dietrich's daughter," Bel says, rising from the bench. "And your friend."

"I've never seen you before."

"That's because history changed while I was on an auth mission. Take me to Med like you're supposed to, and we can clear this up."

"There's no such thing as *auth* time travel," Novalie says. "What the eff are you trying to pull?"

"Nothing," Bel says, and I'm impressed how sincere she sounds. "I want to prove I am who I say I am. A rapid DNA will show I'm a Jenny. Compare it with my mom's DNA and you'll see—this is my real time."

Novalie's hands perch on her hips as she stares at Bel and bites a piercing in her lower lip.

"Come on, Novalie," Bel says. "Why wouldn't you want to test me and find out?" I don't detect even a trace of mean-girl in her tone. Amazing. I didn't think she was capable.

Finally Novalie turns to Spires. "Why weren't they taken to Med?"

"Dietrich's orders."

"Dietrich *herself*?" Novalie asks.

Spires nods. "She put us on Security Priority One."

Novalie's face goes slack. "Gods *damn* it."

"Might as well get comfortable," Spires says, gesturing to an easy chair.

"I have a better idea," Novalie says. "I'm going to walk

out of here and we're all going to pretend this never happened."

Spires steps toward her, his hand moving to his gun. "I can't—"

"Don't draw that weapon," Novalie barks.

Spires freezes.

"You know something's not right," Novalie says. "They should be in Med."

"We have orders," Daum says.

A look from Novalie makes him take a step back.

"I'm going to check into this," Novalie says.

Spires draws a sharp breath.

"I'll be careful," Novalie says. "I'm not getting recycled over this, and neither are you. Sit tight and I'll be back."

Daum looks to Spires. Spires stands stock-still and silent, his meaty forehead bunched in a scowl. Finally his empty hand leaves the holster and he nods.

Without another word, Novalie turns and leaves.

"Is this good?" I whisper to Bel.

"Maybe. Maybe not."

It seems like this has promise. I mean, at least someone is going against the status quo, someone who seems pretty powerful, or at least determined and ballsy. I shouldn't get my hopes up, but I've got nothing else to latch onto. Especially now that I know the lock is unpickable—can't pick it if you can't touch it.

"Daum, get everyone nutrition," Spires orders.

Daum makes the kitchenette appear again and pushes buttons. I hear whirring noises, then he places a glass under a spigot. There's burbling as the glass fills with a greenish-gray liquid. He takes it to Spires who's back in the easy chair with his feet up. I'm not surprised when Spires doesn't say thanks.

Daum fills two more glasses and brings them to the bars.

"I'll go," I say to Bel.

I meet Daum at the front of the cell and take both glasses. "Thanks."

He nods, then turns away.

"Wait, what is this stuff?" I ask, not wanting to burn an opportunity to build a connection.

He turns back. "Nutrition."

I sniff one. *Ew,* it smells like sauerkraut. "Yeah, but what *is* it?"

"Protein, carbs, fat."

"Okaaaay." I take a tentative sip. It's disgusting. I force myself to swallow the bitter, gritty glop, and it leaves a chalky coating in my mouth. "Gross."

"You'll get used to it." Daum walks away.

"Doubt it," I say under my breath. I really, *really* hope I don't have to.

I give Bel her glass and she downs it without even making a face.

"How can you even?" I set my full glass on the floor.

"Do you always have to be so drama? It's like a smoothie from your time."

"Uh, no. Not even close. What's in it? Don't tell me fruit."

"Labs grow food down here. Nothing goes to waste. This is a mixture of leftover matter."

"So appetizing. *Not.*" I spot my water glass on the floor by the bars. I go over and chug it, trying to wash the vile taste from my mouth. It doesn't work.

I return to the bench and sit beside Bel.

"Drink up," she says. "That's all you're going to get."

"Geez, what kind of future did you bring me to? Please tell me there are still Micky D's."

"Out in the world, but not down here."

That's the second time she's said "down here," like we're underground or something. "What do you mean, *down here?* Where are we?"

"In the old BART tunnels under the city."

"What? *Why?*"

"After the White War, when researchers discovered the wormhole here, a small Resistance colony was established to keep the wormhole secret from the ASPs."

"Asps? Like snakes?"

"A. S. P. American Syncretic Party. ASPs for short. They evolved from what you know as Nazis."

"*What?*" Did she really say Nazis? "What the hell are you talking about?"

"In this time—at least in my version of it—the ASPs run everything from the government on down. Everything except these tunnels and the wormhole. They believe there are a dozen scientists here working to relieve the pressure on the San Andreas fault. They have no idea about the wormhole or the hundred-plus members of the Resistance."

"*You,*" Spires barks, coming toward the cell. He's pointing at me.

My heart jumps into my throat. "Yeah?"

"Turn around and put your hands on the wall." Spires's tone leaves no room for negotiating.

I stand and put my hands flat on the cold cement, glancing at Bel for guidance. She looks scared, which scares the crap out of me.

"You with the red hair," Spires says. "Middle of the cell."

Bel presses her lips in a line, then gets up and leaves my field of view without even a glance at me.

I hear the cell door open, then the swishing of movement. After a moment, the door clanks shut and I steal a peek. Bel's outside the cell with her wrists bound in front of her.

"Novalie said take her to Med," Spires says, thrusting Bel toward Daum.

"What about me?" I ask.

"Shut it," Spires says. "Daum, we're still Security Priority One. No tagging or talking to anyone."

Daum leads Bel away, leaving me with the more challenging mark. I'm sure I could have gotten something out of Daum. Cracking Spires may be beyond my ability.

At least Bel is going to Med. Fingers crossed she can get to a computer.

Spires hasn't told me I can move yet. How long is he going to make me stand here with my hands on the wall?

"Excuse me?" I call. "Can I sit down?"

He doesn't answer.

I try something else. "Could I have some water?"

Still nothing.

I'm getting tired of this real quick. What's he going to do, shoot me for taking my hands down?

I turn and Spires isn't even looking. He's sitting at the desk with his back to me.

I'm tempted to curl up in a ball and wait for Bel to do her thing, but I know better than to count on her, or anyone but myself. I can't afford to waste any time. "Hey," I call.

He's a statue.

"*Hey*," I say louder. "I really do need water."

He doesn't twitch. It's like I'm not talking at all.

I sit on the bench and lean back against the wall. I can't believe Bel left me hanging with "Nazis." What happened to the world? I have to find a way to get Spires talking. I need answers.

CHAPTER FIVE

FLYX

It was close, but I managed to pull the reports, cover my virtual tracks, and log out on time. Anyone who logs out late, Remo looks at tight, and no one wants that, even when they're innocent.

At the STARS office, I drop my transfer drive and Dietrich's hist-report, and grab my personal from Remo. He grunts without looking at me, so I know I didn't trigger any alerts.

Trying not to look like I'm in a hurry, I leave the office, strapping the personal to my wrist as I go. The sec it's engaged, I tag Daum.

FLYX: whr u?

where are you? appears on the screen. There's a split second when I can stop transmission if there's an error, but there isn't, so I let it fly. The algo's are getting better. Used to be every other word was jumbo.

No response from Daum. I have zero patience. I tag again.

FLYX: D u there?

He's supposed to be off shift now. Why isn't he tagging back?

I stop at the junction, not sure which way to go. Daum could be at Middies, but that's the wrong direction if he's still at Detention.

Wait, what am I thinking? Even if Daum's at Detention, Allison wouldn't be—per proto, arrivals go straight to Med. I'll bypass Daum entire.

I check which Med tech is on duty—*Sharrow*. Who the soot is that? It's got to be Rista switching up names again. It's not like there could actually be someone I don't know.

I tag Rista.

FLYX: r u wrkng?

I wait. Two minutes, three minutes. Rista doesn't respond. Maybe that's good. Maybe she can't because she has a patient—one Allison Bennett.

I can't keep static. I start pacing. Six steps forward, six back. Six forward, six back. After three minutes I tag Rista again. Then Daum again.

Still nothing.

I can't continue pacing like the caged animals in those horr-awful vid-histories of "zoos." I have to do something. I key in a new message to Rista.

FLYX: need info new arrival Allison Bennett. on my way to Med now

I bust toward Med, toward one Allison Bennett, my odd-clothed girl from past history. Toward what feels like my future. Halfway there, my wrist tingles with a tag. Finally.

DAUM: not supposed to be tagging. Security Priority One. what's got you nettled?

FLYX: need info on girl came through wormhole this a.m.— Allison Bennett

DAUM: how can you possibly cog that?

FLYX: it's *her*, my odd-clothed girl

DAUM: come to Med. I have three minutes, no more

FLYX: almost there

My feet fly across the cement, my heart racing faster than it should be. I feel like I'm in a dream, like this can't be actual. Am I about to meet the girl from my maginings?

At Med, Daum's waiting outside the door.

I rush up. "Tell me."

"You first. You're not need-to-know, so how do you?"

"Is she in there?" I point to the door.

"No, but she should be."

"Then what are we doing here?"

"Two girls came through the wormhole. I brought the other one—not Allison. This one claims she's from this time, that she's Dietrich's daughter, but I've never seen her before."

"*Bel?* What are you playing at? We used to steal her lunch in Prime."

"No idea what you're talking about."

Rot. History must have changed. But how, without me knowing? Maybe I was too preoccupied with my odd-clothed girl. I've got to be more careful. I'd better find out what Bel knows. "So Bel's in Med with Rista now?"

"No, with *Sharrow*."

"Who's Sharrow?"

"Sharrow? *Your girlfriend?*"

"I don't have a girlfriend."

"Real funny," Daum says. "I gotta get back to Detention."

"Is that where Allison is?"

"Why do you care?"

I knew it. "I'm coming with you."

"You cracked? Spires would unseat my head and suck my spinal cord out my neck. What he'd do to *you* would be worse. Take a resp and line up your progs. I'll tag when I can." He takes off at a jog.

My head's swimming. What the soot happened to history? I can't ask Bel, not with someone named Sharrow there who thinks I'm her boyfriend. There's only one other way to cog what's going on.

I race back to STARS, trying to cipher a story that will convince Remo to let me back in the TIC. I arrive winded without a single good idea.

Stalling, I go to grab a drink, but don't have my bottle. I bank my personal to the potable and grab a one-time instead. After filling and draining it twice, I bin it and settle on telling the truth. I face the entrance mask and bank the door to STARS.

Remo looks up from his desk. "What the eff are you doing back here?"

I cross the office and sit on the arm of the chair opposite his desk. "I think I effed up."

His pierced brow bunches in a way that looks painful. "Whatdja do?"

"Must've missed something on my last shift, because now there are hist-changes—sally ones—that aren't logged because I didn't see them."

He leans on his elbows, his tattooed fingers splayed on the desk. "Like what?"

"Like apparently some girl I've never heard of named Sharrow is my girlfriend."

"Eff me." Remo leans back in his chair. "Sharrow's gonna be torqued."

"So she *is* my girlfriend? Daum told me she was, but..."

"She's your girlfriend all right. Some months, now." He

hands me an empty transfer drive. "Get your hind in the TIC and figure what the eff is up."

"Affirm." I drop my personal on his desk and head for the back hall. That went way better than I imagined.

"Make it fast," Remo calls.

I raise my hand, acknowledging. I had radiation sickness before. That's something no one wants to go through twice.

CHAPTER SIX

Spires leaps to his feet as the door opens and Dr. Dietrich strides in. She glances my way, then zeroes in on Spires.

"Where is she?" Dietrich demands.

"I...I," Spires stammers. It's odd to see him rattled.

"My orders were crystal," Dietrich says. "So where is the other one? *Where's my daughter?*"

She believes Bel's her daughter? What happened to change her mind? I take advantage of Spires's slack-jawed silence and pipe in. "They took her to Med."

Dietrich wheels around to face me. "What?"

"Bel—your daughter—is my sister. They took her to Med."

"They took her to Med?" It's like she's having a hard time keeping up. Like she's the stressed-out twin of the woman from before.

"Yes, a while ago," I answer.

"And you're her sister." She's catching up.

"Half sister. My only family in the world." I make my

voice crack with emotion—I hope that's not laying it on too thick.

Dietrich turns back to Spires and holds out her hand. "Your weapon."

Spires looks like he's about to pee himself. He steps forward, extending the butt of his handgun.

Dietrich grabs it. "Open the cell."

"Ma'am?" Spires's voice cracks. I almost feel sorry for him.

"Do it." Dietrich gestures with the gun toward the cell door.

Spires narrows his eyes at me, like this whole thing is my fault, which throws cold water on my almost-sympathy. He crosses to the cell door and opens it.

"Zip her hands," Dietrich says.

Spires comes toward me, jaw bulging from clenched teeth, and pulls a zip tie from his pocket. I hold my hands in front of me and he loops the plastic strip around my wrists, pulling so tight it pinches. But I don't give him the satisfaction of a reaction.

"Come with me, Allie," Dietrich says. "But watch yourself. I won't hesitate to use this gun."

"Yes, ma'am." She seems confident with the gun. I'm not going to underestimate her.

"Spires, stay there," Dietrich says.

"What?" His voice is tinged with panic.

"You disobeyed me."

"But Novalie gave the order."

Dietrich closes the cell door, locking Spires in.

It's stupid satisfying to see him on the other side of the bars, but I'm careful not to let it show. I don't need to make him more of an enemy.

Dietrich motions me across the room and through the

outer door onto a small landing with a staircase going down. The walls are plain gray, and there's nothing here but the stairs and rails. Or at least nothing I can see. Who knows what's hologrammed.

Dietrich gestures with the gun to go down the stairs ahead of her. I take them slowly—it's a long way down. She doesn't touch me, but she's so close behind I hear her breathing. I know the muzzle of the gun is inches from my back, and I don't doubt she has the nerve to shoot me. But my read is she'll only shoot if she has to, and I'm not going to give her any reason.

At the bottom of the stairs is yet another room with gray walls and a cement floor. These people have no imagination.

"Keep moving," Dietrich says.

I walk toward the only exit. A closed, gray door—what else would it be?

I stop at the door but I can't open it—there's no handle, no doorknob. No buttons or control panel. No window or security camera to someone on the other side.

Dietrich steps forward. I note the gun's now in her left hand—it was in her right before. If I'm going to make a break for the wormhole room, now's the time. I glance back toward the stairs and calculate the odds of making it without getting shot: pretty much zero.

If I'm going to run, I have to take the gun.

Dietrich looks me in the eye, her expression erasing any impression that she can't handle a gun in her left hand. So much for disarming her.

Still pointing the gun at me, she puts her right hand up to the blank wall. At her touch, a door appears and slides open. More hologram tech.

We step through the door into a BART station. It's old

and abandoned, with trash and recycling bins tipped over, debris covering the floor and benches, walls plastered with graffiti. I immediately feel at home.

Across the cavernous space I see the trough in the floor for the trains, though there aren't any train cars in sight. By the looks of this place, I doubt one would be operational anyway.

Dietrich directs me left, along a graffitied wall.

This graffiti's like no street art I've ever seen. The colors are vibrant even in the dim light, and some of the images look like they're sticking out of the wall—I'd guess another type of hologram.

I follow the wall, my boots clacking on the concrete, Dietrich clipping along behind me. Making sure to keep my face pointed straight ahead, I scout for an escape route, but only out of habit. I have no desire to get shot. Besides, even if I found an exit and ditched Dietrich, I'd be trapped in this time.

My best bet for getting back to 1906 lies with Bel. And now that Dietrich believes Bel's her daughter, my odds are looking better.

At the end of the station, Dietrich holds the gun on me while I climb down steel rungs into the train trench, which is a bit awkward with my hands bound. She foregoes the rungs and drops gracefully to the bottom. Duh, why didn't I do that?

To our left is the opening to the train tunnel, so dark I can't see two feet inside. I turn to Dietrich for direction, and her steely eyes glare at me from behind the barrel. Did I read her wrong? Did she bring me down here to shoot me?

"Go ahead," Dietrich says. "In the tunnel."

I don't move. Instead I take a breath and steady my diaphragm so my voice doesn't shake. "Where are we going?" I'm stalling, trying to figure out options. I'm not much of a fighter, but I'll challenge her for the gun before I let her shoot me in the back.

"Med. Get going."

I try to read her—she's calm, voice smooth, face placid. She might be telling the truth.

"Med is through there?" I glance into the tunnel. "It's really dark."

She rolls her eyes in a good likeness of Bel, steps around me, and waves her empty hand. Yellow lights illuminate the tunnel. Every inch is covered in graffiti, even the floor where it peeks between piles of trash.

"Go on, move it," Dietrich snaps, annoyed. Annoyed is good. Way better than murderous.

I start walking, a little more sure she's not going to shoot me. If we really are going to Med, that's good—Bel should be there. Hopefully she's gotten into the computer system and gained access to the wormhole machine.

Dietrich steps up to walk beside me. "What can you tell me about my daughter?"

This is a good sign. "Um, what would you like to know?" I hedge, wondering what she's after. The gun's down at her side now. Definitely a good sign.

"How old she is, to start."

"Eighteen, I think."

"You don't know?"

"I only met her recently. I didn't even know I had a sister until our father found me in 2018."

"Your father." Her voice sounds pinched, like she's trying hard to control her emotions. "He's called Raskin, correct? Tell me about him."

"Okay, uh, he said he was from 2152, same as Bel. He's tall with brown hair, and he wears dark glasses because his

eyes are messed up. I only saw them once and they were...
bloody looking." I shiver at the memory.

"Did he say what was wrong with them?"

"He didn't talk about it, not to me. Maybe Bel knows."

"I'll be sure to ask her." She's silent for a few paces. "I'm
curious why he and Bel were time-traveling."

"I only know what he told me." I weigh my options and
figure there's no harm in the truth. What little I know,
anyway. "He said there were only a few time travelers in his
time—this time—and that some people wanted to get rid of
them. He set out to prove time travelers were useful by
pulling a heist in 1906 and bringing the valuables here. The
catch was, we had to do it without anyone being able to tell
history had changed."

"So where are these items?"

"Uh, things went a bit sideways right before the big
quake."

"Sideways?"

"There was a problem and we had to abort the mission."

"What problem?"

Now I have to veer into a lie because Bel doesn't know
—can't know—the truth, and Dietrich will definitely ask her
to corroborate my story. "I'm not sure why Beck told us to
abort. Something about governors." I remember Haze
telling me *Beck* was a governor. "*Rogue* governors," I
amend.

"Governors...." She seems to be saying this to herself.

Silence fills the space between us. I don't dare pursue
the conversation, since I know next to nothing about governors. I'm literally crossing my fingers that I haven't said
something wrong already.

At the end of the tunnel, we emerge into another BART
station as trashed and abandoned as the last. I'm dying to

know which station it is, but I don't see any signs or maps or identifying characteristics.

"We're almost there," Dietrich says. "Are you doing okay?"

This is the first time she's shown any concern for my welfare. I need to build on that. "A little tired. I'm not used to time-traveling."

"They'll be able to help you at Med," she says. "I'm sure they're taking excellent care of Bel as we speak."

"Can I ask you something?" I venture, hoping to build more of a bond. Plus I'm curious. "At first you were sure Bel wasn't your daughter. What changed your mind?"

"Why do you want to know?" There's a fresh edge to her voice, but I think I can push a little bit more.

"I was hoping you could tell if there is someone in this time related to *me*. I mean in addition to Bel. Because now she has you...and I have no one." I'm hoping her motherly instincts will kick in and she'll group me with Bel as someone related to *her*.

"They'll test you in Med." Not quite the open arms I was hoping for.

Bel asked for a DNA test to prove Dietrich was her mother. Did they run one? Is that what triggered Dietrich's about-face? No, Dietrich came looking for Bel in Detention, not Med, so it had to be something else. Maybe it has to do with those records Bel was sure her mother kept. I'll have to ask Bel. I've pressed my luck with Dietrich far enough.

She stops at the end of the station and holds her hand up to a graffiti-covered wall. A door appears and *whooshes* to the side, revealing a wide hallway. We cross the threshold, returning to flat, boring gray. The walls, the floor, even the lights are dull and oppressive. At least the graffiti had some life to it.

We walk silently down gray hall after gray hall, passing through multiple doors with invisible access panels. Each hall, each door, the same. No sounds, no people, no relief to the gray.

I wonder how long before I start to feel suffocated from having no sunlight, fresh air, or color.

Dietrich stops at yet another gray door. "This is Med."

The door slides open. I guess I expected Med to be white and sterile with maybe the addition of some red crosses or something. But we're standing in a waiting room that is totally and completely green. Like all the shades of green I've ever seen gathered in one place. There are two rows of plastic contoured chairs in a Saint Patrick's green, the floor is some spongy material in an emerald green, and the walls are a neon lime spotted with random-sized teal polka dots. If I was allergic to green, I'd need an epi-pen.

I follow Dietrich across the room to a window in the wall—a window with green-tinted glass. There's a girl on the other side of the glass who looks green, too.

The green glass slides away revealing a girl who thankfully isn't green, at least not completely. She has pale peach skin and amber eyes. But her hair is green. Icy mint green. On closer look, she's got freckles across her nose and cheeks similar to Daum's, but hers are green. Of course they are. Green eyeliner, too.

"Hi, Mom," the girl says.

I look at Dietrich. *Mom?*

"Hello, Sharrow."

CHAPTER SEVEN

The mint-girl—Sharrow—is Dietrich's daughter.

That makes her Bel's sister. Is she my sister, too?

No, that wouldn't make sense. Dietrich doesn't know Beck in this time, so Beck can't be Sharrow's dad.

Dietrich says, "This is Allie. Do a complete work-up."

"Affirm," Sharrow says.

"You have another new patient here, correct?" There's no discernible change to Dietrich's tone, but I can tell this question is important to her, so I bet Sharrow can, too.

"Affirm. Another girl I've never seen before. Bel something." Sharrow shoves a clipboard through the window and I groan. Apparently even in the future, doctor's visits require endless paperwork.

Dietrich holds her palm over the clipboard. It "dings" like a text, then she passes it back through the window. Cool! Paperwork in the future *is* better.

The window slides shut, then a door opens.

Sharrow appears in the doorway wearing a skin-tight bodysuit like the guards' in the same mint green as her hair.

It looks like something a ski racer would wear. Kinda hideous. But I covet her teal-green combat boots.

"Please come in," Sharrow says like she's inviting neighbors in for tea.

Inside, it looks a bit more like a medical facility, at least in terms of everything being white. There's a large counter in the middle of the room, like a kitchen island. Cabinets and countertops line the walls, and there's a variety of machines hanging on tracks from the ceiling. Six white-sheeted beds are distributed throughout the room. One of them is occupied.

"Mom?" Bel sits up in the bed and the sheet falls to her waist. She doesn't have a shirt on. Or a bra.

Instinctively I fold my arms across my chest, but Bel doesn't.

"*Mom?*" Sharrow pivots to Dietrich, her eyes wide.

"This is your sister," Dietrich tells her.

"But...but," Sharrow stammers. "I don't have a sister."

"You don't remember because history changed," Dietrich says. "The rapid DNA should have confirmed it."

"I...it...I haven't seen it yet—it wasn't complete," Sharrow says.

"Shouldn't it be ready now? Go on and check," Dietrich says.

Sharrow looks from Dietrich to Bel, then to me. "Sit there." She points at the next bed over from Bel's. "I'll be right back."

I cross to the bed and sit on the edge, knowing too well what Sharrow must be feeling. I wonder if Bel knew she had yet another sister, but I can't read a thing on her face.

"You believe me now, that I'm your daughter," Bel says to her.

"I apologize about before." Dietrich says. "You were

right—I didn't know it at the time, but there are records kept in a vault that's impervious to time-change."

"Thank gods." Bel swings her legs out from under the sheet. She's totally naked but she doesn't seem to care. "Can we get out of here now?"

Sharrow returns, looking like she's in shock. "It's true. I don't understand."

"I'll explain later," Dietrich tells her. "Get her something to wear."

Sharrow nods. It looks like she's in pain as she leaves the room.

"Mom," Bel says, her voice urgent. "I had to leave Dad in 1906. I had no choice." Bel shoots me a glance that makes it clear she blames me.

"Not now," Dietrich says.

"No, you have to listen. I need to go back for him," Bel says.

"As soon as it's possible."

I breathe a sigh of relief. It doesn't matter if Bel broke into the computer system or not. Dietrich is going to *let* Bel go back to 1906. Maybe this is going to turn out okay after all. As long as Bel doesn't try to leave me behind.

"You'll need to be patient," Dietrich continues. "The president's coming with a delegation. Anything out of the ordinary's on hold until after that."

Sharrow comes back and hands Bel something made of dark gray fabric. I wonder if the color is commentary, or if it's the only option available.

Bel unfurls the fabric—it's a bodysuit like Sharrow's. She slips it on and zips it to her throat. The zipper vanishes and I wonder if it's behind a flap of fabric or if it's another hologram.

"Sharrow, lock Allie so Bel and I can leave."

Lock? "Excuse me?"

Sharrow reaches up to a machine hanging above my bed and pulls down a tube with something on the end. It looks like a dentist drill. She comes closer, grasping my shoulder. I shrink away, but she pushes me onto my back.

"Wait, what—ouch!" My neck stings where she pressed the drill-thing. "What did you do?"

"It's an ordinary paralytic," she says.

"A *what?*" Terror wells in my throat.

"I'll contact you later," Dietrich tells Sharrow, then she and Bel head for the door.

"*Wait.*" I try to sit up but I can't. "Bel? Bel!"

Bel doesn't even glance over her shoulder.

"Bel!" I shout again. But she's gone. I'm dizzy and my legs feel like lead. "I feel weird."

"It's harmless. Much more humane than physical restraints." Sharrow snaps on blue gloves, grabs a pair of scissors, and snips the zip tie on my wrists. Then she starts on my dress.

My arms fall to my sides of their own accord. The ceiling swims and nausea pools in my stomach. "Are you going to kill me?"

"No! Why would you think that? I'm removing your clothing so the doctor can examine you."

"I don't believe you." I try to lift my arm to ward her off, but I can't move it. My instincts are telling me this is all wrong, that I need to get the hell out of here, but my body won't connect to my thoughts. "I can't move my arm. I can't move anything."

"You can still talk, and blink, and breathe. You'll be fine. Just try to relax."

"I *can't move.*"

"I need to you calm down," Sharrow says, cutting up the front of my blouse.

"I don't want to calm down! I want you to make this stop. I need to get out of here." I feel tears running down into my ears. "Help! Someone help me!"

She pulls open my blouse and starts cutting the corset. "Try to calm yourself. This isn't good for you."

I'm gasping. I can't get enough air.

"What's going on?" someone says.

A figure approaches and leans over the bed.

I scream—half of his face is exposed tendons and bone. I can see his teeth through a gap in his cheek. He looms over me, and I try with everything I've got to get away, but I can't move at all, which panics me more. I'm hyperventilating, my vision going black around the edges.

He pulls down a tube from the machine and presses it to my neck.

The fear dissipates and I melt into the bed, like my body is turning from solid to liquid. I feel all warm and gooey. I notice my eyes are wet and I blink.

The man above me meets my gaze. "I'm Calix, your doc."

Now I see that what I thought was exposed tendons and bone is actually a realistic tattoo. Half of his face looks like a picture from a medical book of a head without any skin. His light brown hair is loose and wavy, and swoops back away from his forehead. His lips are smooth and pink, then he smiles, showing perfectly straight, perfectly white teeth. I look up at his brown eyes—they are smiling too.

"Better now?" he asks, his voice sliding over me like warm caramel.

I try to nod. I don't know if my head is moving. I think I might love him.

CHAPTER EIGHT

FLYX

I nside the TIC, I have to be fast, but I still have to log.

Flyx Hansson
Jobrep 2153.08.08.1612
Review previous compare and rep
1613 pull 2153.08.08 and 08.07 logs
1614 re-run compare series

While that's churning, I pull up my Lifereps. Search for "Sharrow" yields zero results. I scan through random dates and everything matches what I recall—no surprises. So my memory's fine, as far as I can be sure.

I ration whatever change created Sharrow and erased Bel must have happened after I left the TIC yesterday, and somehow I missed it during this morning's shift. I wonder what else I missed.

The task is still running. Taking longer than usual. Or maybe I'm more impatient than usual—I'm already feeling woozy from being in here again so soon.

Finally, the compare series completes, and, *rake me,* the list is long.

1650 rev sig-points per protocol

1701 note 13 major anomalies, 157 minor anomalies

In addition to my Allison Bennett, there are eleven people in the -A record who aren't in -B. *Twelve people* disappeared from history.

Kaitlin O'Connell born 1990.02.13

Gracie Cuinn Webb born 2052.12.15

Haze Mei-yin Fong born 2067.09.30

Vee Kelly born 2070.12.21

Charles Belfast born 2071.03.04

Lora Elizabeth James born 2086.06.18

Noah Ibsen born 2096.01.18

Mouse Delacruz born 2101.04.01

Fontaine Solange Minot born 2109.10.09

Bel Raskin born 2134.11.17

Beck Raskin arrived 2150.05.24, birthdate unknown

The only major anomaly from -B log is the appearance of Sharrow Marie Gabler, born 2134.11.28 to Piers Dietrich and Wohl Gabler.

So Sharrow comes into existence, and a dozen people vanish from the histories, but I only noticed the one girl who shows up in my Detention. *Eff me.*

I copy my findings to the transfer drive, but I can't take the time to Liferep—I've already been here too long. My head's pounding, stomach roiling. I've got to get out before I vomit. Or worse.

I stagger to the door and grasp the handle, but it won't turn. I try again, but still nothing.

I can't get it open.

I'm hit with a wave of dizziness and my stomach rebels. I brace my hands on my knees and gravy, barely missing my feet. Propping myself against the wall, I try the handle again, but it's useless. The damn thing is stuck.

I hit the emergency button. But nothing happens.

What the mother-effing eff?

This makes no sense. The emergency is on a completely different relay from the door—they should never both be null sametime. Unless the ASPs discovered us. But that doesn't make sense either—the regular lights are still on. What am I missing?

I try the door again, but the room is closing in, my peripheral vision going dark.

No, I can't pass out. I can't die in here.

I pound on the door, even though no one will hear me. Then my knees turn to pulp and the floor rushes up at me.

CHAPTER NINE

I float in my body as Calix and Sharrow work on it. I don't care what they're doing to me. It's a brand-new feeling, this not caring. I like it. Mostly.

The thing is, I *should* care. I should be worried. I should be *terrified*.

I grab onto that spark. But it's no fun. It would be so easy to let go of it.... So I do, letting the empty floaty feeling swallow me.

"Tunes?" I hear Sharrow ask.

"Nat," Calix says. "Jeronemy?"

"Perf."

Music eases into my awareness like a soft breeze. Some sort of synth. A voice but no words, at least not that I recognize. It's like the voice is one of the instruments.

I look up at Calix. How could I have thought his face was gruesome? It's perfect. It's beautiful. His eyes...I want to swim in them. No, not swim. I want to dance.

So I do.

I open myself to the music and let it take me where it will.

Calix smiles at me. "Phee, isn't it?"

Phee. Fee, fi, fo, fum, I smell the blood of an Englishman.

I giggle and it tickles in my stomach.

I close my eyes and dissolve into the music.

MUSIC. A deep pounding beat. It makes my head throb. I want to cover my ears, but my arms weigh four thousand pounds.

Why won't my eyes open? And why does my tongue feel like sandpaper?

"*Allie.*"

Is that real or in my head?

"Allie, open your eyes."

I'm voting real. I need to open my eyes. It shouldn't be hard. I focus all my energy on my eyelids.

There's a scraping sensation and then there's light. The music stops, but there's still a faint pounding in my skull.

A shadow. A hand comes into view.

Cool, soothing liquid slides over my eyeballs. I blink and green hair comes into focus. It's mint-girl...Sparrow. No, Sharrow.

"Drink," she says.

I feel a straw part my lips. I suck and water bathes my mouth in glorious wet. I keep drinking until she takes it away.

"Did you have a good trip?" she asks.

I'm confused. Where did I go?

"Let's get you sitting up."

There's a soft whir and I feel the bed move, pivoting my body into a sitting position. I can see the room now and I remember—they gave me drugs, they did stuff to me. What did they do?

I look down, relieved to find a sheet covering my nakedness. I can feel my body now. I'm back in it. I wiggle my toes and I see the sheet move—thank God.

"What—?" My voice comes out a croak.

Sharrow puts the straw back in my mouth.

I swallow and try again. "What did you do to me?"

"Nothing invasive. But you thought we were trying to kill you." She laughs. It's a nice sound. "All we did was routine tests."

"So did I pass?"

She grins. "I don't know. You seem healthy to me." Despite her smile, her eyes seem sad. I feel like I should know why.

"Did you do genetic testing? Do I have any relatives in this time?"

"Only Bel. She's your half sister. Weirdly, she's also *my* half sister—same mom."

Sharrow doesn't look too happy about that. *That's right.* She found out about Bel—that's why she's sad.

"It's funny," she continues. "I've always been an only child, then suddenly I have a sister my age."

"I grew up an only child, too. Me and my mom. I only found out about Bel..." How long has it been? "About a week ago." It feels like a lot longer.

"Do you think you're up to walking? I'm supposed to get you moving as soon as possible."

"I can try. You promise you're not going to kill me?"

She laughs again, and this time her face lightens a little. "I promise."

I look around but don't see a guard. Maybe they've decided they can trust me. Or maybe there's a guard hidden by hologram, or a surveillance system that shoots tranquilizer darts.

Sharrow pulls back my sheet and I'm totally naked. My instinct is to cover up, but I remember Bel acting like it was no big, so I try to pretend I don't care.

"Welcome back." *A man's voice.*

I snatch the sheet back over me as the man with the tendon face comes around the bed. The doctor.

I remember him. It makes me warm, and a little embarrassed.

"Feeling better?" He smiles at me with his perfect teeth.

I shrug, and it's strange, like my shoulders aren't used to doing what I ask. "I'm okay."

"You passed your physical," he says. "Now we need to get you on your feet."

"We were about to do that," Sharrow says, holding out her hand. "Ready?"

"Uhhh, *no.*" They want me to stand buck naked in front of him? I mean, he is a doctor, but I still don't feel right about it. I clutch the sheet to my chest.

"What's wrong?" Sharrow asks.

"I changed my mind." I look from her to Calix and back.

"Are you feeling dizzy? Sick to your stomach?" she asks.

I shake my head.

"Privacy," Calix says. "She's not comfortable with her body."

"Hey!" I say, insulted. "My body's fine. I'd just rather have a robe or something."

"We don't have robes," Sharrow says. "But you can wrap the sheet around you."

How am I supposed to wrap the sheet around me without exposing myself first?

"I'll step out," Calix says. "Let me know if you start to feel ill, affirm?"

I nod and watch him leave, then stand and wrap myself in the sheet. I'm a little wobbly, but not too bad.

"See if you can walk to the desk," Sharrow says. "I'll be right beside you."

I walk to the desk and back, feeling more like myself with each step.

"Good, you're doing great," Sharrow says. "How about we try a bath? That always helps shake off the gloops."

"The gloops?"

"That's what I call it when I come out from under the drugs."

"You've had them, too?"

"Of course. As medical practitioners, we have to experience all drugs and procedures before we admin them to others. It's part of training."

That makes a lot of sense. I like that.

She walks ahead of me, puts her hand on the blank wall, and a door opens. I follow her into a bathroom. This time it's an actual *bath* room with a glass tub. The sink and toilet are in a wall shelf, like in Detention.

"You can use the toilet while I draw the water," Sharrow says.

"Uhhh....sure." I walk to the toilet and sit down, with only my sheet for privacy. It's not like I haven't peed in front of other girls, but this is awkward. What changed to make a future where everyone is naked in front of each other?

I head to the tub, thinking it's pretty cool that it's clear. Except that means no privacy. Shocker.

I grab the handrail to steady myself as I climb up three

steps. At the top there's a white towel draped over the rail. I drop the sheet and lower myself into the warm water.

The tub is contoured to my back, like it was made for me, and the hot water is amazing. I already feel my body relaxing.

Sharrow hands me a bar of soap. "Let me know if you need anything else."

I reach up and touch my tangled mass of hair. "Shampoo? Conditioner?"

"The bar works for everything."

She goes to the side of the room and holds her hand up to the wall. The wall opens and a platform slides out with a vanity, a mirror, and a cushioned bench. She sits on the bench and angles herself to the side so she's not looking at me directly or via the mirror. I guess she's giving me as much privacy as she can while making sure I don't drown.

I dunk under the water to wet my head, then suds up the bar and rub it in my hair. I dunk again to rinse, then lean back against the tub as my worries and responsibilities bubble up in my mind.

Top on the list is finding Bel. It's not that I'm worried about her. It's that I don't trust her. At some point, Dietrich will let her time-travel, and I need to make sure she doesn't leave me behind.

As good as the bath feels, I have to get to work.

I climb out and dry off, then wrap the towel around me.

Sharrow motions me over to the vanity. "I have a jumper for you."

Ugh. Can't I wear jeans? After 1906, I'm sick of dresses. Even a ski racer bodysuit like Sharrow's would be better than a jumper.

"I guessed on size, but it's stretchy." She hands me a gray wad of slippery fabric.

I unroll it. Apparently a "jumper" is a bodysuit. I should be more careful what I wish for.

Sharrow takes my towel. I angle my body away from her, step into the suit and slide it on. It's tight, but not uncomfortable.

"No bra?" I won't miss the corset, but I can't imagine not wearing a bra, especially with this tight leotard thing.

"Don't need it. Pull the zipper all the way up. You'll see."

I zip the suit up to my neck and it squeezes my torso—like it's *actively* constricting. "What the..." The squeezing stops, and the suit feels supportive, but still comfortable. I guess they got some things right in the future. I wonder what the shoes are going to be like.

"Would you like some help with your hair? It looks pretty tangled."

"Sure, okay." I'm anxious to get to Bel, but walking around with a tangled mop of wet hair is probably not necessary.

I sit at the vanity. Sharrow accesses a keypad on the vanity surface, then there's a buzzing above me. I look up and see a square panel descending toward my head.

"What's that?" I ask, trying not to sound alarmed.

"The dryer."

It stops a foot above me and blows warm air down.

Sharrow pulls a comb from a drawer and starts working on the knots. It feels like a million years ago that Vee and Haze were doing my hair at the Palace Hotel. It's impossible that it's barely been one day. My heart clenches at the memory, but I channel that into resolve. I'm going to fix this. I'm going to get them all back.

"Thanks, this is good," I say, pulling away from Sharrow. "I need to talk to Bel."

She holds the comb mid-air. "Your hair's still wet."

"It's fine. Besides, it hurts behind my left ear." I rub the spot and feel a lump. I don't remember bumping my head.

"Oh, I forgot to tell you," Sharrow says. "That's your implant. The swelling should go down by tomorrow."

"*You put an implant in me?*"

"It transmits your location and vitals. It's not integrated or anything." She says this like it's normal.

"Back up. What did you do to me? And why?" I probe the spot with my fingers, but don't feel any stitches.

"The implant is harmless. We all have them. Please don't be upset."

"Too late. You shouldn't have done that without my permission. And what did you say about it being *integrated?*" I don't like the sound of that.

"I said it's *not* integrated. Some implants are tied into brainwaves that enable them to communicate non-verbally with tech, like your personal. But not everyone has that. You don't. I don't."

"Brainwaves communicate with *what?*"

"Tech. Like the personal communication device." She holds out her arm, showing me her wrist.

"What am I looking at?" I don't see anything but her skin and the sleeve of her mint-green suit.

She touches her wrist with her other hand and a watch becomes visible as she's removing it. "When it's clasped, it camouflages to whatever it's touching. You get one of your own."

"Seriously?"

She returns hers to her wrist, and it vanishes. "Come on, let's get yours."

I follow her out of the bathroom and perch on the edge of a bed while she grabs something from a cabinet.

She brings over a silvery iridescent watch-like device with a blank face about three inches square. The band shimmers as it bends, like a translucent eel writhing in her hand.

"It goes on your right arm," she says.

I hold out my wrist and she encircles it with the band. I feel a snap, then it tightens and morphs to the color of my skin.

"Freaky." I hold my arm out and squint. Since I know the device is there, I can sorta see the ghost of an outline, or maybe that's my imagination. I run my fingers over it.

"Don't take it off, even in the shower," she says. "You'll need it everywhere you go."

Why would I need a watch I can't see... "Oh! This how you open doors and stuff, isn't it? I thought the sensors were reading your handprints."

She smiles. "Your personal is how you gain access to everything, plus you can use it to communicate and to get info. Like, say I want to know where my boyfriend is." She taps the inside of her wrist. "Where is Flyx?"

She holds her wrist out so I can read the message: STARS.

"He's in the stars?" I ask.

She lets out a tinkle of a laugh. "No, that stands for Sequestered Time-log and Review Station. Where he works. But he's not supposed to be on duty right now." She frowns for a microsecond. "But I'm sure it's nothing sally. Here, I'll show you another use—I can message him."

She taps on the device twice and then opens her hand. A keyboard, glowing blue, is projected on her palm. The fingers of her left hand fly across the keys, and letters appear in the display. "stil mtg fr dnr? thers smone I wnt u 2 mt"

I blink and the jumble of letters transforms: *Still meeting for dinner? There's someone I want you to meet.*

The message vanishes and "sent" appears on the display.

"You can also dictate-record." She taps her wrist once. "Tag Flyx." There's a faint beep. "My new friend is Allie. We'll be at the Donut Shoppe, then at the club." After a moment, it shows "sent" like the last one. "Phee, right? Now you try. Ask it a question."

For a girl who's never had a smart phone, this is some serious bling. "Okay...what do I do?"

"Tap it once on the face—the inside of your wrist. Then say your question out loud."

I'm about ask where Bel is, but realize I'd have no idea how to get there. Instead I tap and say, "What year is it?"

"2153" is displayed on the inside of my wrist.

Oh my God, is it really 2153?

CHAPTER TEN

I t's 2153. 2153.
    A shiver ripples through me. I knew I was in the future, but somehow the exact year makes it more real.

"2153..." I say, not really a question.

Sharrow smiles. "Affirm."

"What's it like? Are there flying cars?"

"I wish. It's not that exciting. But I'll show you around. We can head to the Donut Shoppe right now."

"Hells to the yes!" There's no reason I can't eat something before finding Bel, especially if that something is a maple bar.

"I guess that means you want to go?" She grins. "Come on, I'll show you how to bank the personal, though yours isn't going to work for much yet. Until they reset your parameters, you'll need me to get around. My mom made me your auditor."

"What's that, like a babysitter?"

She frowns and a little crease forms between her eyes. "Sure, I guess. Bel, too."

"You have to babysit her, too?"

"No, *she's* been assigned to *you*. We're both supposed to help you get adjusted. Come on, we'll meet her at the Donut Shoppe."

Yes.

"Here's how you open doors." Sharrow puts her hand to the wall about shoulder height near the door, and the door opens to the green waiting room.

I start to walk, then realize— "Don't I need shoes?"

"Sorry, I forgot. Wait here." She jogs across the treatment room and disappears into the bathroom.

The door to the waiting room is still open. I could walk out of here.... I peer across to the outer door. Will my personal open it? If it does...

I step into the waiting room, and the door closes behind me. Crap! Sharrow's going to know I tried to leave. Although I didn't. Not really. It was more like instinct. Logically, I know Bel is my ticket back home, but apparently no one told my legs.

I hold my personal device up beside the door to the treatment room, but of course it doesn't work. Crap, crap, crap!

I look around, and the waiting room chairs are the only things there. I run over and sit in one as the treatment room door slides open. I cross my legs and try to look casual.

Sharrow doesn't look pleased. "I asked you to wait."

"Sorry. I figured I'd need to sit to put on the shoes. I didn't even think about the door closing. Then I couldn't open it again."

"Like I said, your access is limited. So if I tell you not to move, don't move. You don't want to get on the wrong side of a door."

I sense this is metaphor as well as literal. "Sorry. I won't do it again," I say, intending to heed her warning, though I know myself better than that.

Sharrow's expression softens. "I forgot to ask what size shoe you wear, but I don't think it matters." She holds out socks the same gray as my jumper.

I take them. "Where are the shoes?"

"That's all you've been auth for now."

"I'm supposed to walk around in socks?"

She laughs. "Slips are a little more than socks. They're adaptive to give support, like your jumper."

I pull the socks on. They squeeze my feet lightly and feel pretty good, though they don't seem good for going outside. Maybe that's the point—to keep me from trying to leave.

We cross the squishy green floor. Sharrow holds her hand to the wall, and the door swishes open. Stepping into the gray hallway, Sharrow turns left, the opposite direction I came from with Dietrich.

"What's the deal with these hallways?" I ask as we turn left down another passage. "Like, did you guys build them or were they part of the original BART system?"

"I have no idea."

Well that's helpful. I try again. "So how do you know your way around down here when it all looks the same?"

"Habit? I don't know. I never really thought about it."

Wow, I hardly know what to do with all this useful info.

We stop at another closed door and I sigh, expecting to enter yet another gray hallway. Instead, the door opens to a much larger passage covered in graffiti. The color feels like rain after a drought. We step through the doorway onto cement, and I feel the cold through my socks.

"Almost there," Sharrow says as we head to the right.

All I can think is that Bel had better know her way around this place or I'm going to need an ally who does.

"This is it," Sharrow says, pointing to Donut Shoppe spray-painted bold amidst the other graffiti. Beside it is an artistic rendering of a donut and a steaming cup.

I'm caught off guard, remembering the flyer with the steaming cup of coffee that Jake made for his aunt's café. I'd give anything to be sitting at that café with him right now.

Quickly I shove down thoughts of Jake. They only make me sad, and I can't do sad.

Sharrow puts her hand near the drawing of the mug, and a big rectangle of the wall slides away, making a doorway.

"How do you know where to touch?" I ask, squinting at the wall. "Can you see a panel or something?"

"No, you have to memorize where to bank the personal. Basically if you can see the door, or know where it is, the masks are always to the right at about this height." She holds her hand at shoulder level. "You'll get used to it. After fumbling around like a dimmy for a bit."

We go inside, and the door swishes shut behind us. I turn to see if it disappeared, but on this side, I can see it plainly.

I follow Sharrow while scoping out the place. With a name like "Donut Shoppe," I expected a retro 1950s coffee shop or an ultra-modern interpretation of one. This is more like a factory—large open room, cement walls and floors, high ceiling laced with pipes and ducts and lights. Machines line three walls like metal soldiers. Sharrow heads to the left wall where a couple of people are filling bottles.

So...vending machines? It's definitely not a restaurant, that's for sure. No hostess station. No menus. Absolutely no smell of food. I'd never guess this was a place to eat, except for the cafeteria-style tables and chairs down the center. The whole thing is dreary as heck.

The people are subdued, too, scattered in clumps, hunched over trays. Their bodysuits—jumpers—are in a variety of solid colors, but that's the only non-gray in the whole place.

"Is Bel here already?" I scan for her red hair.

Sharrow consults her personal. "Not yet. Hungry?"

"I could *eat*," I say, with the emphasis on *eat* as I eyeball the people filling bottles. "Please tell me you have something that's actually food."

Sharrow looks puzzled, then her eyebrows shoot up. "Oh! You're not a fan of the liquid nutrition."

"It's not my favorite," I say. "But I could go for a donut."

"There *is* food, but the donut thing is a joke. Some old-timer thought he was being clever."

"Very funny. *Not*."

"Whoever named this place was sadistic," Sharrow says. "But there is carrot cake."

"Any chance there's tacos?"

"Of course."

Yes! I've never had a taco from a vending machine, but there's no way it's worse than the drink I tasted in Detention.

"You'll want to stay clear of this section." Sharrow indicates the machines along the left wall. "This is all liquid nutrition. The solids are over there."

These people sure know how to make things sound appetizing.

I follow her to the bank of machines along the right wall, which don't look any different.

"Tacos, right?" Sharrow bellies up to one of the larger machines. "I'll do mine, then you can have a go."

There's a touch-screen like I've seen at the newer Micky D's. The items displayed are tacos and burritos. Sharrow chooses taco, hard shell, quantity two. On the next screen her options are bovine protein, poultry protein, vegetable protein. She selects bovine.

Ew. "Why doesn't it just say 'beef'?"

"Because technically it's not beef."

"Okaaaay. What is it?"

"It's lab-grown bovine tissue that approximates the nutritive composition of beef. No actual cows are involved."

Bovine tissue? Gross. Vegetable protein sounds infinitely better.

On the next screen is a checklist of toppings, most of which I recognize, like lettuce and onions. But some of the stuff only sounds food*ish*—cheddar dairy composite, soured non-dairy cream, mixed vegetable matter. She presses the button that says "all." Not the choice I'd have made. Maybe it masks the bovine flavor.

The machine whirs and clicks. She taps her toe, waiting.

I realize I didn't notice where she put her personal up to the machine. "Where do you access it?"

"The touch-screen."

"It detects your personal?"

Sharrow gives me the side eye. "Why would it?"

"So they can debit your account or whatever?"

"They don't track that. They don't track any resources—clothes, showers, accs, equip. When resources run low, there's an announcement and everyone reduces. Besides, nothing's ever wasted. All the food, water, and printable compounds are recycled and reused."

Double gross.

The machine ejects a plate with two tacos, and Sharrow takes it.

"Your turn," she says.

"On second thought, I'll just have that carrot cake."

Sharrow shrugs. "Fine by me."

I follow her past machines whose touchscreens show pictures of pasta, stir-fry, sandwiches, salads, and various stew and soup options that look seriously disgusting. Along the back wall are more drink dispensers and a cold-case of snacks and desserts. Sharrow points to a row of plastic boxes with cake slices in them, and I grab one.

"Want some kombucha?" she asks.

I look to see if she's joking. She's not.

"No thanks. Ever," I say, also not joking. That stuff's nasty in any year. "Water would be good, though." *Hopefully.* Not sure about the whole recycling thing.

She hands me an empty plastic cup and shows me how to access the water dispenser. Then she grabs a cup for herself and fills it with brown sludge I can smell three feet away.

I take a fork—also plastic—and some napkins from containers on the counter, and we head to an empty table. The people we pass all look more or less our age. They stare at me while trying not to look like they're staring. Sharrow ignores them, so I do, too.

At the table, Sharrow plops her plate down and sits. I take the spot facing her.

"I'm starving." She picks up a taco and takes a giant bite.

I hear the crunch of the shell and watch her cheeks bulge as she chews, and I have to admit I'm a little jealous.

Or at least I would be if I knew the taco actually tasted like a taco.

I remove the plastic lid from the cake and scrape off a bit of white icing with my fork. It tastes okay. It's pretty much like any day-old cafeteria cream cheese icing, but I can't help wondering if it's some sort of non-dairy lab-grown composite-thing instead of actual cream cheese. I fork a bite of the cake. Also not terrible.

Sharrow's polished off one of the tacos. I scope the other one. It *looks* like a normal taco.

She sees me eyeing it. "Change your mind? You're welcome to it."

"I...don't know." How long am I going to be in 2153? If it's more than a few days, I'm going to have to eat something besides cake.

"Try it." She slides the plate across the table. "I'm dying to know if it tastes like actual animal flesh."

Animal flesh. She makes it sound more disgusting than lab-grown bovine protein.

"You've never had...*animal* before?" I ask, considering the taco.

"Nope, never."

"The world doesn't have animals anymore?" Geez, what's happened since 2018?

"The world has animals. We just don't eat them."

I sniff the taco and I'm flooded with memories of taco night at Bibi's house with all the girls talking and squabbling, rug-rats fussing, dishes clanking. My traitorous stomach growls.

"Oh, what the heck," I say, grabbing the taco and taking a small bite. So far not gross. I chew, letting the flavors cascade over my tongue.

Sharrow leans toward me. "Well?"

"Tastes like a taco." I take another bite, this time my usual mouthful.

"But does it taste like cow?"

"Sure, I guess," I say around the food in my mouth. "As much as any taco actually tastes like beef." I wash it down with a swig of water. There's a slight chemically aftertaste like the water in the detention cell. Still infinitely better than kombucha.

I down the last of the taco, relieved. Whatever else has changed, at least there're still tacos.

"She's here." Sharrow points.

Bel's standing at the liquid nutrition machines. She turns, and our eyes meet. I can't tell if she's friend or foe. I clench my stomach, ready to do battle. I need to fight for all I'm worth to make her an ally or I'm seriously toast.

CHAPTER ELEVEN

B el comes toward us across the Donut Shoppe, strutting her curves in the gray jumper, make-up done, hair in flowing curls. When she arrives at the table, she tosses her hair back like some sort of supermodel. I snort, thinking how ridiculous I'd look if I tried that.

"*What?*" Bel looks down her nose at me.

"What?" Crap, she thinks I was snorting at her. Way to start off on the wrong foot. "Sorry, I didn't mean—"

"Whatever." Bel sits beside Sharrow and sets an opaque plastic bottle on the table. "All right, let's get this over with."

Sharrow's happy expression fades. I know the feeling.

"I guess, uh," Sharrow says. "We should make a plan."

"A plan for what?" I ask.

"My mom, I mean *our* mom," she glances at Bel, "said to show you around. I was thinking the club next. But I don't know what Bel wants to do."

"This whole thing is nox. I don't know why *I* have to do it." Bel takes a swig from her bottle.

Sharrow couldn't look more disappointed. "Mom said we should get to know each other."

Bel rolls her eyes.

Some things never change.

"Tell me about the club," I say with forced enthusiasm. "Bel, did you used to go there a lot? What's it like?"

"How should I know?"

I'm confused. "But this is your real time."

"Not hardly." Bel glances around the room, then back at her bottle.

Then I realize—since no one knows her now, she probably feels as out of place as I do. Maybe more. I almost feel sorry for her. Almost. More importantly, maybe I can use that.

I try again to get Bel to engage. "What's changed since you were here before?"

"I have no idea. I barely got here."

"Was this place the same?" I gesture to our surroundings, pretending not to notice her snotty tone. "Was it called the Donut Shoppe?"

"Affirm."

"And the liquid nutrition is the same, right? I mean you knew about it when we were in Detention," I say. "Are there are different flavors? Because the one I tried was naaaaasty."

Bel is silent, staring at the table.

"There are quite a few flavors," Sharrow says.

"I'd try it again if there's something closer to a strawberry shake." I imagine it—a super cold, thick strawberry milkshake—and my mouth waters.

"We used to have real strawberries," Sharrow says. "But something went wrong with the crop. We do have blackberries. They say they're hardier for growing down here or something. What about a blackberry shake?"

"You grow food down here? Underground?" I ask. "How?"

"Hydroponics, grow lights, fertilizer," Sharrow answers like it's normal. "There's a whole farm wing dedicated to producing as much protein and vegetable matter as possible. Of course, some things we have to get topside, but we keep it to bare minimum to maintain the illusion of only a dozen people living here."

"A farm wing? I'd love to see that. Wouldn't you, Bel?"

"Forget it. It's off limits for you, anyway."

"What *can* I see?" I remember the newspaper from 2152 that Beck showed me. "How about those synth-pets?"

"Pets?" Sharrow says. "We don't have animals down here."

"Not even robot ones?" I remember the picture of the Newfie dog robot.

"I wish," Sharrow says. "That would be phee. Do you have those in your time?"

"No, I..."

Bel shoots me a look that clearly says *stop talking about this*. I don't know why. But I go ahead and change the subject. "How about that club you mentioned?"

"Sure, if Bel—"

"Fine. Whatever," Bel says.

I catch Sharrow's eye and shrug. *Isn't it fun having a sister?*

"Where do we put this?" I ask, gathering trash from the table. "I expected it would be more environmentally conscious in the future, but there's a metric crap-ton of plastic."

"All the plastics get melted down and used to print new stuff," Sharrow says, picking up the remaining items.

"Still, it seems like such a waste," I say, following her away from the table.

"For most stuff it takes less energy to throw all the material in the processor than it would take to clean reusable items," Sharrow says. "Though there are some things we use more than once. Like drink bottles. We'll get you one later."

She shows me where to dump the recycling, then I turn to look for Bel. She's still at the table looking at her fingernails. She seems so sad and alone. But it won't last. Other things may have changed, but she's still the same Bel. I'd bet a hundred tacos she'll be Queen Bee in no time.

The three of us exit the Donut Shoppe into the graffitied tunnel.

"Up for a shortcut?" Sharrow asks, looking mischievous.

"Sure," I say.

"Whatever," Bel says.

We follow Sharrow—who's practically jogging—down the graffitied hallway. It opens into another BART station. I look for any indication of which station it is, but again, there are no signs. I'm about to ask Bel, but one look at her sour expression silences me.

Sharrow goes to the end of the platform and pulls something from a box on the wall. "Put these on." She hands gloves to me and Bel, then puts on a pair herself.

What the heck?

I follow her up a ladder and onto a catwalk that spans the trough where the trains used to go. She stops halfway across and faces the mouth of the tunnel. "Watch what I do, then count to ten and jump exactly the same way. One at a time." She takes a flying leap, her arms out like Superman.

I look below to see her zipping away on a giant slide.

"Sweet!" I turn to Bel. "You want to go next?"

"No."

"You are coming, though, right?"

She lets out a huge sigh. "Just go, already."

I completely forgot to count to ten, but I steel myself and leap. The landing on my stomach isn't comfortable, but I don't care—this is such a rush! The sides of the tunnel are flying past—there are lights overhead at intervals making a strobe effect. This is the coolest shortcut in the history of ever.

It's getting hot where my suit touches the slide. It's not exactly painful, *yet*. I hope the slide isn't much longer.

Ahead, I see a brighter area where Sharrow is standing off to one side, and I realize I have no idea how to stop. But before I can panic, the slide flattens out and I slow to a stop.

"That was amaze-balls!" I say, getting to my feet.

Sharrow grins, and we both laugh.

I peel off the gloves and look up the slide for Bel. "I hope she's coming."

"Me too." Sharrow takes my gloves and drops them in a box.

"So. I guess having a sister isn't all you imagined, huh?"

She smiles, but the smile doesn't go all the way to her eyes.

Bel arrives at the bottom of the slide, gets to her feet, and drops her gloves in the box without a word.

"Wasn't that cool?" I ask. "Did they have that in—"

"*Sluff it.*"

Sharrow's eyes go wide. "Okay, this way," she says, uber-cheerfully. She heads for the side and climbs the metal rungs to the platform

Bel and I follow. We're in another graffiti-covered tunnel. The art is crazy-cool. I think how much Jake would love it. Is it weird to miss someone who doesn't know you exist?

We're not in the graffitied tunnel long enough for my taste when Sharrow accesses a hidden door to yet another gray hallway. We traipse down it to an intersection with another gray hallway, and turn left. This hall is different—it has closed doors spaced regularly along either side, but nothing to indicate what this place was once used for. Offices, I'm guessing, or maybe back entrances to stores in a mall or something like that.

After a left turn at another intersection, I hear a faint beat, like faraway music playing with the bass cranked up. Now the closed doors flanking the hall each have little lights above them, some red, some green. The music gets louder the farther we go.

The hall dead ends in a door. It sounds like the music is coming from the other side.

Sharrow keys something on her personal, then looks from me to Bel. "It'll be crowded. Stay close."

Bel rolls her eyes. You think she'd be tired of that. I know I am.

Sharrow banks her personal, the door slides open, and the music hits me like a shockwave.

Bel and I follow her into a crowded room lit with black-light. Neon colors glow on the walls, like the graffiti in the tunnel, except these are *moving*, pulsing with the music. Even the floor—where I can see it between dancing feet— has undulating waves of pinks and greens.

The music isn't like anything I've ever heard. It's more like irregular, high-pitched wails than actual music. But beneath the wails, if you listen, there's more to it—a clinking, shaking rattle, another rhythm not quite as deep, and a top layer of bright background melody, with an accompanying harmony. It reminds me of when a foster mom took me to the symphony and all the different instruments were warming up at the same time.

We head directly onto the dance floor amidst the mass of gyrating bodies. I catch glimpses of lighted bracelets and glowing patterns on skin. It's a sec before I realize—their *tattoos* are glowing. Insane!

Despite the crowd, no one touches me as I pass, which seems to defy the odds, if not the laws of physics.

On the other side of the dance floor, we exit crazy-town into a seating area. I rub my eyes with my knuckles to clear away the after-images. There're a smattering of tables down the middle. Couches and booths on the perimeter. The lights aren't strobing, and the music's not as loud. I feel like I can breathe again.

I stick close behind Sharrow as she weaves through the tables on a mission. Some tables are occupied, and it's hard not to stare at the glowing tattoos. Sharrow glances back at me, and I notice her freckles and eyeliner glowing iridescent green. It looks like her pink lips have a faint glow, too. Does that mean her eyeliner and lip gloss are tattooed on?

I feel so plain—I swear I'm the only one without lit ink. Then I look back at Bel, and she's not glowing. I wonder if the tattoo thing is new since her time.

Sharrow stops at a corner booth and puts her hands on her hips.

"What the soot?" she says to the empty booth. "Where is he?"

"Who?" I ask.

"Flyx. My boyfriend. I haven't been able to reach him all day, but I assumed he'd meet me here as planned."

"Stood up, huh?" Bel says. "Shocker."

Sharrow bursts into tears and runs away.

"Sharrow, wait!" I call.

"Let her go." Bel slides into the booth. "She'll be back."

"Why'd you have to be so mean?" I scoot in on the opposite side of the table.

"If she thought *that* was mean, she needs to toughen the flick up."

"I know you can be *meaner*. But why be mean at all? She's your sister. She just wants to get to know you."

"Whatever."

I don't know why I even bother. It's not like knowing *I'm* her sister makes any difference.

"Let's at least take advantage of this time," I say. "Tell me what the plan is."

"What plan?

"Going back to 1906. When do we leave?"

"My mom said I can't go until after this inspection or whatever."

"How long is that going to take?"

"What's your hurry? It's not like it matters."

"What are you talking about? We have to hurry—"

"*Hello.* Time travel."

"But—"

Her words rattle around in my brain. The earthquake that killed the crew happened more than two hundred years ago. Does it make any difference if we leave now or in a week? Or a month? We can still go back to before the building fell, before Bel shot Maxen. So I guess I have to admit logically that Bel's right—it doesn't matter when we leave. But my gut refuses to agree.

CHAPTER TWELVE

I lean across the table toward Bel so I don't have to shout over the noise of the club. "I still want to go back as soon as possible."

"Enough, she's coming."

Sharrow arrives at the side of the booth, the wisps of hair at her temples damp, like she splashed water on her face. "We can get out of here," she says.

Bel gets up without meeting Sharrow's gaze. I had a tiny hope Bel would apologize. Right.

I smile at Sharrow as I slide out of the booth. I'm about to ask if she's okay, but it looks like she might dissolve into tears again, so I don't say anything.

Instead of weaving back through the tables, Sharrow leads us in the opposite direction, away from the dance floor, to an alcove with a couple of low couches. From the looks of it, this is the front entrance. We must have entered through the back door.

On the other side of the door is yet another hallway, this one with white walls, white ceiling, blue-gray indoor-outdoor carpet, and florescent lighting. It's completely generic, like it could be any office building, anywhere, any time. On the plus side, at least it's not gray.

Sharrow stops at a junction with three other hallways branching out. "Sleeping quarters?" she asks. "Unless there's something else you want to see."

"Fine by me." I'm exhausted. The last time I slept in a bed was in 1906.

"You coming?" Sharrow asks Bel.

"I don't exactly have a choice. I don't have my own room now." There's a determined edge to Bel's voice that tells me it probably won't be long before she remedies the situation.

We head down the right-most hallway, passing more closed doors. I'd kill for a sign to clue me where we are. We could be in the basement of a high-rise in the Financial District or an office building in SoMa, for all I know.

"This is a lav," Sharrow says, pointing to a normal-looking door with an actual doorknob. "There's a shower room you can access from inside the sleep room."

She continues down the hall, past other real doors, which she ignores. At the end, she banks her personal and an invisible door slides away, revealing a large, low-ceilinged room. The walls are lined with metal lockers, like a gym locker room. The middle of the room is filled with single beds—maybe forty or fifty—mostly empty.

"Welcome to the Mids' quarters," Sharrow says.

"What are mids?" I look at Bel—she's wrinkling her nose.

"People ranging from age ten to twenty," Sharrow says. "There are other sleeping quarters for twenty-plusses, one for parents with juvies, and another for olders."

At Bibi's, there were shared rooms, but nothing like this. "You don't live with your families?"

"Not after age ten," Sharrow says, like I asked if she still wears diapers. "Centralized communal living is tons more efficient than duplicating functional spaces for cooking, sleeping, etcetera." This sounds rehearsed, like propaganda. She checks her personal. "Okay, you're in beds thirteen and fourteen. Not far from mine."

Without a word or glance, Bel heads into the room like she knows where she's going.

Sharrow and I exchange a glance. Mine is meant to convey "Sorry she's such a bitch." I'm guessing Sharrow's means something like "Yeah, I know."

"Over here," Sharrow says, heading for the left side of the room. "Your locker corresponds to your bed number. Thirteen."

"Lucky thirteen," I say ironically. "Lucky me."

"Is that unlucky in your time, too? I guess some things don't change. But Bel claimed fourteen, so you're cement."

She pulls open the door to locker thirteen. The inside is bare except for a stack of gray clothing I'm assuming's more jumpers, and a second stack in soft turquoise. Sharrow pulls the top article off the turquoise stack and hands it to me. "This is your sleeping singlet."

"Where do I change?"

"Right here. Bin your dirty jumper by the door." She points to a receptacle by the door we came in.

I wonder what happened to those self-cleaning fabrics I saw in Beck's newspaper—I'd much rather not strip naked in front of a bunch of strangers. But I tell myself to get over it. No one here cares.

"My locker's twenty-four." She points to the back wall. "I'm going to get changed, too."

She turns away, but I need to say something.

"Sharrow?"

She turns back. "Yeah?"

"I'm sorry about Bel. I know it's weird to suddenly have a sister, especially one like her."

"The worst part is having to share my mom." She looks pained.

"I get it. I mean Bel and I share a dad I barely know, so that's not the same. But if I had to share my mom..."

"I'll get used to it. Not like I have a choice." She gives a shallow smile and heads away.

My heart aches for her. And for me. With just that one mention of my mom, the image of her popped in my mind clear as a photo—my young mom in 1906, so vibrant and in love. The image morphs into her standing under the falling bricks as the building came down. Her life—and my history —ending in an instant. Thanks to Bel.

Molten rage fills my stomach. I feel the pressure building. If we can't get back to 1906 to save them, it's going to erupt all over Bel, and I won't be sorry to watch her burn.

I turn toward my open locker so my back's to the room, peel off my bodysuit, and step into the singlet. It's softer than the jumper, sleeveless, and only goes to my knees. I grab the jumper off the floor, then close my locker to see a face staring at me.

A *guy*. The one with the blue hair.

"Hey," he says. "I don't know if you recog. I'm Daum."

"Yeah, what are you doing here?" I hug the jumper to my chest, realizing he was probably right there while I changed.

He looks confused. "Uh, getting ready for bed?"

I'm an idiot. I'd assumed it was all girls. My cheeks burn and I know my face is red.

He points at the jumper I'm clutching. "I can bin that for you."

"Sure, thanks." I hand it over, then feel really exposed.

It's not like the singlet gives much coverage. I fold my arms over my chest.

"Sorry about before. In Detention. Wish I could have done more."

"It's okay."

"Well...'night." He heads away.

After a moment he glances back, gives a little wave. I wave back. I guess it's not so different from passing a boy in the hall at the school lockers. Except for the naked part.

I spot Sharrow in the middle of the room with Bel. I head toward them, not looking at the occupied beds. Even if they don't care about privacy, I can at least be respectful.

"I'm sorry," I hear Sharrow whisper. "It wasn't up to me. Do you want me to message Ops and see what other beds are open?"

"Forget it," Bel says, in her loud whisper. "It's not like you can actually do anything to fix this. I'll right everything tomorrow with Mom." She huffs to Bed 14.

I look at Sharrow and shrug. "Sorry."

"Don't apologize for me!" Bel snaps.

"Shhh!" someone scolds.

"Sluff off!" Bel retorts.

Sharrow winces. She looks mortified.

I grasp her shoulder to give it a squeeze. She startles and I pull my hand back. "Sorry, I didn't mean to—"

"It's okay," she whispers. "It surprised me."

For as open as they are about changing clothes and peeing in front of each other, apparently personal space is different. At least for Sharrow. "I'm sorry," I whisper back. Seems all I do is apologize.

"No, it's my fault. I should have told you when I gave you the personal."

"Told me what?"

"Before touching someone, we ask for consent, and register it on the personal."

"You do *what?*"

"Hold out your right hand."

She extends her right hand and grasps my forearm, placing our personal devices next to each other. "Consent to contact?"

"Uh...yes?"

"You have to say 'I consent.'"

I nod. "Okay, I consent."

There's a quiet beep.

"There," she says, letting go. "We're good for casual. We'd have to get consent again for anything intimate. And if we go more than five feet apart, it resets and we have to do it over."

"Okay...." This is bizarre. But in a way it makes sense this would evolve after so many issues with people getting groped and date raped and stuff. And it totally explains why I walked untouched across the dance floor. "I'll definitely ask now that I know. And thanks for everything you've done. I really appreciate it."

"No prob." She glances behind me, and I follow her gaze back to Bel's red head poking out from under the covers. "Set your alarm for oh-eight-thirty so we have time for breakfast."

"Um, how do I do that?"

"Shhhh!" someone says.

"Never mind, I'll wake you," Sharrow whispers. "Goodnight."

"'Night."

I pull back the covers of Bed 13 and slide under. The sheets feel like they're made of the same stuff as my suit. I turn on my side and shut my eyes, trying to ignore the homesick feeling prickling behind my eyelids, but failing.

"ALLIE. ALLIE, WAKE UP."

I bury my face in my pillow.

"Allie, you're going to be late."

"Bibi, it's Saturday."

"*Allie, wake up!*"

I roll over and squint against the light. *Crap. It's not Bibi.*

"I've been trying to wake you for twenty minutes," Sharrow says.

"Why didn't you shake me or something?" I ask, rubbing my eyes.

"Consent, remember? Come on, I've got your jumper. Hurry, or we're going to be late."

"Late for what?" I roll out of bed and follow her.

"Testing."

"The doctor said I passed."

"That was only the physical." She activates a door in the back wall and we enter a bathroom with multiple sinks, toilets, and shower stalls.

"Wait, I could still get recycled?" *Now* I'm awake.

"That's an affirm. Sorry."

"Bel, too?"

"No, she's in the clear."

"What? That's not fair. Where is she, anyway?"

"Gone when I woke up. Come on, you need to change. No time to shower," she says, handing me a gray jumper.

I take off my singlet, forcing myself to keep my gaze on

the floor. If there are other people—guys—in here, I don't want to know. I step into the jumper and zip it to my chin.

Sharrow tosses my singlet in a basket then pushes a button on the counter. "Two toothbrushes, vanilla cleanser." There are mechanical sounds in the cabinet, then a drawer pops open. Inside are two toothbrushes, bristles up, each with a perfect line of white paste. She takes one and holds it under the faucet, which automatically turns on.

I grab the other toothbrush and use the next faucet over. As I brush, I can't help flashing on the bathroom at Bibi's with all the preggers girls and baby mamas crowded along the counter brushing teeth and washing faces. For a moment, the sadness feels like it's going to swallow me.

When Sharrow finishes, she inserts the toothbrush into a slot marked with a recycling symbol. I spit, rinse, and do the same, then make the mistake of glancing in a mirror —*ugh*. I try to smooth my hair as we exit.

Sharrow power-walks through the room ahead of me. I catch up as she reaches the door.

"No time for breakfast?" I'd kill for a cup of coffee—or whatever they have with caffeine.

"Nope. You'll have to settle for liquid nutrition."

"There wouldn't be something like coffee, would there?"

She turns to me with a broad smile. "Now I know we can be friends."

CHAPTER THIRTEEN

"We've only got about two minutes before you're late," Sharrow says as we head away from the drink station.

I quicken my pace and slosh coffee from my newly issued bottle down the front of my jumper. It's so hot it stings, so I pull the front of the jumper out, away from my skin. Perfect. It'll be stained *and* stretched out when it dries. That'll go great with my hair.

We race down an access tunnel and emerge in a corridor I don't recognize. Sharrow rushes to a blank wall and opens a door. I hurry through behind her.

The room is small and very purple, with lavender walls and a dark plum couch. One wall has a big white circle painted on it.

And sitting on the couch—

"Bel? I thought you passed already," I say.

"Nafe. I'm *giving* the testing." She's not wearing a gray jumper like yesterday. Instead, her bodysuit is sapphire blue, and has a flouncy miniskirt attached. Her hair is styled with a swoop of bangs tucked behind her ear, and her nails are the same blue as her jumper. I note with some jealousy she's wearing chunky navy blue patent leather boots.

She looks me up and down and crinkles her nose. Yep, I know I look snazzy.

Bel turns to Sharrow. "You can go."

"It's okay, I don't mind—"

"I said *go*."

"Okay." Sharrow looks at me, and I see how crushed she is. "I guess I'll see you later, Allie." She steps out and the door hisses shut.

I turn on Bel. "You didn't have to do that."

"Sluff it. You have more important things to worry about."

"What I'm worried about is getting out of here. Did you find out how long the inspections will take?"

"I told you, time makes absolutely no difference. So ease out."

"But—"

"If you're going put me in traction about it, I'll have my mom send you back to Detention. Or recycle you. Doesn't matter to me."

"You'd do that?" I don't know why I ask. I know she would.

"If you relax and don't cause me any heartburn, you can stick around and see what the future is like. Or you can go the other way."

"I'll take Option A. But if I'm 'giving you heartburn,'" I say with air quotes, "then why not let Sharrow do my testing?"

"Reasons."

"What reasons?"

She rolls her eyes. "Not that it's any of yours, but I have things to research, and here no one looks over my shoulder."

She didn't have to tell me that. Maybe this is progress. "Can we start now? Does that meet with your approval?" Without waiting for my answer, she banks her personal to the right of the white circle. It splits down the middle, the two halves slide apart, and she goes through.

I follow her into more purple—a lilac classroom with long fuchsia tables topped with white computers. The chairs are standard armless metal chairs, if you don't count the purple plaid fabric on the seats. It's all or nothing with these people—plain gray or crazy color. There's soft background noise that sounds kinda like the ocean. I'm guessing it's supposed to be relaxing, but it puts me on edge.

"Sit," Bel says.

"Anywhere?"

Again she rolls her eyes.

Fine. I pull out the nearest chair and sit facing the computer screen.

"Pay attention to the vid-histories. You need to know this stuff." She trounces to a lone desk at the front of the room and sits at the computer like she's the teacher.

I scope the keyboard, relieved it's similar to what I'm used to—QWERTY layout with some weird keys across the top. There's no mouse or trackpad, so I press "enter," then glance back up at Bel. She's already engrossed in whatever's on her screen. I wonder what she's up to.

I look back at my own screen, which now displays "2025" in white on a purple background. Then a video begins. It looks like a protest rally. It's weird there's no sound. Then I realize there are headphones in a cubby of the desk. Duh. I put them over my ears.

In the mid-2020s, the Nazi movement existed in small, independent pockets, primarily underground. Though they occasionally came together in public rallies under the banner of "Nationalism," they weren't an organized entity, and were never viewed as a political power.

These separate groups grew, unnoticed and unchecked, until a pivot point in 2049. During a rally, violence erupted between African Americans and white supremacists. Blood was shed on both sides, but one incident stood out—three black men laughing while beating a white man to death. The vid went viral, and there was a mass outcry that resulted in the unification of white supremacist groups across the nation. This culminated in the formation of a third political party—the American Syncretic Party, or ASP.

Syncretic. I remember that vocabulary word. It means non-partisan, which is kinda ironic when their name has "party" in it.

Now the screen shows another rally, this one huge. There's a sea of signs and banners in the crowd, all depicting coiled snakes and the letters A S P.

The ASP neo-Nazi group grew exponentially, and began running members for governmental positions. They started with school boards, city councils, mayoral candidates. From there, they progressed to state governments, then their first national Senate seat.

By the 2080s, ASPs were a presence in both the House and the Senate, and several had taken unsuccessful runs at the presidency. ASP ambitions for the White House were finally realized when a mediocre non-ASP presidential candidate, Theodore Tuttle, named an ASP, Carl White, as his Vice Presidential running mate.

Thanks to this cross-party alliance, Tuttle was elected easily in 2108.

At first, it was business as usual. But then Tuttle was assassinated in what is now believed to be an ASP coup. As soon as Vice President White was sworn in as president, he instituted marital law, closed the borders, and replaced all White House non-elected positions with ASP leadership.

The screen shows a casket draped in an American flag in a cemetery filled with black-coated mourners. The new ASP president, a tall, thin man with salt and pepper hair and strange rimless glasses, stands at a podium giving a speech I can't hear. The video cuts to a border crossing, barricaded and guarded by armed soldiers, then a city with tanks patrolling deserted streets.

The nation was taken by surprise. Overnight, citizens lost the freedom of speech, the right to vote, and the precept that all people are created equal. Mass deportations began: tourists, migrant workers, recent immigrants, and anyone who could not definitively prove US citizenship. Despite their Nazi origins being rooted in racism, the ASPs did not consider race in the deportation policy, nor was it part of their platform. But religion was a different story. All religious observance—by members of any religion—was banned. Churches, mosques, and synagogues were closed, and religious schools were decreed secular. Anyone caught preaching or teaching religion was detained without trial.

Public outcry led to an organized rebellion the ASPs called the Uberlegen Uprising. That culminated in the

White War, where President White and his ASP army handily quashed the rebellion.

The video shows fighting between military and civilians, civilian bodies littering the streets. It flashes from one street to the next, one city to the next, all the same. Then it dramatically pans through black smoke to an American flag flying over the White House. The camera zooms in on the flag showing the field of stars has been replaced by a coiled snake. A shiver travels up my spine, despite seeing something similar in every alien invasion and Nazis-won-the-war movie. I guess life imitates art. Or people just aren't very original.

On the world stage, President White and the ASP government were widely criticized, but no one stood against them. Eventually the world went mute—no one wanted to be denied access to the emerging scientific and technological advancements of the ASP government. To stay in the good graces of President White, the world became selectively blind and deaf to ASP atrocities, in particular the means by which medicine was advancing— through human experimentation, genetic manipulation, and selective breeding.

The year 2119 marked another pivot when The Massive, an earthquake of the greatest magnitude ever recorded, struck San Francisco in a disaster of epic proportions. Even supposed "earthquake-proof" buildings succumbed. The result was massive loss of life, and total destruction of the city.

My mouth drops as the camera pans the devastation.

My city is hardly recognizable, far worse than photos of the 1906 quake aftermath.

The camera zooms in on hundreds of birds in the street fighting and squawking. I hear someone yell—presumably the camera guy—then the birds take flight and I see the horror. The birds had been fighting over human bodies.

The dead numbered so many, it was impossible to remove the remains, particularly given the volume of debris, the instability of the surrounding structures, and the threat of aftershocks. So President White declared San Francisco uninhabitable and off-limits. Due to the bio-hazards and other dangers, the city was believed to be unsalvageable, so what was left of the city government relocated inland to the newly built New Francisco.

Geologists, seismologists, and a host of scientists furiously studied the quake and determined it had not relieved all the pressure along the San Andreas fault. They predicted that Los Angeles—on the southern end of the fault line—was in imminent danger. If they couldn't find a way to relieve the pressure, it would only be a matter of time before LA succumbed to the same fate as San Francisco.

A small group of researchers, tasked with finding a way to relieve the pressure, was allowed into the ruined city to study the fault. In the process, they discovered the wormhole and immediately realized its potential—using time travel to destroy the ASP empire. They couldn't allow the wormhole to fall into the hands of the ASPs, so they kept their discovery secret and began a small movement with the hope of changing the world.

This is the movement you are now part of.

Welcome to the Resistance.

CHAPTER FOURTEEN

FLYX

I wake up shivering and reach for the coverlet, but there isn't one. This isn't my cot.

I sit up. The room spins and I fall back against the pillow.

I'm in STARS. Recovery room. Remo must have pulled me out of the TIC.

"Remo," I call, voice weak. "Remo!"

I hear someone coming. Carefully, I turn my head toward the doorway. It's Daum.

"You *stink*," he says, scrunching his nose.

I take a whiff. "Ugh." What did I do, gravy on myself? Then I remember, yeah, I basically did. "What are you doing here?"

"You're welcome." He tosses a fresh uniform at me.

"Did Remo tag you to come nettle me?"

"Something like that."

"Why the soot didn't he take me to Med?"

"Sincerely? You'd want to be at the mercy of a girlfriend you don't remember? When you feel like compost and smell worse? Remo did you a *favor*."

I shrug. I know I should be concerned about this Sharrow person, but all I can think of is Allison. I swing my legs over the side of the bed and suck in a resp to steady my stomach.

"Whoa, you okay?" Daum asks.

"I need to find Allison Bennett. Do you know where she is?"

"Last time I saw her was last night in Middies."

"Is she okay? How'd she get out of Detention? Tell me everything."

"I don't cog anything. Yesterday I spent working off demerits for disobeying orders during a Priority One."

"That's rot."

"Nah, I got lucky compared to Spires and Novalie."

"*No.*"

"Yeah."

Oh gods. The blood rushes from my head, and I grip the mattress. "Allison—was she recycled, too?"

"Negative. She remembered me."

Phew. "But you don't know where she is now?"

He shakes his head. "Sharrow would. She's Allison's auditor."

"I can't ask Sharrow."

Daum snorts. "Guess not. Too thorny."

"But *you* can. Please? I'm desp. You've got to help me."

"Kidding, right?"

"You owe me for covering your hind with Janell last month."

"Neg. Huh uh." Daum looks away. That's when I cog I've got him. I wait. One, two, three... "Fine. You win." He keys something into his personal.

While we wait for a reply, I get a whiff of myself. *Eck.*

No way I can meet Allison Bennett like this. "Send me her locay when you get it? I need to shower."

"Good call," he says, fanning his nose.

CHAPTER FIFTEEN

Welcome to the Resistance.

So dramatic, and again completely unoriginal.

The computer screen goes black, displaying a white logo that says "ResistGov."

Then it fades to purple, and white letters spell out "Press ENTER for safety protocols."

I stretch and finish the dregs of my coffee. Bel's focused on her screen, not paying any attention to me, so I think a little snooping is in order.

I open a new window and list the directory, but there's nothing useful. No schematic of the compound, nothing about a time machine or a wormhole, no information about the tests I'm taking. There's plenty about recycling, but nothing about recycling *people*.

I'd bet good money the info is in here. I sure could use Jake's hacking skills.

Jake. I imagine looking into his eyes...and him looking back and not knowing me. I'm pretty sure my heart would crack in two. I can almost feel it fracturing just thinking about it.

Enough. I need to quit feeling sorry for myself and do something.

I scour the directory again, but I still don't find anything. I need to get out and do some real snooping, the kind I'm good at.

A message window pops up on my screen.

FLYX: hello? is this Allison Bennett?

Is Bel messing with me? I glance up, but she doesn't look any different. I type a response, going easy on the keyboard so she doesn't hear.

GUEST: who is this?

FLYX: I need to find Allison Bennett. is this Allison?

GUEST: who are you

FLYX: a friend

GUEST: tell me your name

FLYX: Flyx but you don't know me

GUEST: then how exactly are you my friend

FLYX: so you ARE Allison

GUEST: maybe, but don't dodge the question. how can you be a friend if I don't know you

FLYX: I'm a loggie. basically a history monitor. I look for changes to the timeline and I saw you. well, not *you*, exactly. I saw evidence of you. in 2018 you were reported missing, last seen in the San Francisco Public Library wearing a Victorian costume

Wow, that's right. But that doesn't mean he's a friendly. Maybe he's spying on me. Maybe this is part of the test.

GUEST: what do you want

FLYX: to know if you're okay

GUEST: I'm fine

FLYX: good. do you think we could, I mean I was hoping, I'd really like to meet you. in person

If this is a test, I don't know what the right answer is. Probably *no*. I'm kind of intrigued, but I have to be smart...

FLYX: Allison, are you still connected?

GUEST: I'm here

FLYX: this place has gotta be weird for you. I wanted you to cog you have a friend. you're not alone

Relief washes over me. I didn't realize how alone I felt until he said that. Bel may be my sister, but she isn't exactly my BFF.

GUEST: a friend would be good

FLYX: have you eaten?

GUEST: only coffee

FLYX: be there soon. act like you don't know me

GUEST: that won't be hard

There's a tingly feeling in my belly as I clear the messages. A mix of nerves and excitement, and a little hunger given the mention of food.

I return to the purple screen and press *enter* to watch the safety protocols.

An image appears of a man in a black suit with medals on it, like a military uniform. There's a coiled snake on his hat. The voiceover starts up again.

The ASP military wears uniforms similar to these, though members of the party can look like anyone.

The screen goes purple again, and words appear in bold:

Safety Protocol One: anyone, anywhere, anytime can be the enemy.

Then the screen shows a graffiti-covered wall. It could be one I've seen, though I don't recognize it.

Hologram technology has been deployed throughout the complex to protect our true nature in the event of an inspection.

The image morphs into a closed door on a white wall. Then morphs again into a plain gray wall with no door visible. Now the camouflage makes sense.

"Allie!" Bel shouts, loud enough I hear it over the narration.

I take off my headset. "What?"

"Aren't you done yet? I'd like to get out of here before the day's completely over."

"Uh...." I hit enter several times, advancing the presentation. How many safety protocols are there? I'm up to eight with no end in sight. "How do I know when I'm done?"

"You need to get through math before we can leave."

I keep advancing the presentation until I come to a purple screen that says "Aptitude Test #1: Math."

"Starting math now."

"Do it fast. I don't want to eat lunch in here."

"'K." I'm uneasy missing all those safety protocols, but I don't go back.

Math has never been hard for me, and I blow through the questions. Thank goodness it's cake because I'm distracted thinking about the arrival of my "friend," Flyx.

I realize I'm expecting a guy, but I have no idea what kind of name Flyx is. It could be a girl. Or, there could be more gender identities in this time. Maybe it's evolved to where you don't have to choose one gender if you don't want to. That would be kind of cool, so long as they got the language part figured out. I feel bad when I choose the wrong pronoun.

The doors hiss open and I look up.

Definitely a guy. A really hot guy.

His silver-white hair is buzzed on one side and hangs to his jaw on the other. It perfectly matches his silvery jumper.

"Flyx," Bel says. "What are you doing here?"

"Hey, Bel. I could ask you samewise." The door slides shut behind him, and he looks over at me. "Allison?"

His eyes are a piercing bright blue, almost too blue. He's got a white tattoo—I didn't know there was such a thing—in a triangle design under his left eye, and his dark brows are striking next to his white hair. His jaw is square, his nose and chin slim and perfect, his mouth a bit pouty like a model. Then he smiles. Not a big smile. Barely an upturn at the sides of his mouth, and now I'm pretty sure I'm melting.

"Are you Allison?" he asks.

Oh God, why can't I say anything?

"Allie, you're drooling," Bel says.

My cheeks flare. "I, I'm Allie. Allison, I mean. Yes. That's me."

"*Please*," Bel says. "You're embarrassing yourself."

"Ease out, Bel," Flyx says.

Then it dawns on me— "Bel, he *knows* you."

She frowns, then turns to him. "Do you *know me* know me?"

"I know you," he says. "Sorry no one else remembers you. That's bleak."

"Why do *you*?" I ask.

"He's a loggie," Bel says, her voice dripping with contempt. "He monitors the past. He doesn't travel like a real Jenny."

"*Bel*," I scold. The one person who remembers her and she treats him like dog crap on her shoe.

"She's right," Flyx says to me. "I monitor history in the TIC. It's basically a wormhole that doesn't go anywhere. The side effect is I'm out of time like a Jenny, so I remember my old timeline when something changes. Like when someone I know disappears from history." He lifts his chin at Bel. "Good to see you, too, pal."

"Spare your drama. We were never friends."

Flyx makes an exaggerated sad face, and I bite my lip so I don't laugh. Then he walks to my table. His expression transforms into a full smile and he's so hot I have to bite my lip harder.

"So yeah," he says. "I know Bel." The way he says it implies that he's not surprised by her attitude.

"What are you doing here?" Bel demands.

"Liquid nutrition." He holds up a bottle. "I was tasked to bring it to Allison. If you want, I can sit with her while you get lunch." He turns to me and winks.

Bel narrows her eyes, like she's trying to figure out what the trick is. "Not necessary. You can go."

Flyx holds out the bottle to me. I grasp it and my finger nudges his hand. Oops—I'm touching him and didn't ask for consent.

But he doesn't mention it, and doesn't pull away. "Nice to meet you, Allison Bennett," he says.

We're frozen there, looking at each other, still both holding the bottle.

"I said you can go," Bel says.

Flyx nods, still looking at me, like he's trying to tell me something, but I'm not sure what. Finally he lets go of the bottle and heads for the door.

I watch him walk, his wide shoulders, his cute butt.

He activates the door but then turns back to me. Quickly, I pull my gaze up to his face. He grins like he knows I was looking at his butt! *Nooooo.*

"'Bye, Allison."

I don't trust my voice. I nod.

The door shuts, and I let out a breath.

"Really, it's like you've never seen a guy before," Bel says.

"Shut up, Bel." I unscrew the lid from the bottle and take a sniff of the contents. Mmm, smells like coffee. I wasn't expecting that.

"Aren't you done testing yet? I don't want to be here all day."

"You could have left for lunch. He said he would stay."

"Let's call that *no way in hell.* Hurry up and finish, okay?"

I turn my attention back to the screen, then take a swig from the bottle—it's a coffee *milkshake.* Cold, thick, espresso-y deliciousness. If this is "liquid nutrition," I officially change my mind.

I go back to my test and a new message pops up.

FLYX: Allison, you there?

GUEST: here

FLYX: I couldn't stop staring at you. you're even prettier than I imagined

My cheeks blaze, and I hope Bel doesn't notice. I've never blushed this much in my life. I hate to admit Bel's right—I'm acting like I've never seen a guy before.

Get it together, Allie. Act normal.

GUEST: thank you for the drink. it's really good

FLYX: thought you might like it since you mentioned coffee

GUEST: I'm not used to the liquid nutrition. it's not really a thing where I'm from

FLYX: most of them are pretty odious. I'm glad you like this one

GUEST: yeah, thanks for bringing it.

Dang it, I already said thanks. I try to delete my last message but it won't let me.

FLYX: I wish Bel would have left so we could talk

GUEST: me too

FLYX: how about we meet later

My heart does a little flutter.

GUEST: sure but I don't know where I'll be

FLYX: I'll find you

The chat window vanishes and I'm left staring at the test, my heart beating fast. What is wrong with me? I don't even know this guy. And he looks at least two years older than me.

I like *Jake*. I try to bring up a picture of him in my mind, but I can't. Oh my God, am I losing my memories? I think of Bibi, and her image pops right into my mind. Same with my mom. Why not Jake?

Maybe it's because I feel guilty.

But why should I feel guilty? Jake doesn't know who I am. In his reality, we never met because I was never born.

I tell myself there's no reason to feel bad about being interested in Flyx. But of course that's the moment an image of Jake pops in my head, and my heart constricts.

"You've got to be done by now," Bel says.

"Almost." The faster I finish, the sooner I can see Flyx again.

CHAPTER SIXTEEN

Bel activates the door to the Donut Shoppe and I follow her inside. Sharrow's mint-green hair draws my attention like a beacon. She's at the first table, head down, by herself.

"Hi, Sharrow," I call.

She looks up and smiles. "Hi, Allie."

"Oh gods," Bel says. "Sit with your perky twin while I get food."

She leaves without asking if *I* want anything. So very Bel.

I go to Sharrow's table and sit across from her. "What's that?" I point to the mug in front of her.

She grimaces. "Soup. It's horr-awful."

She thinks kombucha tastes good, so the soup must be really bad.

"Sorry Bel was so rude earlier," I say.

"Sluff Bel," Sharrow says. "How'd the testing go?"

"Easy." I kind of want to tell her about Flyx. Partly to find out what she thinks of him, but also because it would be nice to have a friend to share stuff with. "Sharrow, there's someth—"

"Flyx!" Sharrow leaps up and runs toward the door.

Then I remember—last night Sharrow mentioned her boyfriend. She said his name was *Flyx*.

No.

Her boyfriend's been flirting with me? And I've been flirting back?

No, no, no. That's so wrong.

Flyx stands frozen as Sharrow rushes to him.

"Consent?" She extends her hand.

"Uh...sure." He grasps her arm. "I consent."

She flings her other arm around him and pulls him into a hug. He makes eye contact with me over her shoulder. He looks distressed, I guess because I found him out. But he also looks confused.

Sharrow drags him to the table, grinning huge. It's like she's a different person.

"This is who I've been wanting you to meet," she says, and I'm not sure if she's talking to him or me. "Flyx, this is Allie, the girl I told you about. Allie, this is my boyfriend, Flyx."

Flyx looks at her, definitely both distressed and confused. "Uh...I'm sorry, are you...*Sharrow*?"

"That's not funny." Her voice is minus half its animation.

"I don't know how to tell you this, except to say it," he says. "Something happened to the timeline. And, well, I don't remember you."

"Wait...*what*?" Sharrow says.

"What?" I say at the same time. Maybe he's not a two-timing jerk.

"I'm really sorry," he tells her. "If there was anything I could do to change it..."

Sharrow looks crushed. I feel terrible for her. And for me. Whether he knows her or not, Sharrow likes him. That means he's off limits, at least in my book.

Bel returns to the table with a tray. She sits, then looks up at Flyx and Sharrow. "Are you going to stand there calling attention to yourselves?"

"Nice to see you again, too, Bel," Flyx says.

"You know *Bel?*" Sharrow drops Flyx's hand like a hot coal, and bolts for the door.

"Sharrow!" I jump up, but Bel grabs my arm and pulls me back down.

"Leave it." Bel's spindly fingers dig in. Why is she exempt from asking for consent? I yank away from her grasp.

"Aren't you going after her?" I ask Flyx.

He looks at me, stricken. "I would, but I don't know her. I'm sure I'd make it worse."

"What are you still doing here?" Bel says to Flyx.

He shakes his head slowly, his expression pained. Then he looks at me. "Allison, do you want something to eat?"

My stomach's in knots. There's no way I could eat. But I need to get away from Bel. "Sure." I half expect Bel to tell me I can't go, and I really, really want her to try it. The wrongness of everything is making me itch for a fight.

But she doesn't say anything. She looks away, ignoring me, so I go with Flyx to the wall of food machines.

"What do you feel like?" he asks.

"I feel like shit!" I blurt. "Sorry. It's just...."

"I know. It's not fair."

"She was so...wounded." A hollow sadness fills my chest, and I train my focus on the food machine in front of me. Spaghetti. Ugh. "I don't think I can eat. You go ahead."

He looks at me, his blue-blue eyes now clouded. I believe him that he doesn't remember Sharrow, and that he feels terrible about it. And I realize—none of it's his fault. History changed because of Bel. And because of me.

"I'm not really hungry either," he says. "How about some juice?"

"Sure."

We walk to the back where the desserts are. I eye some cookies while he fills two cups with an amber liquid.

"Let's sit where we can talk," he says.

I grab a box of cookies and follow to a deserted area near the liquid nutrition machines.

He picks the most remote table, and I take the chair opposite him. Our cups of juice and the box of cookies sit untouched between us.

"So, you go by Allie?" he says. "I can't help thinking of you as 'Allison Bennett, my odd-clothed girl.'"

"Your *what*?"

"That's how they described you in the newspaper from 1906. It said 'an odd-clothed girl appeared in the street as if from nowhere.' That was the first I knew of you, even though I didn't know it was you-you yet. It stuck."

I think back to that day I tumbled onto the street in 1906. I'd been in the wormhole so long I was loopy, and Sink came to my rescue. I had no idea there was a reporter there.

"I didn't know it made the paper."

"Written records are the only way I can monitor history."

"Oh." I sniff my cup, making sure it's not kombucha, then take a sip. Apple juice. It's so normal it makes me think of Bibi's, and I'm hit by another wave of sad. I shake it off and focus. "Before, you said you saw an article about me missing in 2018. That one had my name, but the 1906 one couldn't have."

"I wasn't a hundred it was the same person, but I found a common thread and I rationed it probable. There's this guy, Steinbeck Raskin—"

"Beck! How do you know about him? They said there was no record of him in this time."

"There are records. Most people don't have access to them, but I do. And I saw that he was operating in both of those times—2018 and 1906."

"There was record of him in 2018 connected to me? How? A custodian saw us in the library, but I never said Beck's name."

"Raskin wasn't mentioned in the newsarticle about *you*. He was in an article about a different girl. I put two and two together."

Why would Beck be in the paper in 2018? And with which girl? Haze? Maybe it was Vee—she and Beck were mysteriously missing the night we played parlor games. What were they up to, and how did they end up in the news? "The girl—was her name Vee?"

"No, Kaitlin O'Connell."

"*Kaitlin?* Was it about her acting? The role she was offered?" I want so bad for it to be that, but I flash on Haze giving Kaitlin the memory loss drug, and I know too well what that drug did to Beck.

Flyx is avoiding eye contact, looking at his cup, the ceiling, anywhere but me.

I don't want to hear it. But I need him to say it. "Tell me."

Flyx looks at me, like he's sizing me up. Then he nods. "Kaitlin died."

I swallow back the bile in my throat and clench my teeth, trying to get my rage under control. Damn Beck. *Damn* him. I make myself stop shaking. "Did it say how?" I'm surprised my voice doesn't sound as strangled as I feel.

"The newsarticle said she overdosed on a combination of drugs and alcohol. It said it could have been accidental, but most likely...not."

I clench my teeth again to keep from screaming. Her poor family. They thought she committed suicide, when really Haze killed her. I can't blame Haze, though. She was Beck's victim as much as Kaitlin. My eyes fill with tears and I fist them away. "What did it say about Beck?"

"He's mentioned by code name so loggies can cross reference with the list of auth missions. That way I know her death is permissible—the result of GENterference—and not to rep it as an anomaly of concern."

"*Permissible?* How is it permissible?" I'm so pissed I want to flip the table, scream, rage at someone. But that won't do any good. The only way to fix this is to go back and save Kaitlin. But I can't do it on my own. I lean toward Flyx over the table. "Kaitlin was murdered. By Beck. And it's *not* permissible. I can save her, but I need help."

He stares at me, his face unreadable. Is he going to help me? Or did I just screw up big time? Then he looks over my shoulder. "Rot, looks like Bel's coming. Hold out your right hand."

"Why?"

"We can private-message." He holds his right arm near mine, placing our devices together. "Huckleberry protocol twenty-eighteen." There's a low beep.

"What?"

"To message me say 'Huckleberry,' like Finn," he whispers. "Then the year you're from, twenty-eighteen." He stands and faces Bel as she arrives at our table. "You don't have to say anything. I'm leaving." He takes his cup and walks away.

Bel frowns. "What was that about? Never mind. I don't care. Come on, we're going."

"No, I don't think we are." I'm clenching my fists so hard my hands are shaking.

"Excuse me?"

"Sit down, Bel."

"What—"

"*Sit.*"

Slowly she lowers herself into a chair. "What's gotten into you?"

"Kaitlin is dead."

Bel rolls her eyes. "Of course she's dead. She died like a hundred years ago."

"The drug Haze gave her—it didn't wipe her memory. It killed her."

"No it didn't. Why would you even say that?"

"I know it's true because...." I can't tell her I killed Beck with the drug. Not if I want her to take me back to 1906 with her.

"Whatever that Flyx guy told you, he's lying. I'll have his job—"

"It wasn't him, I swear." I can't let Flyx get in trouble because of me.

"Then what were you talking about, all huddled together?"

"Uh..." Crap, what can I say? I blurt the first thing that pops in my head. "Milkshakes."

"Milkshakes? *Milkshakes?*"

"We were talking about liquid nutrition and it led to milkshakes." I shrug. "Sue me—I like milkshakes."

"Well, you're wrong about the memory loss drug. So drop it. I mean it." She stands and looks down at me. "My mom wants to see us. But I have an errand first, and since baby-bird *Sparrow* flew off in a huff, looks like you're coming with me."

I bite back my defense of Sharrow, reminding myself I need Bel on my side. I grab my juice and unopened box of cookies from the table. "What should I do with these? Seems a shame to waste them."

"Who cares. Bin them."

I finish the juice and drop the cup in the recycle bin, thinking again how it's such a waste. Then I remember I have a drink bottle now. Actually two—one Sharrow gave me with coffee, the other Flyx brought me. I wish I hadn't forgotten them in the testing room.

I can't bring myself to throw away the cookies, so I ignore Bel's glare and return them to the food case.

"Come on, already," Bel says.

My gut reaction is to slow my stride, but I don't give in to it. "Can we stop by the testing room? I left my drink bottles there."

"They'll be there tomorrow when you finish testing."

"But I thought I was done. Does that mean I could still be recycled?"

Bel doesn't say anything, but the look on her face is answer enough.

CHAPTER SEVENTEEN

B el is two steps ahead of me as we exit the Donut Shoppe. It's rude, but I let it go. Besides, I could do with seeing fewer eye rolls.

I follow up a flight of stairs into a BART station, but this one's not abandoned. Yes, it's covered with graffiti, and there are no trains, but there are people. *That's* different.

"Which station is this?" I ask, hoping to finally get my bearings.

"Trying to plan your escape?" Bel smirks.

I forget sometimes that Bel and I think alike when it comes to some things.

"Just curious," I say, probably unconvincingly. "So what is this place?"

"The mall. If there's something you want—vids, games, mods, accs—this is where to get it."

I look around, reminded of the flea market on Treasure Island my mom took me to once. This place is less crowded —there's maybe thirty people here, total, everyone tatted up and metaled out. It's funny they call it a mall. Maybe they think it's retro-cool like Donut Shoppe.

Bel leads me past racks of jewelry and scarves to a brightly lit section where three people are lying on tables getting tattooed. She approaches a woman who's working on a guy laid out on his stomach, yellow bodysuit bunched down around his knees. The guy's already covered in ink, but apparently there's an inch or two of blank skin on his butt. I *so* don't want to see that.

I keep my gaze on the woman so I don't have to look at the butt. Her brown skin is covered with geometric patterns in that orangey color that makes me think of India, and her black hair is in long cornrows with copper disks woven in. Her jumpsuit is a dusty pink, which honestly looks terrible next to her hennaed skin.

Without stopping work or looking up she says, "No time today. Come back tomorrow."

"I don't want ink," Bel says, her tone tinged with disgust. "I'm here for info."

"I give tattoos," the woman says. "Not information."

"Even when Dr. Dietrich asks?" Bel says.

The woman is silent a long moment, working on the tattoo. Then she turns off the tool and looks at us for the first time. "You are not Dr. Dietrich."

Bel says under her breath, "Dammit, I forgot." She stands up straighter. "Tryda, you don't remember me, but I'm Bel, Dr. Dietrich's daughter."

After a beat, Tryda looks at me. "And who does that make you?"

"I'm—"

"She's not important," Bel says. "I have a question from my mother I need to ask *privately.*"

Tryda stares at Bel. Time stretches, and I'm surprised Bel isn't berating her. Then I realize Tryda's making a decision, and Bel is letting her. The way Tryda is looking at Bel makes me think she's searching for something. Maybe a physical similarity to Dietrich?

Finally, Tryda nods and stands. "Gheil, I'll be back."

The guy on the table turns his bushy bearded face toward us. "Affirm," he says. Then he looks right at me and I gasp.

His eyes are black. Like unnaturally black. So black you can't see the difference between the iris and the pupil.

He smiles, showing teeth filed to points, and chuckles like he's pleased he shocked me. Jerk.

We follow Tryda into a narrow corridor that must have been an access tunnel once upon a time.

Several feet in, Tryda stops and turns to Bel. "How can I help Dr. Dietrich?"

"She may need you to remove some tattoos."

Tryda nods. "Describe them."

"Green freckles and eye liner."

She's got to be talking about Sharrow.

"Pale skin?" Tryda asks.

Bel nods. "My mom needs to know how long it will take for the person to look normal again."

"Complete removal, four days. Faster if I obfuscate with nat-look pigment."

"We'll be in touch if we decide it's necessary," Bel says.

"You might want to know before deciding," Tryda says, "that both options are painful."

Bel shrugs. "I don't think that matters."

Really? It doesn't matter?

"Anything else?" Tryda asks.

"That's all," Bel says. "Unless Allie wants a tattoo. What about a butterfly on your forehead, Allie?"

Tryda and Bel both look at me.

"No, I'm good."

"You sure? You'd fit in so much better," Bel says.

"*You* don't have any face tattoos. Shall we get matching ones?"

"Touché," Bel says.

I see Tryda crack the barest hint of a smile, but it vanishes quickly. "I must get back to work." She gives a nod that's almost a bow, then heads back the way we came.

"I have one more errand." Bel says. "But I was serious about the butterfly—we have time if you change your mind."

I follow her back into the mall, past the tattoo area, more jewelry, and tables of board games I don't recognize. I smell chemicals as we approach someone getting their hair colored.

Again, Bel marches right up to the person working. "Hey, Rista. I mean, is your name Rista?"

The girl doesn't look up from what she's doing. "Yeah?"

"I love the color of your hair," Bel says. "But I'm not sure how it would look on me."

Bel sounds sincere, but she can't be serious. This girl has *green hair*. Not minty like Sharrow's, but super green like AstroTurf.

Rista glances at Bel. "It would be fine with your skin tone. I'll be done in ten if you want to wait."

"What if I color it then change my mind? How hard would it be to get my current color back?"

Rista looks up, tipping her head to examine Bel. "It's nat now?"

"Completely."

"I could strip out the green and dye it something similar to your color in a few hours. It would look close to your nat, but not a hundred."

"Thanks, I'll think about it," Bel says.

"How have I never seen either of you? You new or something?" Rista asks.

"Yeah, I'm Allie. Nice to—"

"We need to go." Bel gives me a pointed look, then strides off.

I shoot Rista an apologetic look, then catch up to Bel. "What's the deal? Why so rude?"

"Getting all nicey-nice is a waste of time."

You'd think it would be worth the effort to be civil to people she deals with on a regular basis. But then a possibility occurs to me. "Do these people exist in your other timeline? When we set things right, are they going to be erased?"

"What does it matter? I'll never actually change my hair, so who cares if I'm nice to some color-drudge?"

"*She* might care. She's a person—isn't that good enough reason to be nice? Besides, why burn a bridge by being a—" I swallow back the word. "By being mean."

"I'm not burning bridges. Not ones I use. My mom and I are topsiders. We don't deal with these people."

"So you're not like 'these people.' You're special—a topsider. That's why you don't have any visible tattoos, isn't it?"

"Someone's observant."

I knew she was up to something, prodding me to get a tattoo. She wants to make sure I'm one of "these people" rather than one of *her* people. I wonder if Sharrow knows that Bel and her mom are trying to turn her into a topsider. And how she'd feel about it.

We head down some stairs into another tunnel faintly lit by overhead panels. We're back to gray and boring, and I miss the graffiti.

The tunnel ends in a regular door—no holo-camo-whatever. No, I take that back—Bel banks her personal to an invisible sensor. There's a click, then she turns the knob. The door opens into another tunnel that looks identical to the one we're in.

Once I'm through, Bel makes sure the door latches shut. Then, without looking at me, she starts down the hallway, picking up her pace.

Two more doors and tunnels later, we climb stairs again. At the top, we enter a hall like the one by Middies—white walls, white ceiling, blue-gray indoor-outdoor carpet, florescent lighting—typical office building circa 2018.

This place is either total graffiti or total blah, and never any sunlight. If I lived here, it wouldn't take long for me to start clawing my way out.

Bel stops in front of a door that looks no different from the others. I'm sure it's going to open into yet another blah hall. But then she smooths her hair, stands up taller, and banks her personal.

CHAPTER EIGHTEEN

As the door slides open, I note Bel looks nervous. That's different. I wonder if I should be nervous.

Sharrow's on the other side of the door, red-eyed and somber. "Hey," she says, like she was expecting us. "Come in."

Bel walks past without a word and disappears from view.

"You okay?" I ask Sharrow, but she won't look at me.

Given the surrounding hallways, I was expecting an office, but we're standing in a living room—*Dietrich's* living room, I assume. To our immediate right, there's a leather couch and two armchairs clustered around a coffee table. The couch is flanked by side tables with lamps that emit a homey, yellow light, and the wall above has a wide painting of a lake. The only decorations are a fake plant and a stack of books on the coffee table. To the left is a kitchen with breakfast nook. Beyond that is an open arch to a dim hallway. Straight ahead is a closed door.

"Where'd Bel go?" I ask Sharrow.

"Lav, maybe? Or Mom's bedroom?" She's still not meeting my gaze. "Nice, isn't it?" She gestures to the room.

"Sure." I glance around and notice the door we entered has disappeared, a blank yellow wall in its place.

"Have a seat. I'll get us something to drink." Sharrow crosses to the kitchen.

I don't want to sit, and I don't want a drink. I'd rather find out what's going on. I ignore her instructions and follow into the kitchen.

Sharrow loads mugs onto a tray. There's a chrome toaster in the middle of the tray, but the slot for bread has a handle poking out of it. Seems odd, but I don't ask. She seems so sad, I skip past the small talk.

"What's wrong?" I ask.

"Nothing. I'm fine."

"You don't seem fine. Nobody would be in your situation. It really sucks."

She winces. "It's...whatever." She grabs the tray and heads toward the living room.

I follow. "If you need to talk..."

"Move those?" She points with her chin to the books on the coffee table.

I grab the stack. The top book is a collection of Edgar Allen Poe. He gives me the creeps. I put the books on a side table.

Sharrow sets the tray down. "You can sit on the davenport. It's more comfy than the chairs."

That weird word again—that's what Bel called the sofa in Kaitlin's house.

"Tea?" Sharrow offers. "It's my fave. I made it really strong."

I remember her fondness for kombucha. "No, thanks."

She presses down on the handle. It recesses into the gap and a spigot pops out the side, complete with a cartoon-like wisp of steam spiraling up. She puts a mug under the spigot and presses a button, filling the cup. Then she sits in the armchair nearest me, cradling her mug in both hands and blowing across the top.

I want to ask why Dietrich wants to see me, but first, Sharrow deserves to know Bel's plotting something.

I lean forward, my voice low. "There's something you should know."

She peers over the rim of her mug. "Yeah?"

"Bel was at the mall asking questions about removing tattoos and hair color. I think it was about you—trying to make you a..." I struggle to recall the term. "A topsider."

Sharrow brings the mug away from her face without taking a drink. "Rot. I was hoping with Bel here I wouldn't have to go through with it."

"Go through with what?"

"Bel's already taken my mom, my boyfriend. The least she could do is— *They're coming.*"

I lean back on the couch and fold my hands in my lap as Bel and Dietrich enter through the archway.

Sharrow is concentrating on her tea again.

Dietrich smiles. "Tea—how nice. Thank you, Sharrow."

"Mm hmm," Sharrow says without looking up.

"Hello, Allie." Dietrich says, filling a mug. She's wearing a navy blue pencil skirt and jacket, with a cream blouse. She sits beside me on the couch, sips her tea, then places her mug on the coffee table.

Bel claims the empty armchair. She's still wearing the sapphire blue jumpsuit, but she's replaced the flouncy skirt and blue boots with a wide brown belt and knee-high boots. I wiggle my toes in my "slip" socks, wondering when I'll graduate to boots.

"Thank you for coming," Dietrich says, crossing her long legs at the ankles. "You're all sisters, of a sort. I thought it would be good for you to get to know each other."

I nod, glad she's decided to group me in with Bel and Sharrow. But I can tell there's more to this gathering than sister bonding.

"Allie," Dietrich continues. "Why don't you tell us a little about yourself?"

My inner debate lasts about half a second. "Why don't you tell us why we're really here?" My gut says I'll get more out of being direct than by playing along.

"*Allie*," Bel says.

Dietrich laughs. "I should know better with a Jenny. Well played, Allie." She sips her tea, and I feel a little proud of myself. "We're here because I want first-hand reports of your missions."

"So why is *she* here?" Bel's gaze flicks to Sharrow.

"Geez, Bel," I say.

"I'll leave." Sharrow stands.

"*Sit down.*" Dietrich's tone leaves no room for question. Sharrow sinks back in the chair.

"All right." Dietrich's tone is pleasant again. "You start, Bel. How did you end up going back in time?"

"*Mo-om.*" Bel draws out the word into two syllables. "You already know."

"Only from the hist-reports," Dietrich says. "I want to hear it from you."

Bel huffs. "Fine. My father, Steinbeck Raskin—"

"Who's Allie's father, too," Dietrich interjects, nodding at me.

"The first time I remember meeting him was when he showed up here in 2151. He'd been away on extended missions my whole life, but he had to come back because his vision was failing. He had a new plan to stop the ASPs, but he needed my help because of his eye condition."

Wait, Beck never mentioned ASPs or Nazis or anything like that. He said he was trying to prove Jennys could change the past without affecting the timeline. Was that a cover for his real mission? Or the other way around?

"The plan was complex," Bel continues. "We prepped for the mission for almost a year. Then we went back in time to collect Jennys. My first travel was to 2086."

Dietrich nods. I can't tell if any of this is news to her—she's got a good poker face. "Who did you collect?" she asks.

"Twenty eighty-six was Vee and Haze. There was a third, Charles, but he wasn't viable, so Beck neutralized him."

"You mean *killed* him?" I blurt.

Everyone turns and looks at me.

"Of course not," Bel says. "We gave him a drug that wipes recent memories so he wouldn't remember us. It also contains a blocker so he can't see wormholes anymore."

"I don't believe you," I say.

"Have your loggie friend Flyx check the records," Bel says.

"I still don't belie—"

"Enough." Dietrich silences me.

Sharrow looks betrayed, and I register that Bel called Flyx *my* friend. Great. Just great.

"Bel, continue," Dietrich says.

"We gathered Gracie in 2067. Noah and Mouse in 2109. Cora was 2100, but she had to be neutralized. That brings us to 2018."

"Allie," Dietrich says. "Why don't you pick up the story there?" It's not really a request.

"Okay." I glare at Bel. "Bel was following me. When I confronted her, she drugged and kidnapped me."

"You're so drama," Bel says.

"Haze and Beck were with her," I continue. "Later I met the others—the ones who weren't 'neutralized.' Mouse, Gracie, Noah, and Vee. Plus the one Bel failed to mention, *Kaitlin.*" The more I talk, the more riled I get. I know I should rein it in, but I don't. "Kaitlin didn't want to go through with the plan—which we were told was a heist, nothing about Nazis—so they gave her the drug. But it didn't wipe her memory. It *killed* her."

"It did not!" Bel shouts.

"Yes it did!" I shout back.

"*Stop*, both of you," Dietrich says.

"But it's true," I say. "Check the records. You'll see."

"It's not! I—"

"*Bel.*" Dietrich holds up her hand to Bel, and turns her attention to me. "What records?"

Uh oh. I can't throw Flyx under the bus. "I, uh....I'm not sure, uh...records in general?" Geez, how lame can I be.

"She's been pally with that loggie, Flyx," Bel says. "One guess who's feeding her this info—which is total lies, by the way."

"Flyx?" Dietrich says. The look in her eye is lethal.

"He wouldn't do that!" Sharrow says.

"Enough," Dietrich snaps. "I'll deal with that later. For now, Allie, tell me about this heist."

I fill her in on the missions and what we planned to steal in 1906—the rhino horn, the photographs, the money and jewels at the Harris mansion—but it's hard to concentrate. I'm watching Dietrich, expecting her to key something on her personal to bring hellfire down on Flyx. She hasn't touched her wrist yet, but I'd bet a dozen Micky D's shakes she's going to. I have to warn him.

"Um, could you excuse me for a minute? I need to use the lav." I know leaving's a risk—it gives Dietrich an opening to alert her goons. But I can't shake the feeling I have to warn Flyx *now*.

I head for the archway that leads to the rest of Dietrich's apartment, fully expecting her to send someone to keep an eye on me. I glance back, but they're all still sitting around the coffee table.

The hallway has five doors, all shut, and I don't know which one is the bathroom. I try the first. Locked.

The urge to contact Flyx is so strong, I half-consider messaging him right here in the hall. But I resist. It would be too easy to get caught.

"I know what you're up to," Bel says behind me, as if on cue.

"Is this the lav?" I point to the second door, all casual so she knows she didn't startle me.

She nods. "You should know, it won't work."

"What won't? The door? The lav?"

"Do you think we're stupid?" An unladylike fleck of spit flew from her mouth with the word *stupid*. "Your personal won't tag Flyx."

"What are you talking about?" I shake my head like she's imagining things, while hoping she's wrong, that Flyx's private messaging system will still work despite any measures Dietrich's taken.

"In fact," Bel says with a snide grin, "you leaving the room sealed his fate faster. My mom is sending guards after him right now. And you can't do anything about it."

"It didn't even occur to me. Now, I really have to pee. Are you going to watch?"

"As if." She flounces away.

I open the bathroom, lock myself in, and turn on the faucet in case Bel decides to listen. Then I sit on the closed toilet, wishing Flyx had told me how to message him without voice commands. I tap the face, trying to remember exactly what Flyx said. *Tag Huckleberry Finn?* No, just Huckleberry. "Tag Huckleberry protocol twenty-eighteen."

DICTATE-RECORD ACTIVE blinks in the display window. Looks like it's working.

"Flyx," I say, my voice almost a whisper. "Dietrich's sending guards. She thinks you told me about Kaitlin. I denied it, but Bel says they're coming for you. I'm sorry."

My words appear on the display, then minimize. "SENT" appears, and I exhale. I hope it reaches him in time.

I wash my hands, then head back to the living room wearing my most innocent face.

"I don't know what happened to Beck," Bel is saying. "He was supposed to be at the exit point. I did everything I could—I killed the younger version of him to clear the way —but I didn't see if he came out of hiding, because Allie jumped me into the wormhole, though I don't understand how because the wormhole wasn't big enough. Then I got the upper hand and brought her straight here, only to find out my life's been vanked."

"What caused you to cease to exist in this timeline?" Dietrich asks her as I retake my seat. "What changed?"

"I'll tell you what changed," I say. "She killed our dad before she was conceived. *That's* why she doesn't exist."

"No, that wouldn't be it," Dietrich says. "Jennys can't have children."

CHAPTER NINETEEN

FLYX

The gym is crowded, but I find an open ex-bike and set my usual. The radiation sickness is completely gone now. Norm I'd be begging Remo to let me back in the TIC, but with Allison here, monitoring history has lost appeal.

I imagine Allison's face, her laughing smile, her nat-beauty. Then I flash on Sharrow and her devastation when I didn't know her. There's nothing I can do about not remembering her, but I feel grave anyway.

I pedal hard, trying to escape my guilt. Of course that gets me nowhere.

My personal buzzes. There's a private-message from Allison—*Dietrich's sending guards.* I clean-delete the message and drop the personal by the bike as I head for the back door.

As I slip into the hall, I hear voices in the gym calling my name. Hopefully they didn't see me duck out and they'll be slowed by my personal registering in the room.

I sprint down the hall, away from the station toward the dead end. There used to be a ladder attached to the wall, leading to the air ducting. It was removed, leaving rough divots in the concrete that work—barely—for holds. I strip off my boots, tie the laces together and sling them over my shoulder, then climb. I tell myself it's like a climbing wall. But it's not—these aren't great holds, and the ground is cement.

At the ceiling, I push the hatch out of the way and haul myself up, then replace the hatch silently.

"Did he go that way?" someone shouts.

Rot—that's close. If they know about this access hatch, I'm crashed. But if I crawl through the ducts now, they'll definitely hear me.

"Checking." A different voice, even closer. I hear heavy boots on cement. I hold my resps. "Dead end. We lost him." The footsteps recede.

That was way too close. I take a minute, allowing them to put distance between us, then crawl as quietly as I can away from the station. It's pitch-dark in the duct without my personal, so I compose a mental map and hope-pray it's accurate.

Finally I reach the hidden access to the roof. I identify by feel the metal sheeting that hides the alcove for the ladder, then carefully slide it to the side. I've coated the bottom edge in waxed duct tape to dampen the sound. The gray tape practically disappears against the sheet metal, so it's unlikely to be noticed if anyone were ever poking around.

I step through, then reposition the metal cover. Almost there now.

I put my boots back on, then feel my way to the ladder. It's a three-story climb and I take it graddie, trying to sort my way out of this gnarl.

By the time I reach the roof, I've got a plan that, if luck, could work.

I pivot aside the hatch and am blinded by sun. I scramble out, replace the hatch, and duck in the lean-to I use during daylight. Drone patrols are rare, but I can't afford chance-takes.

I flop down and drain a water I stashed here. I keep granola bars and nuts, too, after learning hard-way how to safe them from marauding birds, but I hope to be gone long before my stomach gripes.

I open the strong box and dig out my spare personal. I re-built it from a broken one that had been discarded. It took two months to steal the parts and get it working, but it was worth every minute. It's the only thing now between me and consequence.

I'm at the bare edge of signal here, but I power up and it catches. I tag Daum on our private channel.

FLYX: using back-up device. in deep. need assist

Seconds feel like hours while I wait for a response. Finally one pops.

DAUM: here. what's prob?

FLYX: guards after me. dropped personal at ex-bike and fled to roof. need cover

DAUM: call it

FLYX: you go on our usual obs-course run, but don't get eyed. story is I was with you whole time—that I lost personal at warmup and didn't realize. your tracker will corroborate so long as no viewers can say otherwise

DAUM: understood. heading now

FLYX: meet you at the Y-junction in fifteen. tag if there's prob. use this device, private channel only—guards have my primary

DAUM: affirm

I fall back against my bag-sleeper to wait. If luck, this

patches the immediate problem. But I still have to deal with why guards were after me to begin with.

I do have a solution. It's the only option I can cog. But I wish it weren't.

There's a few minutes left before I need to leave to meet Daum, so I tag Allison on the private channel.

FLYX: it's me. thanks for the warning. I'm safe. can you talk?

I wait for her response, picturing her, drop-dead in that old-school way I crave. No mods, no colors. A nat-beauty that makes my heart flip. I want to run my fingers through her long auburn hair. I want to touch her unmarked face, to stare into her clear eyes.

Why hasn't she answered?

I have to go. I can't wait any longer.

FLYX: don't tag back. I have a plan. if it works, I'll be in a cube waiting for you. if it fails…I'm glad I met you, and I just wish

I hesitate. Oh, what the eff—I'm going to say it.

FLYX: I just wish I would have had the chance to kiss you

CHAPTER TWENTY

I remember my mom saying she was surprised she was pregnant because Maxen/Beck wasn't supposed to be able to have kids.

"If Jennys can't have kids, how do you explain *me?*" Bel's leaning forward, practically shouting at Dietrich. "I am *not* a gen-fab."

"Bel," Dietrich says, sounding apologetic. "People are not born with the ability to time-travel. Genetic fabrication's the only way to be a Jenny."

"You're wrong," Bel insists. "My dad passed it down to me."

"And me," I pipe in. "That's what my mom told me."

"That's simply not possible," Dietrich says. "Jennys are physiologically unable to have children. They're genetically engineered that way—it's one of the core mandates."

"Then somebody effed up!" Bel says.

"*Language,*" Dietrich scolds.

There's a tiny buzz against my wrist from the personal. It's got to be a message from Flyx, but I can't exactly read it here. I need a cover.

"Oh my God," I say dramatically, rising from the couch. "You're saying I won't be able to have kids? Ever?" I choke back a manufactured sob and run to the breakfast nook.

"I'm so sorry, Allie," Sharrow says. Tentative footsteps come toward me.

I deposit myself at the kitchen table and slump over, facing away from the living room.

"Give her a minute," Dietrich says.

I hear Sharrow return to the others. There's another buzz at my wrist. I hunch over more and sneak a glance, but the personal is camouflaged. I tap on the face once, hoping it "wakes up" without making any sound.

Yes!

FLYX: it's me. thanks for the warning. I'm safe. can you talk?

FLYX: don't tag back. I have a plan. if it works, I'll be in a cube waiting for you. if it fails...I'm glad I met you, and I just wish I would have had the chance to kiss you

I imagine Flyx's lips on mine, and my heart flip-flops. Immediately I feel lower than dirt. Sharrow still likes him, even though he doesn't remember she was his girlfriend. Plus I like Jake, even though he doesn't remember I exist.

Why does everything have to be so complicated?

Whatever. It doesn't matter.

I'm not going to meet up with Flyx. I mean, I hope his plan works out and he's not in trouble, but I've got other things to worry about.

I stay at the table, eavesdropping on their conversation.

"Bel," Dietrich says. "What year were you born?"

"2134. February."

"And the DNA tests prove I'm her mother?" Dietrich asks Sharrow. "Conclusively?"

"One hundred," Sharrow says.

The DNA tests. "Hang on," I say, turning in my chair to

face them. "Shouldn't it be easy to prove Maxen is Bel's dad with DNA testing?"

"Maxen?" Dietrich says. "That's not the name you said before."

"I knew him as Beck Raskin," Bel says. "But he used to be called Maxen—is that the name you know him by?"

"There was a Jenny named Maxen," Dietrich says. "But I didn't know him well."

"You said *was*, past tense. What happened to him?" Bel asks. "Is he dead?"

"I don't know for certain," Dietrich says. "I know he's not here, in this time. When I took over, I recalled as many Jennys as I could, but some remain unaccounted for. They're presumed dead or lost in history."

"But you'd still have records, right?" I say. "So we can prove he's our father."

"I ran full DNA batteries on you both," Sharrow says. "There were no paternal matches for either of you."

"Even if it were possible for a Jenny to be their father, you wouldn't have found his records in the system," Dietrich says. "I put all the GEN records in the time-vault when I shut down the travel program."

"Don't you think we should—oh, I don't know—get them out of the vault and check?" I say, borderline rude.

"Fine, but it won't make any difference," Dietrich says. "Jennys can't have kids."

"Why are we even talking about this?" Bel says, throwing her hands up dramatically. "None of it matters."

"It does matter," I insist. "I assumed our lives were erased when Maxen and my mom were killed. What if that's not true? We have to know exactly what caused us to be erased so we can fix it when we go back to 1906."

"It doesn't matter because we're not going back," Bel shouts.

"The hell we're not!"

"*Enough*." Dietrich slams her hand on the coffee table. "No one's going anywhere."

"You can't do that," I yell, coming out of my chair.

"Let well enough alone," she says. "You're alive now. All of you. If you try to change things, you might not be."

"Not *everyone* is alive who should be," I shout, pacing, fists clenched. "My parents and the crew are dead. We have to go back and save them."

Dietrich folds her arms. "No. No time travel."

"Give it up," Bel says.

"It'll be okay," Sharrow tells me. "You'll get used to it here."

"I won't! Not in a million years." How is Bel just accepting this? I have to get out of here. *Now*.

I run to the yellow wall, but I can't remember where the door is. I hold my personal up, scanning it back and forth trying to activate the sensor pad.

"That won't work," Bel says.

I run to the other door—the one to Dietrich's office.

"Try to calm down." Sharrow steps between me and the door.

"I don't want to calm down. I can't stay here." I glare at Bel. "It's our fault everyone died. You know we have to fix it. What's wrong with you?"

"Sharrow," Dietrich says. "I'm getting Allie a sedative." She leaves the room.

"I don't need a sedative. I need to get out of here." I go back to the yellow wall and try to make it open.

"We can't go back," Bel says. "The sooner you accept that, the better."

"Please. Calm down," Sharrow says, coming as close as she can without touching me. "I don't want to sedate you."

I look at her. There's something she's not saying. The sedation drug—is it really sedation? Or something else?

Cold fear washes through me. Instantly, I'm calm. I turn to Sharrow. "I'm sorry, I don't know what came over me."

Dietrich comes back in the room with a syringe.

"I'm okay now," I tell her. "It was the shock of the news. I'm okay now, really."

"Still, I think it would be best." She hands the syringe to Sharrow.

"No, I swear I'm fine." If they sedate me, I won't be able to get out of here. "Please, Dr. Dietrich, I understand it's too risky to time-travel. I really do. It was a shock, but I can accept it. I promise I'm okay now."

"I'm afraid I must insist," she says. "It won't knock you out. It will simply calm you down. Now please stand still and let Sharrow do her job."

Sharrow holds the syringe up to the light. There's something printed on it, but I can't read it. "It'll be okay, Allie. Push up your sleeve and hold out your arm." She turns her back to the others. *Trust me*, she mouths.

My heart's pounding like a jackhammer, but I push up my sleeve, hoping I can trust her.

Sharrow holds her personal next to mine. "Medical procedure, extended contact. Consent?"

"I consent," I say, hoping I really can trust her.

"You seem a little woozy. Are you afraid of needles?" She looks at me expectantly.

"Yes, I am," I say, playing along.

"Cold water helps. We'll do this in the kitchen. Mom, can you get some gauze, please?"

Dietrich disappears down the hall. Sharrow ushers me

to the kitchen sink and turns on the faucet, positioning herself so Bel can't see what she's doing. "Hold your wrist under the cold water and look away, okay?"

"Okay." I do as she says, and the next thing I feel is a prick in the crook of my elbow. "Hey!" I jerk back but she holds tight.

Trust me, she mouths again.

Trust her? I thought she wasn't going to give me the shot.

Dietrich comes back with the gauze. I look down and there's a tiny blood spot on the inside of my arm. Dietrich hands me a square of gauze.

"Put pressure on it," Sharrow tells me.

I glare at her while I press the gauze to my arm.

"Come back to the living room," Dietrich says.

"Whatever she says, agree," Sharrow says in my ear as she guides me to the living area, holding my elbow as if she's supporting me. "Act sedated," she whispers.

Act sedated? She stuck me with the needle—I saw the blood.

Dietrich and Bel are standing shoulder to shoulder, watching me and Sharrow approach. I want to rail against them, to give them the full force of my fury, but that will get me nowhere. Instead, I shuffle along, letting my eyes go unfocused.

"Listen to me, Allison," Dietrich says. "You must give up all hope of time travel. You must not speak of it or think of it again."

"Mmm." I say, hoping my acting is on target.

"Look at me," Dietrich barks. "Focus."

I bring my eyes to focus on her, rocking in place as if I'm losing my balance. Sharrow tightens her grip on my arm, steadying me.

"You will be compliant with my instructions," Dietrich says. "You will forget about time travel. Do you understand?"

"Yeah," I say, wavering as I look at her. "I...sure, okay."

"Done?" Sharrow asks. "I should get her to bed."

"Isn't there something *you* want to say to her?" Bel asks Sharrow. "Like 'stay away from my boyfriend'?"

"Sluff it, Bel," Sharrow says, steering me to the yellow wall. "Aren't you coming?"

"I'm staying here," Bel says.

"Is that wise, given..." Dietrich says.

"*Mom*," Bel says. "She's compliant, so I don't see why I should have to sleep in that awful room with all those people snoring and farting."

"*Bel*," Dietrich scolds.

"Well it's true," Bel retorts. "It's disgusting."

"We'll be fine," Sharrow says. "Allie won't give me any trouble, right, Allie?"

"Huh?" I say in a groggy voice. "I'm...fine."

"I'm sorry *you* can't stay, Sharrow," Dietrich says.

"No, it's okay. I understand." Sharrow's chipper reply doesn't match the sadness in her eyes. "What's the plan for tomorrow?"

"I'll message you the details," Dietrich says. "Take her to Middies. She should sleep through the night, but I expect you to keep your eye on her anyway."

"Affirm." Sharrow puts her hand to the yellow wall and the outline of a door appears. She opens it, walks me through, then closes it behind us.

"What the hell was that?" I whisper.

"Not here."

As we hurry through the corridor to the stairs, my mind's reeling, but I stay silent.

When we're well into the bowels of the vacant gray tunnels, Sharrow finally stops. "Okay, we're good here."

"I thought you weren't going to drug me!" I don't feel sedated, but she did stab me with the needle.

"I put it down the drain, but I had to make it look like I administered it."

Phew. "Good thinking." My mind flashes to Kaitlin. "If you had given it to me, would it have wiped my memory?"

"No, I checked the bottle. It would have made you calm, as well as susceptible to suggestion. Like you wouldn't be able to help following commands."

"Like brainwashing?"

She nods. "I didn't give it to you because I want you to decide on your own to give up on time travel."

"But—"

"My mom will *never* let you go. If you don't convince her you've accepted your life in this time, she *will* give you the drug that wipes your memory."

"Why are you doing this? You barely know me."

"I think you deserve a fair chance. But Bel doesn't feel samewise. She'd rather have you out of the way, and...I hate to admit this but, my mom might be inclined to agree with her."

I nod, processing this. I'm grateful she's looking out for me, but there's more to it. "Bel wants you out of the way, too. You know that, right?"

"What do you say we help each other?" She's biting her lower lip, looking at me expectantly. Either she really wants this, or she's a great actor.

CHAPTER TWENTY-ONE

FLYX

Dietrich's glaring at me from behind her desk. I stand across, near vibrating with tension. The only other person here is snake-faced Kraft who's sentried by the door. I clench my core, trying to mask my nerves.

Finally, Dietrich says something. "Kraft, outside."

Rake me. This is sally.

Kraft nods. "Affirm." The door clicks shut.

"Sit," Dietrich tells me.

I perch on the edge of a chair. I'm sure she can see the fear in my eyes.

She raises her chin, staring down at me. "I've looked into the matter of your disappearance. As you claimed, Daum's personal verified his whereabouts. But I don't for one moment believe you were with him."

"But I—"

She puts up her hand, stopping me. "However, I understand you have information about Allison Bennett. I'm willing to hear what you have to say."

I hate that I have to do this. "She trusts me."

"Oh?"

"She's plotting something."

Dietrich shakes her head, like she feels sorry for me that I'm so dim. "Why would I care. She's nothing."

"You might care if she's plotting to time-travel."

I see her jaw tighten. I try not to fidget.

"Tell me what you know," she says, her voice low and deadly.

I swallow. "She asked me to help her."

"If that's all you've got—"

"She *trusts* me. I can play the inside, then tell you everything."

"Or I recycle her and the whole thing goes away." She stares me down, tapping one fingernail methodically on the wooden desktop.

It *would* be gobs easier to recycle Allison. But she's considering my offer, so there's something else going on here. I hold my resps, hope-praying she'll come down on my side.

Finally she nods. "Okay."

"Okay?"

"You're my eyes and ears, as long as you prove useful. You begin immediately. Allie is supposed to be sedated. However I'm not convinced Sharrow actually administered the drug. The two of them are together now. Find out what they're planning."

That's why she agreed—she's concerned about how deep Sharrow is. "Yes, ma'am."

"And there's something else. I need all the GEN program records from the TIC, including genetic profiles. Specifically I'm looking for a Jenny named Maxen to compare with Bel's DNA. Plus everything you can find on governors. My eyes only. Can you do that?"

"Not now. I'm limited by auth-shifts, and this is my

recover-week. But if you auth at-will access, I can go any time, and no one will question."

"See Sharrow first, then go to the TIC. By the time you get there, it will be authorized."

I nod, swallowing down my guilt. But what other choice do I have?

CHAPTER TWENTY-TWO

Standing in the cold, gray corridor, I stare back at Sharrow, trying to see beneath the surface. Her words about helping each other still echo in the air. She seems genuine. Or she's a good con.

"We could both use an ally," I say.

"So do we have a deal?"

She's eager. Too eager? I don't know. But agreeing is the best—only?—option I have right now, so I stick out my hand. "Deal."

She shrinks back. "Not a good idea to shake on this."

"Right. I guess we don't want it 'on the record.'"

"Let's get to a cube where we can do some planning."

A *cube*. "Flyx said he'd be in a cube. If he was able to get out of trouble."

Sharrow frowns.

Damn, I'm an idiot. "Sorry. That was dumb. Insensitive. I wasn't thinking."

"No, it's okay." She attempts a smile. "He's a good guy. Smart. Connected, too. He could help us."

"We can trust him?"

"Absolutely."

"Then let's go."

"Can you ride a bike?" she asks.

Weird question. "Like a bicycle?"

"It's okay if you can't. We can walk, but the bikes are faster. And more fun."

"I could stand a little fun."

WE EMERGE from the corridor in another unidentified BART station. It can't be an accident that none of them have signs. If I knew the names of the stations, I could map out the whole thing easy. I know my way around BART better than anywhere, except maybe the Main Library.

I guess there's no reason I can't outright ask. "Which station is this?"

"What do you mean?" Sharrow asks.

"The name of the BART station," I say, wondering what else it could mean.

"We call them by their functions—testing center, sleeping rooms, cubes..." She looks confused.

"But it has a name, like Embarcadero or Montgomery. In my time, there were maps and signs everywhere."

She shakes her head. "Sorry, I've never seen a map down here."

"If you could tell me even one name, I'd know where I am. Right now I'm....lost."

Sharrow scrunches her brow and scratches her head like a caricature of someone who is trying to remember something.

"Please," I say, wanting so badly for her to be straight with me, to give me one scrap of info I can use.

"Does Powl sound familiar?" she asks. "I once heard an old-timer say Powl Station, or something like that."

"Powell? Powell Street Station?"

She shrugs. "That could have been it. Do you know it?"

"I know Powell really well. Are you saying we're in Powell?" I look around, trying to superimpose my memory of the Powell platforms on the ruins we're in. Powell is big, but not so big it could include *all* the ruined platforms I've seen. Unless... "Are there any other names you remember? Anything at all?"

I don't want to suggest something and create a false memory, so I wait, hoping.

"Maybe...." She scratches her head again. "There was something that reminded me of the moon. Moony, maybe?"

Moony... That could be how they pronounce *Muni*. Which is exactly what I was thinking. I remember the bus and light rail stations being expanded underground around Powell. I'm finally getting somewhere. Now all I need is to know which direction I'm facing.

"That helps a lot," I say. "There's one more thing. Have you heard of Union Square?"

She shakes her head.

"What about Moscone Center? Or Civic Center? Embarcadero?" I don't see any recognition spark in her expression, but I can't let it go. "Daly City? Coit Tower? Chinatown?"

"Sorry," she says. "You could keep saying names, but I've never heard them before."

I was so close. "Thanks anyway."

"Why do you want to know?"

I don't feel like I can tell her the truth—that I want to know which way it is to the wormhole. But actually, maybe it's that simple. "I don't like feeling turned around. I think I could picture the layout if I knew which way it was back to Detention."

"Detention's that way." She points.

I'm so happy I could hug her.

"You good now?" she asks.

"So good." The world feels right-side up again. "Thanks."

"You still want to take a ride?"

I grin. "Let's do it."

Near the mouth of a tunnel, we hop to the bottom of the trough where the tracks used to be. There's a rack of bikes just inside the tunnel.

"Grab a helmet," she says, taking one from a hook on the wall. "They're all same-same."

That doesn't seem very safe. I put one on and, as soon as I click the buckle, there's a hissing noise. The helmet is squeezing my head.

"What's happening?" I say, fumbling to unbuckle the helmet. I break the connection and the hissing stops. "What *was* that?"

"You mean the helmet tightening?"

"Yeah. What the heck?"

She laughs gently. "It does that to make it fit properly."

"Oh, like the jumper." I snap the buckle together again. The hissing and squeezing start up, but stop before the helmet gets too tight.

"This bike looks about right for you." She wheels one from the rack. "You know how to use the brakes? We'll get going pretty fast."

"No problem," I say, taking it by the handlebars and squeezing the handbrakes.

She mounts her bike and rides into the tunnel, cruising fast. I pedal hard to catch up, but she's still pulling away. I decide to let her—I'm a little scared to go any faster. But I have to admit it's fun. I feel like I'm flying. It reminds me of being in the wormhole. I could get used to—whoa!

Sharrow is stopped, waving her arms. I put on the brakes as hard as I can. The bike starts to skid, then I'm flipping—still on the bike—the back wheel over my head. I hear Sharrow yelling, along with my own high-pitched shriek.

The ground is coming, but I don't know what to do about it. I'm trying to decide if there's anything I *can* do when I hit, hard. I'm flat on my back, a tangle of bike on top of me, and I can't get any air. The tunnel overhead's a spinning blackness. I think I might pass out.

"Breathe," Sharrow says, coming into focus above me. "Breathe."

I want to scream *I would if I could* but I can't scream without any air.

My chest is on fire, trying draw a breath. When I can't take it another second, something releases inside me and air rushes into my lungs. My heart's beating so fast it's vibrating. I take deep gulps of air, and finally the ceiling stops spinning.

"There you go," Sharrow says. "Where does it hurt? Is anything broken?"

"I, I don't know."

"Let me take a look. Consent?"

"Y-yes." I hear a beep, then she unbuckles my helmet and tosses it aside.

She puts her fingers through my hair, checking my head, then runs her hands down my arms and legs. "Does it hurt anywhere? I don't feel any cuts or bumps."

"I think I'm okay. Help me sit up?"

She slips her hand behind my shoulder and eases me upright. "Good?"

"You mean considering I just endoed at a hundred miles an hour?"

"What happened? Didn't you see the warnings?"

"What warnings?"

"The rings starting with yellow, then orange, then red." She points and there they are, plain as can be, lining the tunnel.

"I didn't realize." That's probably what made me think of the wormhole.

"That was a pretty bad crash. Maybe we should go to Med."

"No, I promise, I'm fine."

She stands and pulls me to my feet. My head pounds and I stifle a groan. I don't want to go back to Med.

Sharrow tosses my helmet in a recycling bin and puts my bike in the rack, then gestures for me to go first out of the track area. She probably wants to make sure I don't tumble backward, given my prior gracelessness.

If my internal map is correct, we're in one of the Muni stations. We walk to the far side where Sharrow banks her personal to a wall of graffiti. A door opens and we cross into a familiar-looking white hallway with blue-gray indoor-outdoor carpet. Does everything here look the same, or are we back where we were last night?

"Is this near the club?" I ask.

"Affirm. The shortest way to the cubes is through the club."

Finally, I'm starting to get my bearings.

Down a couple of halls, Sharrow accesses the door to the club and loud music spills out.

"Stay close," she says, shouting to be heard.

It's already pretty crowded. Sharrow heads onto the dance floor and is swallowed by the mass of bodies. I tiptoe, but can't see her. She's gone. *Which means no one's watching me.* With my new mental map, I'm pretty sure I can make it back to Detention and the wormhole room. There's nothing stopping me.

I'm back at the door when I catch myself. If I get into the wormhole room—a big if—what then? What exactly can I expect to accomplish on my own?

My instinct was to bolt. But being rational, my best bet is to work with Sharrow, and even Bel.

I turn and Sharrow's standing there, hands on her hips. "What are you doing?"

"Old habits are apparently hard to break."

Her scowl softens. "I get it. So are you going to run, or come with me?"

"Come with you."

She turns back to the dance floor. This time I stay close and follow her through to the other side. She accesses the door we came in last night and we enter the hallway with the lights above the doors. Almost all the lights are red now.

Sharrow looks at her personal. "Last one on the left."

The door she stops at has a red light. She banks her personal, and the door opens to a square room with two couches in the center facing each other. There's a person on each couch—Flyx and *Daum*, the guard from Detention with the blue hair. Why's he here?

Sharrow crosses the room and plops down beside Daum. "Hey," she says as she settles back and crosses her arms across her chest, pointedly not looking at Flyx. I get the impression she's trying to seem casual, like Flyx doesn't matter to her, but everything from the quaver in her voice to her body language says otherwise.

The only place left to sit is beside Flyx. I want to sit by him, but I don't *want* to want that. My heart's racing as I sit on the far edge of the small sofa, hyper-aware of how close we are, despite me trying to put distance between us.

Sharrow steels a glance at us, and it hits me like ice water. I bury my feelings and inch even farther away from Flyx. I can't have her thinking I'm trying to steal her guy—I need her as an ally. No way will I let my stupid crush get in the way of saving my parents and the crew.

"So," Flyx says, slouching back.

We're all silent, sizing each other up.

"What's going on here?" Daum says. "What am I missing?"

I'm not sure what to say. Sharrow and I were planning to talk about how to deal with Bel. She seemed to think Flyx could help. I have no idea why Daum's here.

"Okay, I'll go first," Flyx says. "We're talking about treason."

CHAPTER TWENTY-THREE

"*Treason?*" Sharrow says, shrinking back.

"*What the eff,*" Daum says at the same time.

"Allie needs to go back in time," Flyx says. "Dietrich won't let her. I'm going to help her."

A huge weight lifts from my shoulders, but he should have kept it between us. "I appreciate that, but Sharrow says it's impossible."

"Yeah, are you off the tracks?" Sharrow says.

"But..." Flyx stares at Sharrow. "Then why are you here?"

"To figure out how to deal with Bel," Sharrow says. "Not...*this.*"

"Treason? Really?" Daum says.

"No one's talking treason," I say. "Sharrow says I have to forget about time-traveling, so that's what I'm going to do."

"Allie, you don't mean that," Flyx says.

"What choice do I have?" I stare at Flyx, pleading with my eyes for him to catch my drift. *Now's not the time.*

"Whatever this is or isn't, I'm out." Daum stands.

"Hold up," Flyx says. "I'm asking as your best."

"Why does this have you so twisted?" Daum shakes his head at Flyx. "The girl says she has to forget it. So *do*."

"Yeah, Flyx. Let it go," I say.

"Allie," he says, looking into my eyes. "If you want any chance of going back, we need them. Both of them."

It clicks. I get it now—he's trying to tell me we *can't* plan on our own. We can't do it without them. I nod, making the shift in my brain, trying to figure out how to get them on board. But I don't know them. I don't know what angle to take.

"Give it ten minutes," Flyx tells Daum. "Hear Allie's story. Then, if we aren't of one mind, we all drop it. For good."

Daum settles back on the couch and folds his arms. "Ten minutes."

"Sharrow, you game?" Flyx asks.

She avoids him, looking at me instead. "I'll listen. But I'm not promising anything."

"Time's counting," Daum says.

No pressure. "Okay, well..." I try to figure where to start, how best to convince them in only ten minutes. "Here's the really short version. I had no idea time travel was real until Bel and some other kids from the future showed up in 2018—my time—and took me to 1906 to pull a heist. Then, during the big quake, Bel shot my dad and a building fell, killing my mom and my friends."

"Oh, gods," Daum says.

"After that," I continue, "I got in the wormhole with Bel so we could travel back before the quake and fix everything. But instead, Bel hijacked me and brought me here. And now Dietrich won't let me leave."

"That's terrible," Sharrow says.

I look at her, allowing my true emotions to show on my

face. "All I want is to go back to 1906 and save my parents and my friends."

"I'm really sorry." Sharrow looks like she means it. "But my mom won't budge about time travel. And she has a point —changing the past only makes things worse."

"But I don't want to change the past," I insist. "I want to change it *back*."

"What do you mean?" Sharrow asks.

"My parents weren't supposed to die in 1906. When Bel and I went to that time, we changed history. Now I need to change it back to the way it was. The way it's supposed to be."

"How do you know *this* isn't the way it's supposed to be?" Daum asks.

"Because in this version Bel and I were never born," I say. "Since we clearly were born before, this latest version of history is wrong."

"I can confirm," Flyx says. "I saw it on the compare series. There were a bunch of people who were alive before, then their existence blinked out."

"That's probably my crew," I say. "Do you remember the names?"

"There was you, Bel, and Kaitlin," Flyx says. "Plus like ten more. I remember one of the names was odd. Mouse, maybe?"

"Yes, Mouse!" My heart clenches thinking of her. "Do you remember any others? Haze or Vee? Gracie? Noah?"

"Affirm," Flyx says. "It was definitely your crew."

I swallow back tears. It's not time to get emotional. It's time to do something about it. "They were not supposed to die in 1906. None of them had even been born yet. I have to change it back to the way it's supposed to be."

"I don't know about changing things *back*..." Sharrow says. "Is that any different?"

"It has to be, right?" I say. "If changing things makes it worse, changing things *back* has to be better."

"Has anyone ever tried that before?" Daum asks.

"Not as far as I know," Flyx says. "But Allie's theory makes sense."

"So you're saying you think it can work?" Daum says.

"Not without you," Flyx tells him. "We need your access to the wormhole. And we need you, too, Sharrow, since you're Allie's auditor."

"Even if I agree, you've got bigger problems," Sharrow says to me.

"Bel?"

"That, too," Sharrow says. "But I meant with the wormhole. My mom deactivated it."

"I think I can re-activate it," Flyx says.

"Why on the flat earth would you think that?" Daum says.

"In the TIC—" Flyx turns to me. "That's where I work. It's basically a wormhole. I have access to the operational programming, and—"

"You *what*?" Daum exclaims.

"Never mind," Flyx says. "My point is, if I can compare the TIC—that works—to the wormhole—that doesn't—I might be able to reactivate the wormhole."

"You're going to get us recycled like Spires and Novalie," Daum says.

"*They were recycled?*" My mouth goes dry.

"Oh, my gods." Sharrow sounds scared.

"Are they...dead?" I ask.

Flyx shakes his head. "Memories erased. But don't worry. It's not going to happen to us. I have it covered."

"How?" Sharrow asks.

"I've got everything under control. We're not getting recycled."

How is he so confident? Does he have some inside track? "What are you not telling us?"

"What do you mean?" He cocks his head and narrows his eyes, which tells me I'm onto something.

I shrug, all nonchalant, but I'm actually honed in on his micro expressions for clues to what he's hiding. "You seem so sure we're not going to get recycled...makes me wonder if you have some sort of inside information."

His eyebrows arch for a fraction of a second, telling me I got a hit. He *does* have inside info.

"Wait," Sharrow says so forcefully we all look at her. "Speaking on inside info..." She turns toward Flyx, but avoids meeting his gaze. "My mom was sure you told Allie something about the past. What happened? How are you not in trouble?"

Flyx and Daum exchange a glance.

"I convinced Dietrich it was a misunderstanding." Flyx presses his lips in a straight line, brow slightly furrowed. It only lasts a moment, but it's enough to convince me he struck some sort of bargain with Dietrich. That's how he knows we won't get recycled.

I don't know how he managed it, but it's a big relief.

I check Sharrow and Daum—they look relieved too. I feel like we're close to getting them on board.

"Listen, you guys," I say, looking back and forth between them. "If I don't go back to 1906, my parents and my friends all die, and my life is erased along with them. That's not supposed to happen. I can't let that happen. I have to go back. *Please*," I say, borderline begging. "Will you help me?"

Daum and Sharrow look at each other. The silence is thick, and the moment seems to take forever. Finally, Daum looks at me.

"I'm in," Daum says.

Sharrow looks down at her lap. The silence draws out again.

"Sharrow?" Flyx asks, his voice tender. "Are you with us?"

She meets his gaze, the first time I've seen her really look at him since she found out he doesn't remember her. "I'm with you," she says, and I feel like she means it just for him.

"Are you sure?" I ask her.

She looks at me and nods. "I'm sure."

I lean back, so relieved I'm shaking.

"Phee!" Flyx says. He looks at his personal and his expression goes flat. "I gotta go."

"Now?" Daum asks.

"I won't be gone long. You guys'll be here when I get back, right?" Flyx exits without waiting for an answer.

With Flyx gone, the room feels hollow, like he took all the energy with him. Or maybe what I'm feeling is relief— for the first time since I arrived in this time, I actually have a spark of hope.

"Hey, I'm hungry. Anyone else?" Daum asks.

Sharrow looks at me. "He's always hungry."

"Let's go eat," Daum says.

I can almost always eat, but I'm too drained to go anywhere. Plus I want to be here when Flyx gets back. "No thanks. You go, though."

"Sharrow?" Daum asks.

"Negative. I'll stay with Allie."

"Then how 'bout I bring stuff back? Would you eat then?"

"Absolutely," I say.

"I could change my mind," Sharrow says.

"Back soon." Daum heads for the door.

When the door closes behind him, Sharrow turns to me. "I've been thinking about Bel."

"Yeah?" I'd almost forgotten we came here to talk about her.

"As much as I'd like for us all to be a happy family, I can't deny she wants my mom to be *her* mom, not *our* mom. She doesn't want me around. But I can't cog what she'll do about it, how far she'll go. You know her better. What do you think?"

"I actually don't know her that well. But from what I *do* know, expect the worst. I've seen her be ruthless. She's capable of anything."

"So how do we fight that? Or at least protect ourselves?"

She's including me—that's good. "I wish I knew. All we can do is stay on our guard until we figure out her angle."

"Okay." She looks crushed, but attempts a weak smile. "I need to shower. Back in a few."

She disappears behind a door. I settle into the couch cushions, already bored. The room's got no TV, no books, no games. Not even a deck of cards. I wonder what the personal has.

I tap the face. "Do you have games?"

Query not understood displays on the screen.

I try again. "Start game."

Query not understood

"Open Scrabble."

Query not understood

"Do you have any entertainment?"

Query not understood

I give up and flop onto my back, kicking my feet up on the arm of the couch. I stare at the ceiling, plain white. There are no light fixtures. Instead, it looks like the ceiling itself is lit, like the whole ceiling is a light. Okay, that used up three seconds. What do I do now?

It's a lot harder to avoid thinking—feeling—when there's nothing to do. Now it grips my heart like a fist.

Mom. Jake. Bibi. The crew. My dad.

I've wondered my whole life who my dad was. I finally found him, and then he was ripped away. I picture Maxen's face, his smile. Then that image is replaced by Beck. Older, weathered, angry. Still Maxen, but...not. What happened to change him? Will I ever know?

My throat gets all tight, and my eyes prickle.

The bathroom door opens. I sit up, pushing away the tears with the back of my hand.

Sharrow comes out in her mint-green jumper, hair up in a towel-turban. "Something wrong?"

"Thinking about stuff I don't want to think about. I'm over it."

Sharrow rubs her head with the towel, then tosses it aside. Her hair is even more minty when wet.

"Hey," I say, eager to focus on something that's not my own misery. "What's with all the wild hair colors, tattoos, and body mods?"

Sharrow's brow furrows, but she doesn't seem offended. "What do you mean?"

"Some people have them in my time, but here, *everyone* has them."

She shrugs. "It's a way of showing we have the right to look how we want. To *be* how we want. When people topside can't."

"So why doesn't your mom have any?"

"She interacts directly with the ASPs, so she can't. She has to talk like them, too. But I don't think she cares. She was born into her role—her dad was one of the original scientists who discovered the wormhole and started the Resistance. She's always been really supportive of me not following in her footsteps." She ruffles her mint hair. "At least until now."

"What changed?"

"She's making me play junior diplomat when the president brings his daughters to tour the Zone. She says she needs someone she can trust absolutely. But I don't see why she can't pick Bel. I mean, *she's* her daughter, too. And Bel's already mod-free, plus she doesn't have a job...a job she loves."

I hear the anguish in her voice. I'm not going to tell her the tattoo lady said there's more pain to come.

The outside door swishes open. It's Daum, and I feel a twinge of disappointment it's not Flyx.

Daum holds up two plastic bags. "I didn't know what you'd like, so I got a bunch of different stuff."

"I'll flip the room." Sharrow heads toward the door. "Allie, come over here or it won't work."

I have no idea what she's talking about, but I join Daum and her by the door.

"Stay in the box or we'll get an error." Sharrow points to the ground. There's a rectangle outlined on the floor I hadn't noticed before.

"Keep your hands and feet inside the ride at all times," I say. They look at me like I grew a second head. "Never mind. I'll stay in the box."

Sharrow punches keys on the control panel. The lighting turns red, then there's a hum, and a rumble. Most of the floor—with the couches on it— lowers away, leaving a dark void. There are more mechanical noises, then another square of floor rises to fill the space, this one holding a round table and four chairs.

There's a *ca-chunk*, then the lights go back to normal.

Daum walks to the table and unloads the bags. "Spaghetti, enchiladas, spring rolls, veg salad, pizza. Take what you want."

"I'll take the enchiladas," I say. Closest thing to tacos.

FLYX STILL ISN'T BACK, and I wonder what's taking so long.

Daum, Sharrow and I are sitting around the table playing a card game they pulled from a hidden cabinet. It almost feels normal. Almost.

The game is one I've never heard of where the goal is to take over an alien planet. I've won three out of five rounds so far, and I remember back to playing parlor games with the crew, prepping to go to 1906. I guess I am pretty good at games.

"Occupation," Daum says, laying down his cards.

I lay mine down. "Annexation."

"You took it again," Sharrow tells me.

"Good game." Daum yawns.

It's catching, and I yawn, too, as I gather the cards to shuffle.

"We should get some sleep," Sharrow says. "We have to be at the testing center at nine."

"Flyx said he'd be back," I say. "Maybe we shouldn't leave yet."

"Who said anything about leaving? We flip the room."

"About that..." I've been thinking about it ever since she disappeared the couches. "Why make rooms transform? Don't you have tons of unused space down here? I mean, wouldn't it be easier to have different rooms for different purposes?"

"That's old-school thinking," Sharrow says. "And very American."

"Aren't we American?" I ask.

Daum chuckles. "What she means is, gobs of people don't have much space for personal use, particularly in overgrown urbans like Shanghai and Tokyo. This could be a solution. Plus, smaller spaces are more efficient with resources."

"But why do it here?" I ask. "Aren't you guys isolated from the rest of the world? It's not like your research gets shared. Or am I missing something?"

"No, you're right," Sharrow says. "But we have brilliant scientists here without much to do. My mom sets up research projects and contests so they don't get bored."

"Plus," Daum says, "one day we won't have to hide down here. *Vank the ASPs!*" He punches the air.

"*Flank and vank!*" Sharrow answers, like a cheer at a football game. Only in this game, the opponent is the Nazis and the losers might die.

"I've been meaning to ask you," I say. "How exactly is the Resistance trying to stop the Nazis? The videos weren't super clear on that."

Daum shrugs. "We exist. That's an act of resistance by itself."

"*That's it?*"

"It wasn't always," Sharrow says. "The founders used the wormhole to go back in time and try to prevent the ASPs from ever taking power."

"But that didn't work out so well," Daum says. "They discontinued the program. I've never actually seen anyone show up from another time before you."

"But you stand guard anyway?" I ask.

"Before yesterday, I'd have said it was a waste of time. Guess not."

"Yeah, guess not," I say.

"Aren't you guys dozy? Let's flip the room," Sharrow says.

"We could wait up a little longer for Flyx," Daum says.

"I can do another thirty, max," Sharrow says. "But I'm uber-bored of this game."

"I have an idea," I say. "How about if I tell your fortunes?"

"You can do that?" Sharrow says, eyes wide.

"It's one of my many skills."

"Phee," Daum says. "I'm in."

"How do you do it?" Sharrow asks.

"There are lots of ways," I say. "I could read your palms or tea leaves or—"

"Palms." Daum thrusts his hand out, palm up, on the table. "I consent one hundred."

CHAPTER TWENTY-FOUR

FLYX

In the TIC, I find the data Dietrich wants and copy it to the transfer drive. I'm about to erase the evidence of my log-in when the power goes.

I grip the CTAR, waiting for the back-up lights. But they don't come on. Rake me—it's a lockdown.

Real or drill?

The odds of an unannounced drill at this hour are low-low. More likely, the ASPs are in the Zone. They could be tearing apart our camouflage right now, searching for our soft, vulnerable core.

We train for this, but how can you really prep?

My heart's doing double-time and my resps are quick as I pull the flashlight from the wall and click it on. I try the door even though I know it won't open on lockdown.

I could be here as long as three days. The high-ups figure that's enough time for things outside to resolve, whether it's a false alarm, a nat disaster, or an invasion. Enough time for settling out and seeing who's left: the goodies or the baddies.

I'll be fine, physically anyway—the radiation turned off

with the power, and there're more than enough supplies.

I cross to the emergency box. Everything looks as it should: thermals, flashlight batteries, water, calories. Paperback novels—that's a laugh. And the three-day countdown timer. I push the red button and the ticking starts.

Three days isn't long. It's an eternity. Wondering who is out there, who's in control of the Zone. Who—if anyone—will come to the door.

I sit there on the floor by my box of useless supplies, borderline hyperventilating, runwild with maginings.

If the ASPs have invaded, it's unlikely anyone will come for me. Even if the baddies torture goodies for the locay, the surrounding camo is actual, not holo. Collapsed tunnels, huge cement slabs fallen from the ceiling, flooded sections, dead-ends. Near-impossible to nav.

So I'll spend three days brain-mauling what they've done to my friends, to my home. To Allison. Then, in the end, I'll never know. Instead, I'm sworn to set off the explosives embedded in the TIC, destroying myself, the wormhole tech, and as many of those ASP-bastards as possible.

I curl up, close my eyes, and picture Allison's face.

Tick, tick, tick.

Whoever chose that timer was an effing sadist. I'll go crazy from that sound long before three days.

There's a whirring. The lights come on. It was a drill.

MY GUT'S still tight as I head to Dietrich's office. The public sector is dark and deserted. I've hardly ever been here, and never this late. It gives me the crawls.

When I knock, Dietrich opens the door fast, like she was hovering there, waiting.

I step in, and she closes and locks the door. That's not ominous. Not at all.

She slips behind her sally desk and sits down.

Should I sit? She didn't say to, so I stand awkwardly, trying not to look jumpy.

"You have something for me?" she says.

The transfer drive's in my sweaty palm. I wipe it on my leg and hand it over.

She looks at me expectantly, but I have no idea what else she wants. Why doesn't she dismiss me?

"Well?" she prompts, raising her eyebrows. "Tell me what you found."

"Uh, sure..." I didn't think I had to memorize it. "Let's see...I got everything you requested. All the Jenny personnel and bioinformatics records, including files for the one named Max—"

"*The governors.*"

"Yeah. I got all the info I could find on governors. Assuming you didn't mean the old state government kind." I chuckle. She doesn't.

"Summarize."

"Uh, there were gobs, some in every quake-time in previous timelines."

"*This* timeline."

That's easier. "When you discontinued travel, you recalled and recycled all you could, so there aren't many left."

"How many are still out there?"

"Three, I think. Listed as DOD—dormant or dead."

"Which quake-times?"

"I remember two in 1906 and one in 2018." Easy, because those are Allison's years. "The one in 2018 has an odd name—you refer to him as 'Sink.'"

CHAPTER TWENTY-FIVE

I'm in one of four single beds, the one closest to the door. Sharrow and Daum are both asleep—I can tell by their breathing—and I'm jealous. It's not that the bed's not comfy or that I'm not tired. It's that my stupid brain won't shut off.

There's a full-on circus happening in my head. My mom and dad—the young versions—in one ring, surrounded by the crew, all crying out, reaching for me. Another ring has Jake and Bibi herding a bunch of rug-rats in animal costumes. The middle ring is writhing with Nazis. Beck's at the center cracking a whip, his red eyes leaking blood.

I shiver and roll on my side. I try to imagine I'm back in my bed at Bibi's, the sounds of baby-mamas walking the halls with fussy rug-rats, the smell of soured formula and full diapers wafting under my door. In real life, that always put me right to sleep simply to escape it. But I'm still wide awake, just sadder.

I hear a soft click at the door. In the dim light, I see Flyx step inside. Our eyes lock. My breath catches.

He crosses to my bed and squats down so we're face to face. "Hey, you okay?" he whispers.

"Not really." In more ways than one.

"What's wrong?"

"Can't sleep." I don't want to go into my whole sad story. Or tell him that being that close to him makes me feel all woogly inside.

"Wanna take a walk?"

"Now?"

"Why not? We'll have the whole place to ourselves."

We head away from the cubes and the club. It's silent, that middle-of-the-night hush when it feels like no one is alive but you.

I like the quiet. I never could find much of it back home. Except in the Main.

We walk side-by-side, settling into a quiet rhythm. I'm glad Flyx doesn't feel the need to fill the void with chitchat. I don't like chitchat on a good day.

At the end of a narrow corridor, Flyx banks his personal. I follow him through the door into a BART station, dark, deserted, and cold. I shiver and hug myself against the chill.

"Hang here. I'll get jackets." His voice sounds hollow in the void, and it's creepy, like we're the only humans left after the apocalypse.

He jogs away and I stare up at the dark ceiling, reminded of all the times I couldn't take it anymore at a foster home and I'd sneak out to look at the night sky. Somehow, I can forget my problems, at least for a minute, when there's no ceiling over my head. Plus, stars are pretty.

Flyx returns wearing a black hoodie and carrying a second one. I guess some things never go out of style. It's heavy, and soft, and I smell dryer sheets as I slip it over my head.

"Where did you go earlier, when you left the cube?" I ask, my curiosity winning over my love of silence.

"Not important."

"It was important enough you were gone for hours in the middle of the night. What were you doing?" I'm not going to let it go.

He seems to realize this and sighs. "I went to read through the histories again. When you said your crew hadn't been born yet in 1906, it tickled something in my memory, and I had to tease it out."

"Tell me."

"It wasn't that the crew hadn't been born *yet*. In this timeline, they are *never* born. I've been twisted trying to make sense of it—why would dying make them never be born in the first place?"

"Because—" My brain processes what he said. It *doesn't* make sense. "Okay...let's think this through. For me, my parents were killed before I was born—that tracks. I'm assuming it's the same for Bel, that she hadn't been conceived yet when our father died. *If* he's actually her father."

"He is."

"*What?* How do you know?"

He shrugs, looking sheepish. "I, uh, I checked the DNA records."

"How? Dietrich said they were in a vault."

"Yeah, the vault where I work. I rationed you'd want to know for sure."

"Oh. Thanks." That was nice of him. Though I don't remember telling him about it.

"So," he says, shoving his hands in the pockets of his hoodie. "That explains why you and Bel weren't born. But not the others."

"Yeah." I start walking. I need to think this through, and I can't do that standing still.

Flyx walks close beside me, not quite touching. It's a comfort, having him here. And it's nice he's letting me think, not pressing me to talk.

After a few minutes, something occurs to me. "You said the whole crew disappeared. Does that mean Kaitlin, too?"

"Affirm."

"Not died, *disappeared*?"

"The previous timeline articled her dying in 2018. But this timeline has no record of her existing what-so. She vanished from the histories. She was never born.

This makes zero sense. "What could we have changed in 1906 to make Kaitlin never be born...?"

"I'd guess whatever erased the rest of the crew. For the timing to work, something vanked them all at the same time."

"But what? They were all born in different times.... How could—" My mom said Maxen wasn't supposed to be able to have kids, but by some fluke she got pregnant with me. He was different than other Jennys...the only Jenny who could father children. "*Oh my God.*" The pieces click into place, forming a picture.

"What?"

Could it really be true? "I think...I think maybe..." I swallow. "What if Maxen was *everyone's* father—the whole crew."

It hangs there in the air for a moment.

"If he's the father of all of us—including Kaitlin," I continue. "It would make sense that when he died, none of us were born. Unless you have another explanation that works." I almost want him to, because this makes losing the crew hurt even more.

Flyx cocks his head. "You could be right. It's the only thing that makes everything fit."

I nod, my damn eyes filling again. I fist the tears away, doubling my resolve to get the crew back. Then it dawns on me— "Do you think Bel knows?"

"If she does, that's one way to confirm the theory."

Bel was adamant that Beck-slash-Maxen was her father and had passed down the ability to time-travel. Maybe that's because she knew he had fathered children across time, all of whom inherited the ability. "I need to talk to her. *Now*."

"You can't."

"Try and stop me." I turn and start back.

"Wait," Flyx says, catching up with me. "Bel's in Dietrich's chambers, in the public sector, past a whole lot of security."

"But—"

"How important is it? Can it wait until tomorrow?"

"Yeah, I guess." I clench my fists, frustrated, with nowhere for all that energy to go. I glance at the ceiling again, wishing I could see the sky. "How can you stand it? Never seeing the stars."

"What makes you think I never see the stars?" He raises his eyebrows mischievously.

"Are you serious right now? Because I'm pretty sure I can get through tonight if I could be out under the stars."

"Okay, but it's a climb."

"Bring it on."

MY THIGHS ARE BURNING when we climb out onto a flat roof. There are more stars than I've ever seen, and I can smell the ocean.

"This is exactly what I needed." I feel better than I've felt in days. "Can we check out the view of the city?"

"It's not much to see at night, but sure." He heads toward the edge of the roof.

I only make it a few steps before I trip and fall hard on my hands and knees.

Flyx rushes back. "You okay?" He reaches for me. "Consent?"

I clasp his right hand with mine. "I consent." There's a soft electronic ping from our personals, and he pulls me to my feet.

"You hurt?"

"Just my pride." I let go of his hand and dust off my knees. My jumper is intact and I don't seem to be bleeding.

"My fault. I should have guided you. We can't risk a light. But I know the way." He extends his hand again.

I slip my hand in his, and my heart gives an involuntary skip. His hand is warm and dry, and I hope mine isn't clammy. He guides me across the roof to a wall that comes to my chest. Still holding hands, we look out.

"There isn't a single light," I say, looking across the tangled black shapes that were once the buildings of my city.

"The Massive destroyed everything. There's no one down there. No one alive, anyway."

Seeing this in person punches me in the gut like I'm learning it for the first time. Pier 39, Coit Tower, the Transamerica Pyramid. The Main. Everything I've ever known. Ruins.

"Even earthquake-proof buildings went down," Flyx continues. "Fires burned out of control. Of the million-plus people, only a few thou made it out. That's one reason the city was declared uninhabitable—all the bodies."

I heard that on the history video, but couldn't believe it was true. "They actually left them there..."

"They had to. It was too dangerous to go in and get them. Besides, what would they do with hundreds of thousands of decaying bodies? Can you imagine how much land it would take to bury them? Or how much pollution from cremation?"

I picture streets, stores, office buildings—schools—filled with the dead. I cringe, glad it's too dark to see anything below. Then I realize—this didn't *just happen*. "How long has it been?"

"It was 2119, so...thirty-four years."

"Shouldn't the bodies be pretty much decomposed by now? Or picked clean by animals?" I remember the awful video of the birds. "So why hasn't anyone come back to rebuild?"

"Because *we* can't let them—the Resistance. We can't risk the ASPs finding out about the wormhole. So when they started making noise about coming back to the city, our scientists inflated the test results to show it's still too toxic."

"I guess that makes sense." There's a sadness, a sickness in my belly as I look out at the wreckage. "How far does it go?"

"The entire peninsula, from the remains of the Golden Gate Bridge all the way down to Palo Alto."

"The Golden Gate's gone?"

"All the bridges were destroyed in the quake. No need to rebuild them with the peninsula off limits."

It's impossible to imagine San Francisco with no bridges. "What's the nearest inhabited city?"

"I'll show you." He leads me to the opposite side of the roof. Off in the distance, two patches of light glow in the fog. "That's San Jose to the south, and Oakland to the east.

They both suffered damage, but nothing compared to here."

"What about the new city...New Francisco? Can you see it from here?"

"No, too far inland."

"What's it like?"

"No idea. I've never been anywhere but here."

"Really? Don't you wonder about it?"

"I never thought any more about it than about living on the moon. It's out of reach, out of the realm of possibility."

"You don't get stir crazy?"

"No, not me. Some people do, though. They can leave if they want, but not very many do."

"You can leave?"

"We're not prisoners. But it's not a good life out there. It's safer here, plus people can be themselves."

I guess that's not nothing.

"You ready to go back?" He gives my hand a squeeze and a thrill goes through me.

"Honestly? No. Can we stay a little longer?"

"Sure." He leads me to a lean-to then lets go of my hand to reach inside. He pulls out a blanket and shakes it into the air, letting it drift down. "Help me spread this out?"

I grab a side and pull it flat, then we crawl to the middle and sit cross-legged.

"I'm guessing you come here a lot," I say.

"When I need to think." He repositions himself, lying flat on his back. "View's better this way."

I lower myself beside him.

"Wait," he says. "I'll make you a pillow."

I prop myself on my elbow and he slides his arm around me. I settle back with my head cradled in his shoulder. Lying there beside him, I'm aware of his scent, the sound of his breathing, the heat where our sides press together. My whole body is buzzing, like every cell is awake. I like this feeling, but at the same time I know it's wrong to feel this way about *him*. I try to focus on the stars while my body wars with itself about whether to press closer or scoot away.

"Allison," he says, all low and breathy.

I tell myself not to look at him. But I can't help it. I turn and we're staring into each other's eyes.

"I'd like to kiss you," he whispers.

Quickly, I turn my gaze to the stars. I can't look at him because I want to kiss him, too. I think of Jake, the only boy I've ever kissed. My heart clenches at the memory, and I'm frozen. Caught between missing Jake and wanting to kiss Flyx.

"It's okay if you don't want to," he says.

"No! I mean, *yes*." I turn to him. "I do want to kiss you."

"Do you consent?" he asks.

This place is so weird! I nod.

He moves closer, so close his breath whispers on my lips. "You have to say it."

"I consen—"

His lips are on mine, and a bolt of electricity zings through my body. I wrap my arms around him. He pulls me closer, and I kiss him back, hard. My heart is slamming in my chest. I've never felt like this before.

After a few minutes, he plants little butterfly kisses across my cheeks, then down my neck. My whole body tingles, and my cheeks sting from where his face scraped against mine. Then he presses against me, his mouth hot against my neck. I'm breathing fast, and so is he, and I know I have to stop this.

"Flyx?"

"Mmmmm, yeah?" His voice is husky, and it makes me want to kiss him more.

"Uh, we should probably go. It's getting late." I have no idea what time it is.

He groans. "I hate it, but you're right." He plants a quick kiss on my lips, then gets to his feet and extends a hand, pulling me up. "Thanks for coming here with me. Maybe we could do it again sometime?"

I slip my arms around his waist and answer with a kiss.

CHAPTER TWENTY-SIX

An alarm blares and I bolt upright, hitting the device on my wrist to stop the sound. I register where I am— the cube—and flop back on the bed. It can't be morning already.

"Are you always late?" Sharrow asks, coming out of the lav.

I bolt up again. "But—I set my alarm."

"You're not late *yet*. But you're cutting it close if you want coffee."

I sling my legs over the side of the bed, still wearing the gray jumper from yesterday. "I always want coffee."

Sharrow gives me the side eye. "Especially when you're up really late, huh?"

Guilt floods over me. Does she know I went out with Flyx? She's smiling, so I'd guess not. Which somehow makes it worse.

What was I thinking, kissing Flyx? I *wasn't* thinking. I'm supposed to be Sharrow's friend. And Jake's more-than-friend. I can't let it happen again.

I notice the other beds are empty. "Where are the guys?"

"When I woke up, they were scheming about getting Flyx into Detention to check out the wormhole machine. They should have an opportunity later today, so they went to prep."

"Cool!" I hop up and head to the lav. "I'll be ready in a sec."

SHARROW and I show up at the lavender waiting room with only seconds to spare. Bel got here first again and looks impatient. Today she's wearing regular clothes. Well, regular-*ish*. High-water blue plaid pants and a long-sleeved white T-shirt that shows her tummy.

"What's with your clothes?" Sharrow asks.

Bel smirks. "Looks like I graduated."

"From what?" I ask.

"All this." Bel gestures to our surroundings. I have no idea what she means. "You should be thrilled, Sparrow."

"*Sharrow*," I say.

"Why should I be thrilled?" Sharrow sounds doubtful.

Bel looks smug. "I convinced Mom *I* should be the junior diplomat, not you."

"*Really?*" I say. Bel's the least diplomatic person I know.

"How'd you convince her?" Sharrow asks. She seems relieved. Mostly.

"I *knew* there were records from before the latest history-change," Bel says. "Mom reviewed them and couldn't help coming to the conclusion I'd be a perfect diplomat. I've only been training for it my whole life."

"That's...great." Sharrow's smile is strained.

Just yesterday she told me how she loved her job and didn't want to be a diplomat. But I guess now she's feeling a bit pushed out. Probably because Bel's the one doing the pushing.

"On the bright side, you won't have to dye your hair or get your tattoos removed," I tell her.

"That's right!" Bel says with fake enthusiasm. She strides to the circle on the wall and banks the door to the purple classroom.

Sharrow gives me a look like a wounded puppy. "I guess I'll go to Med. See you later, Allie?"

"Of course."

She attempts a smile, then leaves.

As soon as the door shuts, I head for Bel. As much as I want to ream her about how she treated Sharrow, I skip to the bigger issue. "I need to know something." My voice sounds ominous, even to my own ears.

Bel turns and looks me up and down. "What's wrong with you?"

"Vee actually *is* your sister. Did you know that?" I scrutinize her reaction.

Her brows shoot up, then scrunch down. "What are you talking about?"

"Not just Vee, the *whole crew*. They're our half siblings."

I watch her face and it's like I can see the words registering, her brain calculating. "*Oh my gods.*"

She didn't know.

"How could I have been so blind?" she says. "It all fits. I can't believe I didn't see it before. They wouldn't have all vanished from the records unless..."

"Unless something happened that caused them never to be born," I finish.

"Like me killing Maxen," she whispers. "It's like I killed them all."

"No," I say, though I'd thought the same thing. "The building collapsed. You didn't do that. If that hadn't happened, they'd be like us—time orphans."

"Instead they're...gone forever."

"It doesn't have to be forever...."

She looks at me with so much pain and regret, I think I have her. Then her eyes harden. "We can't. We can't go back."

"We have to. You need to convince your mom. *Please*, Bel. "

"You're wasting my time." She marches to the desk she used yesterday and drops into the chair. "Get to work."

I stare at her, but she avoids looking at me. What's her damage? She should be all about going back to fix what *she* messed up.

Whatever. I'll do it without her.

I sit at the computer and see the name of the test. "*Ethics?* Are you kidding me?"

Without looking up, Bel says, "I'm supposed to tell you that this test requires complete and total honesty. Be yourself." She says this like it's in quotes.

Be myself. About ethics. As if that would ever fly. Talk about a definite fail.

I stare at the screen, delaying. I consider messaging Flyx. I want to—I *really* want to. But that's exactly why I can't. I don't trust myself.

I never should have gone with him last night. I never should have kissed him.

I have to tell him it can never happen again.

But not yet.

I'll tell him in person. With some distance between us.

Might as well get on with the test. I wipe my palms on the legs of my jumper and hit "enter."

Question 1-A: Someone drops a valuable coin but doesn't notice. What do you do?

Easy. I'd slip the coin in my pocket and head to Micky D's, which sounds really good right now.

But of course I'm not actually going to say that. I type in the *correct* answer: I would return the coin.

Question 1-B: In the above scenario, you are starving and the coin is the only way for you to obtain food. What would you do?

Why would that matter? But again I type the answer they want: it doesn't matter if I'm hungry. Returning the coin is the right thing to do.

Question 1-C: In the above scenario, the person who dropped the coin is wealthy and will never miss is. What would you do?

I don't know why I was worried. I've totally got this.

AFTER A BAZILLION QUESTIONS, each with parts A through Z, the screen displays TEST COMPLETE.

"Done," I tell Bel. "How many more are there?"

She looks at me over her screen. "That was the final test."

I wasn't expecting that. "Great! Can I go? I'm starving."

I bet I can find my way back to the Donut Shoppe. The coffee-flavored drink Flyx brought me yesterday has me reconsidering my opinion of liquid nutrition. Maybe they'll have something like a strawberry shake. I'm tempted to fill my bottle and sneak back to the roof. Without Flyx this time. I have a morbid need to see what the city looks like in daylight, and I need to do that alone. Plus avoiding temptation is top priority.

"Uh, hello?" Bel says, standing over me frowning.

"Uh...yeah?"

"Where were you? I was talking, and you zoned out or something."

Oops. "That happens sometimes when I'm hungry. I was thinking about food." Could I sound any more lame?

She goes to the door, shaking her head like she can't believe what an idiot I am.

I follow her into the waiting area.

"Wait here. My mom will be here soon. See ya." She exits though the main door, leaving me alone.

That probably wasn't her best idea. What's to keep me from taking off?

But I shove my instincts down. I'm better off if Dietrich thinks I'm cooperating.

I sit with my legs tucked under me, wishing again I could access a game or music or something on my personal device. Given how many games have been played throughout history on phones and Gameboys, there has to be some sort of entertainment. People can't have changed that much. I should ask Flyx.

I tap the personal to tag him, but stop myself. Nope. Not gonna do that.

The door swishes open and Dietrich enters.

"Allison, I have your test results."

"How'd I do?" I think I did pretty well, and I'm curious how well. Like will she tell me how I scored compared to average?

"Regretfully, your results were not good enough to warrant salvage. You'll be recycled."

"What?" There's no way I heard that right. *"What?"*

"You're being recycled. Now."

No. They can't actually recycle me. "There's got to be some mistake." My heart races and sweat drenches my pits. "I knew the right answers."

"It wasn't about *correct* answers. It was about being honest."

Oh, crap. "Wait, I didn't realize. Let me take it again. I'll do better."

"The   decision   is   final.   You'll   be   recycled immediately."

"No, no, no! You can't do that. *Please.*" What the hell happened? Flyx was so sure I was safe.

For a split second, I see a trace of sadness on Dietrich's face, then it's gone. "Let's go." She grabs my arm and yanks me off the couch—I guess consent doesn't matter when someone's getting erased.

I frantically look for a way to escape as she drags me through the outer door.

"Don't be stupid." She pats a gun strapped to her hip. How did I miss that?

As we head down the hall, I walk as slowly as possible, buying time. I don't see any way out other than getting her to change her mind.

"Doctor Dietrich, please. Think of all the time you've already invested in me. Let me retake the test."

"Not an option."

"No, listen—if you keep me around, I promise to make it

worth your while. I can be really useful. I could spy for you or I could be a diplomat like Bel. I'd be great at that."

"Hardly."

"No really, I have all kinds of skills. I can help you. Let me prove it."

"Stop begging. It's pathetic," she says.

"What can I do to get another chance? There has to be something."

"There's nothing more to be done. We're here."

"What?" We're at the outer door to Med. Wait, that's good—Sharrow's here. She'll help me.

The door opens and Calix is standing there.

Dietrich shoves me toward him. "You know what to do."

"Wait—" I turn to plead with her, but the door closes. I turn back to Calix, remembering how kind he was before. Now his brown eyes are hard. Still, I have to try. "There's been a mistake. I'm not supposed to be recycled."

He takes my arm and pulls me across the empty green waiting room, not saying a word.

"You're a doctor," I say. "You're not supposed to hurt people."

Still silent, he banks his personal and the door slides open to the medical room. It's empty. No patients, no Sharrow.

"Where's Sharrow?" Panic wells in my throat. "Sharrow?" I call out.

Calix leads me toward the beds. If he injects me with the paralyzing stuff, it's over. I have to do something now.

He's a doctor—I can play on those instincts.

"Ow, my ankle!" I drop to the ground, the sudden move jerking my arm free of his grip. My muscles tense—fight or flight? Flight? I won't make it out the door—I'm sure my personal's been deactivated. So fight? Calix looms over me, outweighing me by maybe double. Fight doesn't seem any better.

"Give me your hand," he says.

He reaches for me and my instincts kick in. I grab his hand and squeeze hard to draw his attention while I unlatch his personal device with my other hand. Once I palm it, I moan and fall back. "Owww, it hurts." I roll to my side, facing away from him, and slip the personal into my jumper. I turn back and assess his reaction—I don't think he noticed a thing.

"I'll carry you."

"No, let me try again." I get my feet under me, and as I sense him leaning over to take my hand, I tuck my chin and push up hard, ramming my head into his jaw.

He falls to the ground, slack. Did I knock him out?

I'm not sticking around to find out. I use his personal and in seconds I'm through the door in a fight-and-flight combo.

I bank the personal to get into the hallway, then sprint like I'm being chased, because it won't be long before I am.

I run down hallway after hallway, holding tight to Calix's personal. My luck holds and I don't see another soul, but I'm not sure where I am, or where I'm going.

My luck won't hold forever—I've got to get out of sight. I use the personal to access a door, and find myself in a BART station. I sprint across it and drop into the track area so I can escape through the train tunnel. But the mouth of the tunnel is bricked over. Please let it be camouflage! I hold the personal up, waving it back and forth. I'm on the verge of full-blown panic when a hidden door slides open. I step through and it shuts behind me, leaving me in pitch darkness.

I wave my arms, hoping for motion sensor lights to kick

on, but nothing happens. I remember Flyx using his personal as a flashlight when we crawled through the ductwork, so I push mine higher on my arm, strap Calix's to my wrist, and tap the face.

"Flashlight."

It works! I shine the beam around the tunnel. It's filthy and cobwebby and littered with trash, and the train tracks are still in the ground. They obviously don't use this tunnel. If I follow it, it should lead me away from their complex and out into the city.

But *out* won't get me back to 1906.

Maybe I should head for Detention instead. Sharrow said Daum and Flyx were checking out the wormhole machine today. They could have fixed it.

I turn back to access the secret door in the brick wall, but between me and the wall is a pile of broken concrete that goes to the ceiling. It's got to be a hologram, but I touch a concrete slab and it feels solid. If I didn't know better, I'd never believe there was a passage here at all.

But it doesn't matter—I've already come to my senses. The only thing waiting for me back that way is recycling. And if they recycle me, I'll *never* get back to 1906. I won't even know there is a *back* to get back to.

I turn away from the rubble and head in the other direction. I'll find a way to return when they're not looking for me. As long as I stay alive—and stay me—there's a chance I can get back to 1906.

I head out, wishing I hadn't lost track of my mental map. I don't have any idea how far it is to the next station. Some of the BART stops downtown are pretty close together, but others are a lot farther apart. At least I'm sure of one thing—I'm not in the tunnel that goes under the Bay because my ears aren't popping.

After what seems like a mile, I see the end of the tunnel where it opens into the next station. I turn off the flashlight in case anyone's there, and crouch low while I creep down the tracks. My eyes adjust and I scan the station—I'm the only one here. It doesn't look like anyone's been here in a very long time. The walls are dark with grime and slime, with trickles of water running down them, and the floor's got a layer of trash and dirt that must've been accumulating for decades.

This place obviously doesn't get used by the Resistance. Time to head outside.

I spot one of those kiosks with the map of the routes. I jog over and rub the surface with my sleeve. The star marked "You Are Here" is at Montgomery Station. I know this part of town—right by the Palace Hotel.

I dash for the stairs to the street, but when I reach the base, I hear something—*voices*.

Adrenaline surges through my body, but it's too late to run. A man and a woman are coming down, looking right at me.

"Halt," the woman says. She hurries down the last few steps, followed by the man. They're in uniforms—military. With guns. Their hats have patches of a coiled snake.

ASPs. *Nazis.*

Shit! What do I do? Only scientists are supposed to be in this area—there's no way can I pull off I'm a scientist.

"Who are you?" the woman demands.

I open my mouth to reply. The usual caught-off-guard Cockney accent is about to pop out, but I stop myself— Nazis don't like foreigners.

"Hello," I say, in a perfectly plain, all-American news-caster accent.

They look at me, more puzzled than suspicious, if I'm reading them right.

"Who are you?" the woman repeats. "What are you doing here?"

My brain flips past possible scenarios—who can I be? Why am I here? What do I say?

My mouth hangs open, but nothing comes out.

I can't come up with a single answer.

CHAPTER TWENTY-SEVEN

FLYX

Daum and I pause at the top of the staircase outside Detention. He looks nervous. Being honest, I am, too.

I'm re-thinking, now. Not for me—I'm all in. But I shouldn't risk Daum getting vanked. He has no stakes.

I'm about to nix the mission when he stands up straighter, chin out.

"Don't worry—we got this," he says. Reassuring *me*.

Before I can stop him, he banks the door and steps inside. I can see he's scared, but only a best could glim that. We should be okay.

As per expected, Ogden and Lark are on.

Ogden looks over, surprised but not alarmed, and gives a nod. "What's down?"

Lark alerts, suspicion crinkling the skin around her eyes —she's the tougher sell.

"Orders," Daum says, crossing to the console. He banks his personal and a req populates the screen.

I hold my resps, gauging Lark's reaction. Luck—she glances and her concern fades.

"Og, grab your stuff," she says.

Ogden doesn't question, doesn't even glance at the screen. He grunts an affirm and extracts his pack from under the desk.

Then—*bang-oh*—the two exit. The whole thing took less than a minute.

Daum gives a sally grin. "Doesn't get more cinch than that."

This could have gone so many other ways. But no need or time to dwell. "Let's get doing." No tell how long it will take to cog how Dietrich disabled the machine. "Tools?"

Daum cocks his head. "Not waiting for lockdown?"

The lights turn yellow, a warning tone sounds, and there's a buzz at the door indicating the auto-lock mech has activated. Simultaneously, I get the alert zap from my personal.

"Right," Daum says. "I'll find those tools."

CHAPTER TWENTY-EIGHT

I stand there with my mouth open, staring at the two Nazis.

Come on, brain, engage. Say something!

Calix's personal zaps my wrist and I jump, hugging it to my chest.

The Nazis are probably wondering what the hell is wrong with me.

"I'm a little jumpy. You surprised me." Surely they noted that my "jump" was two minutes after they arrived, *after I said hello*.

What was that zap, anyway? Did someone discover I have the personal? Are they using it to track me? I'm an idiot—I should have dumped both personals back in the tunnel.

"What exactly are you doing here?" the woman asks. Her reddish-pink skin is blotchy, her features pinched like a weasel.

"I'm new." I pause, hoping she'll fill in some details for me. But she doesn't, so I keep scrambling. "I was stretching my legs and got turned around. I guess I'm not supposed to be in this area?"

"You're certainly not," the man says. He's tall and bald with round features, his expression kind. He looks old enough to be my dad. I glance at his hand—he's wearing a wedding ring, so maybe he *is* a dad. Maybe I can appeal to his fatherly instincts.

"I didn't mean to break the rules," I say, trying to project a helpless vibe. "I got lost."

"Who are you?" the weasel-woman insists.

What do I say? "I...I uh..." Suddenly I remember Bel's new job. "I'm an apprentice," I blurt. "I just started my training. Oh, why did I have to wander off? I'm going to be in so much trouble."

"Who are you apprenticing with?" the man asks.

"She's going to be so angry," I say, not giving a name. I look up at the man with my best puppy dog eyes. "I don't want to get in trouble. I have to do well at my new job."

"Answer the colonel," Weasel demands.

I have to give a name—I don't have a choice. "Dr. Dietrich."

"That's a fortunate assignment," the man—the colonel —says.

"*Sir?*" Weasel says. "Look what she's wearing. No apprentice would wear *that*."

"This?" I look down at my jumper. "I'm getting fitted for my new wardrobe. It makes it easier to try stuff on."

Weasel steps aggressively toward me. "Who are you *really?*"

"Stand down," the colonel tells her. He turns to me. "I'm meeting with Dr. Dietrich in a few minutes to discuss the president's visit, and I'm supposed to meet her new apprentice. So the question is, what are you doing *here?*"

"That meeting's now? Oh, no, this is *terrible*. It's a brand-new job and I've already blown everything," I say, channeling my actual distress. "I wish I could undo it. Did you ever make a mistake you wished you could erase?" I ask the colonel.

He looks wistful and chuckles. "A long time ago I did get myself in a pretty good pickle."

"That's where I am now," I say. "You could be my hero and make my mistake disappear."

"*Colonel Marek*," Weasel says.

He holds up his hand, stopping her. I'm laying it on pretty thick, but apparently not too thick for him.

"Sir, *please*," I say. "Can you find it in your heart to point me in the right direction and forget you saw me here?"

He looks at me, his gaze warm and fatherly, a smile crooking his mouth. He's going to let me go!

"Young lady," he says. "You need to face the music."

"But—

"Come with us." He gives Weasel a nod and she grabs my arm like a snake striking.

"I made a mistake," I say, keeping eye contact with the colonel. "And I'm very, very sorry. I've learned from this, and it won't happen again."

He looks away. Not good.

"Shut up." Weasel yanks me toward the stairs.

"Ouch," I say, hoping the colonel will feel sorry for me. No such luck.

"Sir, our recon?" Weasel asks.

"Later."

Weasel holds tight to my arm while we follow the colonel back up the stairs they came from. I think this stairway goes to street level, *outside*. Maybe I can break away.

Nope—at the top of the stairs is another enclosed common area, as rundown as the one below. Weasel's fingers dig in as she pulls me past an orange barrier—so much for my excuse that I was "stretching my legs and got turned around." Coming from this direction, it would have been impossible not to know the area was off limits. Which begs the question, what were *they* doing down there?

Weasel leads me across a cracked tile floor covered with puddles and debris.

"Ew!" I'm in a puddle, my shoe-booties soaked with disgusting water. Weasel's smirking—she did that on purpose.

We cross to a cement wall with one door, no windows. The colonel holds the door open, and Weasel shoves me through into a hallway. We proceed in silence to an area with filing cabinets and other office-y stuff. Ahead, there's a reception desk facing a lobby on the other side—we're entering from the back. There's a woman sitting at the desk. As we approach—the Nazi's boots clacking on the tile—she turns. She sees me and her eyes go wide.

"Officers," she says.

"Where's Dietrich?" Weasel demands.

The receptionist swallows. "*Dr.* Dietrich is in her office. I'll let her know—"

"No need." Weasel turns, yanking me so hard I stumble.

"Wait," the receptionist calls.

Weasel doesn't wait. She marches me down a side hallway with office doors on each side. I hear the colonel following.

Smack at the end of the hall is a closed door with a nameplate that reads "Dr. Piers Dietrich."

Weasel barges in without knocking.

The office is oversized and luxurious. Apparently Dietrich is big stuff. She comes to her feet behind her enormous desk, unsurprised—until she spots me. Then her expression flashes shock, which quickly transforms to fury.

"What's going on?" she asks, her rage barely controlled.

"She says she got lost," Weasel says, "but—"

"Give us the room," the colonel interrupts.

Weasel draws a sharp breath as if to object, then presses her lips together. She gives me a little shove as she lets go of my arm, but I'm expecting this and catch my balance.

"I'll be right outside, sir." She leaves, closing the door.

I look at Dietrich. Under her smooth, poised exterior, I know she's seething. "I'm so sorry," I say, wanting to get my story out before she says something to contradict it. "I know I only started my apprenticeship, and I shouldn't—"

"Enough," the colonel interrupts. "Dr. Dietrich, may we sit?"

She gestures to the two visitors' chairs on our side of the desk, then takes her seat.

"I'm obligated to report," the colonel says, "I found your apprentice below in Montgomery Station. It appears she's too inquisitive for her own good."

"I'm so sorry," I say. "It won't happen again."

"You're right," Dietrich says. "You're relieved of duty. Wait in my chambers while I decide what to do with you." She points to a door at the back of the room.

I stand and the blood drains from my face—as soon as I'm out of the colonel's sight, there's nothing to stop Dietrich from recycling me.

"If I could just explain," I plead. There will be no convincing Dietrich, but if I can get the colonel on my side, it could buy me some time. "This job is all I have in the world. I know I made a mistake—a bad mistake—but it was only because I wanted to do well."

I turn away from Dietrich's scowl to check the colonel's expression. He looks sad, not angry.

"*Now,*" Dietrich barks, stabbing her finger toward the door.

I note the colonel shaking his head. If I keep it up, he might come to my defense.

"Dr. Dietrich, you know how hard I worked to get this job," I say. "I would never throw it away intentionally. I was trying to prove I deserved to be here—"

"By wandering off—"

"By learning my way around. I usually have a great sense of direction, but somehow I got lost. I was trying to be the best at my job I could possibly be, to show that you made the right decision in choosing me. But it backfired. And I can't express how much I regret my choices, and how differently I will do things in the future if given the chance."

I pause, hoping the colonel will jump in, but I don't dare look at him. I can't afford to scare him off.

"Why are you still here?" Dietrich says. "In my chambers now, or I'll—"

"Wait," the colonel says.

Yes!

"Excuse me?" Dietrich's voice is low and gravelly.

"Perhaps we've been a bit hasty."

"I don't think—"

"After all," the colonel says, "a healthy curiosity is a sign of intelligence, is it not? And we know how the president prizes intelligence."

Dietrich cocks her head. "Above obedience, Colonel? I don't think so."

"Yes, of course you're right." The colonel is nodding, agreeing. I hope he's building rapport, not changing his mind. "Obedience is necessary, to be sure. But..." Good, there's a *but.* "With those of particularly high intelligence, *blind* obedience is not the best way to achieve loyalty. Sometimes it's necessary to take a broader view and *inspire* loyalty rather than demand it. In upholding the president's ultimate objectives, we're obligated to be cautious not to throw out the wheat with the chaff."

I don't know this metaphor, but it seems like he's arguing to give me a second chance.

Dietrich shakes her head. "Once my trust is broken, it's beyond repair."

"Surely you can't mean that," the colonel says. "Look at the great examples in history. Broken Japanese pottery made more beautiful by repairing cracks with gold. The rebuilding of the Nazi empire after it was all but destroyed at the end of World War II. Why, your very own success *here* is literally built upon a crack in the earth so great there was thought to be no hope of ever bridging it. Yet here we are, about to show the president the great strides you've made in reclaiming this city."

Dietrich opens her mouth as if to speak, but then purses her lips.

"Piers." The colonel leans toward her, bracing his elbows on her desk. "How do you think the president would handle a similar situation with one of his own daughters, hm? I suggest we use this opportunity to demonstrate that the president—and we as his instruments—are *deserving* of loyalty and obedience. Together, we can turn this curious young woman into an asset for the president and his grand plan."

Thank you, Colonel!

Dietrich looks down at her desk and straightens her pens. When she looks up, her face is placid, but her posture's still rigid. "Let's say I were to give her one more chance. What then if she were to fail?"

The colonel leans back and looks over at me. "I will slit her delicate throat myself."

CHAPTER TWENTY-NINE

Slit my throat?

Apparently I'm a terrible judge of character.

Dietrich looks from the colonel to me, then leans back, her hands braced on the edge of the desk. Her index finger taps the desk four times. Then she looks him in the eye. "I agree her potential warrants another chance. Under the right circumstances."

"What would those be?" he asks.

"A mentor. Someone with a superior sense of duty and adherence to protocol."

"I would be honored—"

"A young woman named Bel Raskin," Dietrich interjects. "A model member of the Party. She'll be an excellent example for our wayward young lady."

"Oh." He casts a look in my direction. "A shame she won't be working with me. But very well."

"Then it's decided," Dietrich says. "I'll make the arrangements and we'll reschedule our meeting for tomorrow."

"Agreed." He rises from his chair.

"One moment, Gav." The way Dietrich says his name verges on condescending. "There's one more thing."

He sinks back into his chair. "Yes?"

"What were you doing in Montgomery Station?"

Surprise flashes on his face, then just as quick it's gone. "It was nothing. Scouting a location for some propaganda footage." He sounds a little defensive.

"I believe that's the purview of *my* office," Dietrich says.

"Yes, yes," he says, as if brushing it off. "I merely wanted to get the lay of the land. Like our young apprentice, here." He pats my shoulder, and I shrink back from him.

"I understand," Dietrich says, an edge to her voice. "However, protocols are important, especially given the magnitude of the impending visit. So have your adjutant contact my logistics manager with a list of your venue needs and security concerns. I'll review and we can discuss tomorrow."

"Of course." He chuckles as he stands. "Until tomorrow, Doctor. And..." He looks over at me. "I still don't know your name."

"Uh, Allie," I say.

"See you soon, Allie." He smiles at me long enough for it to be uncomfortable. Finally, he leaves.

As the door clicks shut, Dietrich turns her full wrath on me. "What on the flat earth were you doing? Do you have any idea what's at stake? Do you know what you risked?"

"You were going to recycle me."

"This is so much greater than one person. There are millions of lives to consider."

"Easy to say when you're not the one person getting recycled."

"Well, you achieved your goal. I can't recycle you now that the ASP colonel has taken a personal interest in you."

The way she says *personal interest* sends a shiver up my spine. How could I have missed how ruthless he is?

"You won't be sorry," I say.

"I'm already sorry."

"I can be useful. Here, I'll prove it. You wanted to know what the colonel was doing in Montgomery Station, right? He told you he was scouting a location, but I heard them call it *recon*."

"Oh?" The change in her expression is subtle, but there. This is new information. "What else did you hear?"

"Well, that was it. But I was only with him a few minutes. I'll learn more."

Dietrich rolls her eyes, then turns and crosses to the door she was pointing at before, the one to her "chambers."

With her back to me, I glance at the outer office door.

"Don't even think about it," Dietrich says.

Busted.

"Get moving." She holds the door open for me.

Her "chambers" turn out to be her apartment, the one we were in before. How the heck? I really am turned around.

Bel is lounging on the couch. She springs to her feet, gaping at me. "What are you doing here? I thought we got rid of you."

"You *knew!*" I lunge for her. But she grabs my arms and does some sort of martial arts move I never saw coming. I land on my back on the floor.

"Stop," Dietrich shouts. "Get control of yourselves. You have to find a way to work together."

Bel's livid. "You said I wouldn't have to deal with her anymore."

"Things change," Dietrich says as I get to my feet.

"I'm out of here." Bel storms to the yellow wall and holds up her hand, but nothing happens.

"We're on lockdown. No one's going anywhere," Dietrich says.

Bel turns on me. "This is *your* fault."

"No," Dietrich says. "There are ASPs on the premises, remember?"

"That's right—our meeting," Bel says. "Isn't that *now*?"

"Postponed. Thanks to Allison."

They both give me the stink eye.

"So what am I supposed to do stuck in here with *her*?" Bel asks.

"Help her go through the clothing you rejected this morning and select at least five outfits."

"Outfits for what?"

"She's going to be your co-apprentice."

"*What the*—" Bel clenches her fists and her face turns bright red, like in cartoons right before the person's head explodes.

"Brief her on the plan," Dietrich says. "I'll be in my office taking care of all the additional paperwork that's now necessary." She gifts me with another angry glare.

"Great." Bel tosses her hair and heads through the archway to the back of the apartment.

Same old Bel. And I get to spend the afternoon trying on clothes with her—oh, joy.

I'm halfway considering if being recycled would be better.

I head for the back of the apartment.

"Allison," Dietrich says. "Aren't you forgetting something?"

I look back and she glances at my wrist.

Dammit.

I hand over the personal I lifted from Calix. She doesn't ask for mine—maybe she forgot I have it.

She tucks Calix's personal in her pocket. I feel pretty bad about taking it. I hope he didn't get in too much trouble. "When you give that back to Calix, tell him I'm sorry."

"That won't be necessary. He was recycled."

Oh God. The bottom drops out of my stomach, and I turn away so she doesn't see my tears.

DESPITE THE FASHION show of ridiculous clothing, the room is tense. Bel despises me, and I like her even less. I'm sure she's choosing the ugliest outfits on purpose: high-waisted pants so baggy that three of me could fit inside; a mustard-yellow shirt with ginormous ruffles around the neck, a brown and orange segmented dress that makes me look like a caterpillar.

She's droning on about the junior ambassador gig—which is completely stupid—and it's all I can do not to tell her to shut her face. I keep thinking about Calix—how could they recycle a doctor? And over something so trivial?

"Our goal," Bel says, finally getting to the punch line, "is to convince the president's daughters that this place is dangerous. Then they'll lean on their father to abandon the idea of rebuilding San Francisco."

"*Seriously?*" I can't keep it in any longer. "How could this possibly be the best plan for stopping the president?"

"What do you think, we're idiots? This isn't the *primary* plan. My mom's got that covered with the president himself —scientists showing falsified readings, doctors with 'proof' of the medical side-effects, vids showing how dangerous the grounds still are."

"Can't all that be emailed or something?"

"Of course it can. It *was*. But this new president is full of himself. He says he's got to see it in person."

"If he already knows it's dangerous here, why would he bring his daughters?"

"Because he's a politician. It's a publicity stunt to evoke support for reclaiming the city. He thinks if he shows his own children in the Zone, everyone will believe it's safe."

"And we're supposed to counter this *how*?"

"We can't put them in actual danger, so we show them around our quarters—"

"The Middie sleeping quarters?"

"Geez, you're such a nafe. We can't let beans see the private infrastructure. Only the carefully curated public areas like this." She gestures to the bedroom painted in suburban beige, accented with pale pink bedding and a few teddy bears.

"So this isn't your real bedroom? It's only for show?"

"It's *my* real room. For you, it's show."

"What about Sharrow? Does she have a room here, too?"

"No, she says she wants to live like the inmates."

"Inmates?" Flyx said people could leave.

"Ease out. It's a figure of speech."

"Okay, so how is showing the president's daughters your bedroom supposed to convince them this place is dangerous?"

Bel rolls her eyes. "The bedroom has nothing to do with it. We're going to show them how we have all kinds of side-effects from living here—rashes, memory loss, deformities. We get to play like we're sick, exhausted, the whole deal. You think you're good for that? Because I can't have you blowing it."

"Acting? I'm absolutely good."

"You'd better be." She looks at her personal. "Lockdown's been lifted. I'm out of here."

"Where are we going?"

"*You're* not going anywhere. You need to study for tomorrow." She crosses to a computer on the little white desk against the wall and keys in something. The screen comes to life.

"Why do I need to study but you don't?"

"I've been studying for days. I'm going out." She fluffs the gold tutu-like miniskirt that's wrapped around her like tinsel on a Christmas tree, then heads out the door. It closes with a click.

I run over and try the door—the knob turns but the door won't budge. It's locked. Only I don't see a lock. If I can't see it, I can't pick it. Someone will have to let me out.

I tap my personal, praying it hasn't actually been deactivated.

The face comes to life—it works!

"Tag Huckleberry protocol twenty-eighteen."

DICTATE-RECORD ACTIVE blinks in the window.

"Flyx, are you there? It's Allie." I keep my voice low, just in case.

FLYX: here

"Are you okay? What happened?"

FLYX: fine, thanks to your warning. Can you meet?

"Uh, things got complicated. Dietrich was going to recycle me."

FLYX: what?!?

"Long story. I got away, but then some ASPs caught me, which was actually kinda lucky. Now Dietrich can't recycle me because they think I'm a diplomat."

FLYX: gods. Where are you?

"Locked in Bel's room in Dietrich's chambers. Can you get me out?"

FLYX: rot, that's public sector. If I'm caught there they'd do worse than recycle me

"I'll see if Sharrow can help."

FLYX: is that a good idea? Do you know for certain she's on our side?

I sit back. Could she have been in on it? Did she know what her mom was doing? "You don't think we can trust her?"

FLYX: wish I knew her well enough to say

"I guess I'd better stay put."

FLYX: if you're in danger, I'm coming anyway

"No, don't. I'll be safe until the president's visit. But after that..." *There's nothing to keep Dietrich from recycling me,* I finish silently.

FLYX: I'm not going to let that happen

You said I was safe before. I push the thought away. I have to. "Tell me what happened with the wormhole machine. Did you get in to see it? Can you fix it?"

FLYX: later, okay? I'll find a way to get you alone, someplace safe

He wants to get me alone. That twists me up. I *want* to be alone with him, but at the same time I know I can't. Not in that way. I really have to tell him. "Tomorrow?"

FLYX: affirm. razing this convo now

Razing?

The words on my personal screen vanish. I try scrolling back, but there's nothing there.

I WAKE up with my face on the keyboard of the computer,

spikes of pain arcing through my back. I check the time on my personal—ugh, it's morning. I rub my crusted eyes, cursing Bel for leaving me to study all night.

There's a sound at the door. I shove the personal under my sleeve, even though it's supposed to be invisible.

Bel enters and eyes me at the desk. "You look like crap."

"Screw you."

"Get changed. We have stuff to do."

After suppressing a growl, I change into a puffy tan shirt that makes me look like a toasted marshmallow. I can't say I like it, but it has long enough sleeves to cover the personal. I don't bother to change the high-waisted black pants I slept in. I slip on chunky black shoes that remind me of combat boots, only without the boot part. They're the best thing in all the clothes yesterday.

In the attached lav, I brush my teeth. I almost leave my hair a rat's nest to spite Bel, but think better of it and brush out the knots.

"Come *on*," she says.

I follow her out of the bedroom. "I need breakfast."

"All you think about is food."

"You left me here all night without dinner. Now I'm not going anywhere without pancakes and coffee."

She looks over her shoulder at me. "Seriously?"

I stop, planting my feet in the middle of the living room. She sighs. "Fine."

Really? I won't believe it until I smell the pancakes.

We exit through Dietrich's office rather than the hidden door in the yellow wall. Dietrich's not there, and we pass through to the lobby. There's a different woman at the reception desk now. She doesn't smile or say anything as we pass.

Bel keeps walking, right past the hallway I came in

yesterday—the one to Montgomery Station. She sees me eyeing it.

"Forget you ever saw that part of the complex," she says.

I follow out a door into a beautiful enclosed garden. It's filled with potted trees and flowers, and a smattering of benches. I look up expecting to see sky, but there's a ginormous dome overhead.

"What is this place?"

She glances at me with a dramatic eye roll. "The atrium. You'd better start acting like all this is familiar or you'll raze our cover, and I'm not going down with you, nafe."

Across the way is a tall brick wall sprinkled with doors and windows. It looks like the outside of a building. If I had to guess, the atrium used to be outdoors.

Bel heads straight for the middle door and enters, letting the door slam on me. I'm expecting this and catch it before it does any damage.

Inside are tables decked out with tablecloths and silverware. A woman in a burgundy waiter uniform bustles over to us.

"Table for two?" she asks.

Bel issues an exasperated huff, but before she can say something rude, I step forward. "Yes, thank you."

Once we're seated, I order the full breakfast special. Minutes later, pancakes arrive along with scrambled eggs—or rather, egg substitute—and "bacon flavored protein strips." It's all surprisingly tasty, and I gobble it like the Cookie Monster from *Sesame Street*. Bel picks at her oatmeal. Maybe it's a skinny-girl thing. I don't care enough to ask.

When my plate's empty and I'm nursing the last of my coffee, Bel pushes aside her mostly full bowl and looks at me.

"So you're ready for today?"

"About that...I'm not clear what we're doing today, specifically."

"You were supposed to study," she seethes.

"I did! The entire stupid tutorial." *Right up until I fell asleep.* "But it said nothing about *today*."

Bel sighs like I'm the dumbest person on the planet. "We're meeting with the ASP envoy to finalize the plans for the president's visit tomorrow. This is the meeting that didn't happen yesterday due to your theatrics."

"What am I supposed to do in the meeting?"

"Listen and keep your mouth shut."

"Okay, no problem."

She looks like she doubts that's true. Given my history, I guess I can't blame her.

CHAPTER THIRTY

The meeting with the ASPs is in a conference room near Dietrich's office. The colonel and weasel-woman sit on one side of a rectangular table. I'm sandwiched between Bel and Dietrich on the opposite side, almost like they don't trust me.

I should be paying attention, but my mind wanders as they talk through the security details of tomorrow's visit. What if Flyx can't get the wormhole machine to work? I need a Plan B. But what? Pray for a real earthquake? I'll be recycled long before that happens.

"*Allison.*"

I tune in to find everyone staring at me.

"I'm sorry. I was..." What excuse can I give? I can't exactly say I was bored and daydreaming about time travel. "I was wondering...." I say the first thing that pops into my head. "What are the president's daughters' names?"

Dietrich's eyes go wide for a split second and Bel hits my leg under the table. Apparently that was the wrong thing to ask.

"How could you not know?" Weasel says, her voice laced with suspicion.

"Oh, I know their names," I say, trying to cover. "I'm wondering what we should *call* them. Like sometimes my friends call me Allie Cat, and I call Bel 'Belle of the Ball.' You know, like that." I giggle, hoping this girlie routine works.

Weasel's scowl deepens. "Nicknames would be highly inappropriate. Call them Miss Liddy and Miss Maisie." She narrows her already-narrow eyes at Dietrich. "Are you sure she's the right person for this?"

Dietrich opens her mouth to speak, but the colonel interjects. "I believe this concludes our agenda regarding the president's daughters. Now would be an appropriate time for the young ladies to demo tomorrow's route."

Bel and Weasel push back from the table, so I do the same. As Weasel exits, Bel gives me a sharp look. I can't tell if she's warning me to keep my mouth shut or cursing me for calling her "Belle of the Ball." Either way, I figure I better stay quiet.

I do pretty well keeping my mouth shut as we go through the tour route on fast-forward. The Atrium, a classroom, lavatories, a game room, a gym. But when we enter the science lab, a "wow" slips out of my mouth.

Weasel wheels on me. "Wow *what?*"

Bel shoots me a hate-glance.

Crap. I backpedal. "I was surprised it looks so good in here. All cleaned up for the visit."

"You don't normally keep an orderly workplace?" Weasel says.

"Allie's exaggerating," Bel says. "Always so drama."

"Guilty," I say.

Seriously, Bel had to cover for me? I'd never let my

attention lapse like that pulling a con. I need to get my head in the game.

"What exactly do you do here?" Weasel asks.

I look to Bel. No way I'm venturing into that territory.

"We monitor pressure in the San Andreas Fault with ground-displacement sensors," Bel says. "This is where much of the experimentation was done previously as our scientists tried to relieve the pressure. But since that didn't work, we're continuing to test theoretical models, hoping to find a way to eliminate the increasing threat."

"Sure you do," Weasel says under her breath.

"You disagree?" I blurt.

"Of course I disagree. The president's entire science team disagrees. That's what this whole visit is about."

"I don't understand why this is even an issue," Bel says. "We've provided all the data and analysis to the president's scientists. The numbers clearly show the pressure is continuing to build. Without relief, there *will* be another catastrophic quake. It's too dangerous to return to the city."

"*You're* here," Weasel says. "Why isn't it too dangerous for you?"

"Our work *is* dangerous," Bel says. "But we know the risks when we sign on, and we believe it's more important to ensure the public's safety than our own."

"Your work? What exactly do you do?" Weasel asks.

"I told you, we monitor the pressure and—"

"I heard the party line. I want to know what *you* do. Show me," Weasel says.

"You know we're under strict orders not to perform work while we show the president's daughters the facility."

"I want you to show *me*," Weasel says. "Consider that an order."

"I don't take orders from you," Bel says, standing up to Weasel both literally and figuratively.

"The girls aren't going to care about this lab," I say, trying to divert them from their pissing contest. "Don't you think they'll be more interested in our bedrooms and clothes and stuff? I mean, that's what I'm more interested in."

"You're right, Allison," Bel says, sending a shockwave through the universe by agreeing with me. "That's why it's last on the tour, right after the boring lab. We want to end on a positive note."

"Let's go there now and get this over with." I start for the door, motioning for them to follow.

"Why, is there something else you need to do?" Weasel asks, like that's a crime.

"Lunch. I'm hungry," I say, figuring that's a safe answer.

"Do you ever *not* think about food?" Bel says.

BACK AT DIETRICH'S OFFICE, I shrink under the colonel's scrutiny as Weasel delivers her report and Dietrich concludes we're ready for tomorrow's visit. I keep my gaze unfocused as we say goodbye, clasping my hands behind my back to avoid shaking the colonel's hand. He gives me the willies.

Once they're gone, Bel turns on me. "What the heck is wrong with you?"

"What?" I thought I did a great job.

Dietrich glares at me. "What did you do?"

"Nothing," I say.

"You were supposed to keep your mouth shut," Bel says. "You could have razed everything."

I'm about to argue, but I get an idea. It's a long shot, but I don't have anything else. "You're right, Bel. I'm sorry. I'm just so stressed out by all this. You know, if I could blow off some steam, I'd do a lot better tomorrow."

"So go to the gym," Bel says.

"Exercise equipment never works for me. The only thing that helps is dancing." I really hope they can't tell I'm lying. "Plus I need to see my friends."

"What friends?" Bel snarks.

"Sharrow and Flyx and Daum." I turn to Dietrich. "The ASPs are off the premises, so it should be okay for me to go to the club as long as I'm back by morning, right?"

Dietrich frowns.

I plow forward before she can say no. "I know how important tomorrow is. We can't risk me blowing it. I promise, going dancing with my friends is exactly what I need. Please? It's not like I can get into any actual trouble, right?"

Dietrich cocks her head like she's considering it. I can't believe this might be working.

"Mom," Bel says, "you're not actually—"

"Actually, I am," Dietrich says. "I think it would do you both some good."

"*Both?*" Bel and I say at the same time.

"Both."

"Thanks!" I say before Bel can argue. "See you in the morning."

"No, I want you back in my chambers by midnight," Dietrich says. "I need you fresh for the tour."

I'll take what I can get. "No problem." I head for the door.

"Bel, don't let her out of your sight, understood?"

"Understood," Bel says, sounding a lot like Eeyore.

Bel exits into the reception area.

"Why are we going this way?" I whisper.

"The more convenient route is closed thanks to you."

"Your mom was going to *recycle* me. What would you have done?"

"There are worse things than being recycled."

"Like what?"

Bel turns and I follow her down a short hall. There's a drinking fountain and three doors labeled "women's," "men's," and "janitorial." She opens the janitorial door. It's a supply closet. "Get in."

Is she punking me? "Uhhh, no."

"What happened to being anxious to see your friends?" She says "friends" like it's a euphemism. "*Fine*. I'll go first." She pushes past me and steps inside the closet with the brooms and buckets. "Satisfied? Now come on."

This must be more camouflage. I step in and Bel pulls the door shut.

It's dark, then the flashlight on Bel's personal comes on and she holds it to a wall. The wall pivots outward and she steps through the opening.

I follow the glow of her personal into the dark space. The door swishes shut behind us, and a greenish florescent light comes on—the hum reminds me of the Main, bringing a wave of homesickness.

We're in a small room—a laundry room—with a utility sink and stacked washer-dryer on the left, a narrow table and laundry basket on the right. No windows, no other doors.

I'm hoping this is double-subterfuge to throw off the ASPs. The alternative is she's going to stuff me in the dryer.

Bel crosses to the washer-dryer and squeezes into the gap behind it, disappearing from view.

I poke my head behind the unit and see an opening in the wall. I squeeze behind the machine and look through the opening down into a dark, narrow shaft that smells like sewer. Bel's head is outlined in the glow of her personal as she descends on metal rungs embedded in the wall.

She looks up. "Come on."

"No way." I hold my hand over my nose and mouth.

"You're the one who insisted we go dancing."

"I changed my mind."

"Too late," Bel says. "You can't get out of the laundry room without my personal. So follow or stay there. Up to you."

Looks like I'm climbing into the sewer pipe.

I breathe through my mouth as I climb down the rungs. My tongue feels like sandpaper, but I don't dare breathe normally.

I know Bel's punking me—climbing down a sewer drain is too disgusting to be a standard route, plus someone like Spires would never fit. Bel's probably enjoying the heck out of making me go this way. At least she's not immune to the stench.

"Take your time," Bel says, dripping sarcasm.

When I reach the bottom, she's already walking away down the dark, reeking tunnel. I jog to catch up, trying to avoid the trickle of liquid on the ground. Thank God I have real shoes now.

"Where are you taking me?" I ask.

"What, doesn't this look like a club?"

After what feels like four hundred miles, Bel stops. It doesn't look any different here than at any other point. Maybe her personal has a nav system? She holds it to the wall and a doorway appears, and we head down another dang tunnel.

"Are we actually going somewhere or are you screwing with me?" I ask.

"Hold your dogs, nafe. We're almost there."

Hold your dogs? I don't ask.

After another couple of minutes, she stops and banks her personal again. This time, we step into an actual hallway and a chemical smell envelops me, clearing the sewer from my nostrils. *Hair color.*

"You brought me to the mall?"

"I thought you might want to get that butterfly tattoo now," she says.

I'm totally mature and stick my tongue out, though in reality the idea of a tattoo is growing on me. I wouldn't get one on my forehead, and it probably wouldn't be a butterfly, but having something colorful that reminds me I can be who I want to be? That has some appeal. Especially if I lived in this time.

Bel taps her personal. "Tag Sharrow to meet me in the club."

"It's barely afternoon. Will anyone be there?" I ask.

"What's it matter? It's not like you know anyone."

When we get there it's nearly empty, as I suspected. It doesn't even seem like the same place in the cold overhead lighting. Bel strides toward the back like she's on a mission. Sharrow's there, sitting in a booth.

"What's up?" Sharrow asks. I try to read her, but her face is a blank.

"She convinced Mom to let her go dancing," Bel says. "Can you keep an eye? There's something I need to do."

Sharrow shrugs. "Sure."

"Don't go anywhere else, and don't let her out of your sight, even in the lav."

"Why, what's she going to do?"

"Just comply, okay?" Bel says. "I'll be back at 11:30." She turns and hurries out.

I'd love to see what she's up to, but right now I need to find out whose side Sharrow's on. Plus I seriously need a break from Bel.

CHAPTER THIRTY-ONE

I slide into the booth beside Sharrow and stop a little closer than social norm. It's time to get to work and see what she's about.

I angle my mouth toward her ear. "I need to ask you something," I say, voice low. Without the music and crowd cover, I don't think it's paranoid to assume someone might be listening.

"What are you doing?" she says, edging away.

"Can anyone hear us?" I whisper.

"Hang on." She keys something on her personal, then synth music with a deep beat starts playing from it.

"How'd you do that? Are there games and stuff, too?"

"Of course," she says, like I'm from another planet.

"Will you show me how to access it?"

"Sure. But what did you want to ask me? Seems serious."

I lower my voice, despite the counter measures. "Did you know your mom was going to recycle me?" I watch her face carefully.

Her eyes widen. "No! What happened?"

Phew. She didn't know. She wasn't in on it. "She said I failed the tests."

"Oh my gods. Oh no. No, no, no." She leans back, shaking her head. "She's going to tell me to do it, and I can't. I can't do it."

"Don't worry," I say, feeling bad I doubted her. "We'll get the wormhole machine working, and I'll leave."

"There's no time. Once my mom makes up her mind—"

"She won't recycle me until after the president's visit."

She looks confused. "What? Why?"

"I'll explain, but right now let's get hold of Flyx. If he fixed the machine, maybe I can leave tonight."

WE DECIDED it was safer to talk with Flyx in a cube, despite Bel's order to stay in the club. On the way, I told Sharrow about the ASPs, and she agreed that I'm only safe temporarily. I have to get out of here before her mom has the chance to recycle me.

While we wait for Flyx, Sharrow shows me how to access all kinds of entertainment on the personal, then she settles in to watch a "vid." But I'm too antsy to do anything but pace, my anxiety rising with every lap.

Finally, Flyx shows up with Daum.

"Did you look at the machine?" I blurt.

"Hi?" Flyx says.

"Sorry. I just need to know—did you see it? Can you fix it?"

"It was genius," Daum says, flopping down beside Sharrow. "He managed to get us alone in Detention during the lockdown yesterday."

"*Yesterday?*" I look at Flyx. "Last night, you said you didn't know anything."

"Because I didn't," he says, propping himself on the arm of the couch. "Nothing that would help. I can't fix it. There's a part missing."

"What about the other machine?" I ask. "The one where you work."

Flyx shakes his head. "I looked at it again today to be sure. It's a dead end."

I refuse to accept the resignation on his face. "But you can find the part for the main machine."

No one's looking at me. They're all staring at the ground.

"Come on, you guys," I say. "Whoever removed the part knows where it is."

"My mom," Sharrow says. "And there's no way she'll give it to us."

"But she wouldn't have removed it *herself*," Daum says. "There should be records showing who she assigned to do it."

"It doesn't matter." Sharrow says. "Even if you find out, no one will go against my mom."

"We have to try," I say. "Find out who it is and let me talk to them. I can be very persuasive."

"It won't work. No one wants to risk getting recycled," Sharrow says.

"Including me!" I shout.

Sharrow recoils, but I'm beyond apologizing. My life is on the line.

"What about you?" I turn on Flyx. "Are you too afraid to go against Dietrich? Are you giving up?"

"No, but I don't know what else to do." He crosses his arms.

Everyone is silent. I turn away, pacing again. There's got to be a solution. Something we're missing.

"It keeps coming back to Dietrich," Flyx says, breaking the silence. "Unless she allows time travel, you're docked."

"So we get her to allow it," I say.

"She's dead-set," Sharrow says.

"We have to change her mind," I insist.

"I told you," Sharrow says. "She doesn't change her mind."

"I don't accept that." I pace faster. There's something itching my brain, just out of reach. How do we convince Dietrich to change her mind when she *never* changes her mind? If it's absolutely against her nature, then— "Wait! Dietrich *did* change her mind. About Bel."

"That's right," Daum says. "She didn't believe Bel was her daughter, then suddenly *bang-oh*."

"What changed her mind?" I ask, wishing I'd remembered to ask Bel.

"She saw a report from herself. She makes them in case of history-changes," Flyx says.

"There, that's our solution!" I'm practically giddy. "We make a report where Dietrich tells herself that time travel is allowed."

"Okay, but *why*?" Sharrow says. "She'd still have to have a good reason to allow it."

"Okay...." I pace more, thinking. What does Dietrich want? She's in the Resistance—her goal is to stop the Nazis.... Bel said Beck's mission in 1906 was related to stopping the Nazi's.... "I've got it," I exclaim. "Dietrich wants to stop the ASPs, right? So the report says that an operative in 1906 has the solution, but he can't travel. The only way to get the information is for someone to go back." I feel a grin stretching my face. "And that someone is me."

"Then she'll *have* to fix the machine," Daum says, mirroring my grin.

"That's all good, but..." Flyx isn't smiling. "There's still one major problem, and I have no idea how to get around it."

"Don't worry," I say. "I have lots of experience with cons and forgeries. With samples of Dietrich's writing, and Sharrow's help with style, we can definitely create a report she'll believe."

"That's not it," Flyx says. "The problem is Bel."

"What do you mean?"

"Even if the report convinces Dietrich that history changed and she doesn't remember...Bel will know we're lying."

"*Oh, shit.*" He's right.

"What?" Daum asks. "You have to spell it out for me."

"Bel's a Jenny," I say. "She keeps her memories, and the minute something is different from what she remembers, the con is blown."

"Rot," Sharrow says.

"Total rot," Daum says.

"Hang on..." Maybe I can fix this. "Besides Bel, are there other Jennys who could blow our plan?"

"There are other Jennys and loggies," Flyx says. "But none close enough to Dietrich to realize—they'd assume she changed her mind."

"So..." I say, looking from Flyx to Daum to Sharrow. "What if I convince Bel to go along with us?"

"A sally if," Sharrow says.

Flyx sucks in a breath. "Affirm. But if Allie can get Bel on side, this plan could actually work."

"Right?" My heart's beating fast. "We do the report tonight...."

"And I upload it tomorrow during shift," Flyx says.

"Not tomorrow," Sharrow says. "Everything's on lock-down for the president's visit."

"That's right," Daum says. "You won't be able to get into the TIC until the following morning."

"We might not have till then," I say. "Dietrich could recycle me as soon as the president leaves."

"Don't worry, I have a workaround. I'll get it in the system," Flyx says, locking eyes with me. "You focus on Bel."

I have no idea how I'm going to recruit Bel, so for now, I focus on something I know how to accomplish. "Let's get that report written now, while we're together. I'll work on Bel later tonight."

"Is anyone else hungry?" Daum asks.

I think he and I are kindred spirits. "Always."

"I'll get food," Daum says. "You like tacos, right?"

"More than life itself," I reply.

IT ONLY TOOK an hour to create the report. Turns out we didn't need my forgery skills because everything's electronic, but we really needed Sharrow's knack for the way her mother phrases things. I think we nailed it, and I'd be over the moon, except I still have no angle on Bel.

"We should get back to the club," Sharrow says.

"You guys go ahead," Daum says. "I can't handle the noise tonight. I'm going to Middies."

"I wish I could go with," Sharrow says, stifling a yawn.

"Why don't you?" Flyx says. "I can stay with Allie until Bel shows."

Butterflies whirl in my stomach at the thought of being alone with Flyx.

"Negative," Sharrow says. "Bel said to keep my eye on her. I can't pass that off without incurring her wrath."

I'm a little disappointed, but mostly relieved. Being alone with Flyx would be a bad idea.

Back in the club, we sit around a table sipping fizzy drinks that taste vaguely like raspberry. The place is full now, and the lights strobe to the wild music.

I should be tired, but I'm buzzing with nervous energy. I have a plan to go back and save my parents and the crew. But it all hinges on me winning Bel over, and I don't have the first idea how.

"You okay?" Sharrow asks me.

"Fine, why?"

"You're jiggling your leg enough to rock the club."

"And holding your drink so tight I'm afraid you'll crush it," Flyx says.

"I guess I'm a little tense," I say with a nervous laugh.

"I know what you need," Sharrow says. "Dancing."

"No way. I don't dance."

"Come on," Flyx says. "There's nothing to it."

"It's like what you're doing with your leg, but with your whole body," Sharrow says.

Flyx reaches his hand across the table. "Consent."

Sharrow extends her hand, too. "You told my mom you needed to dance. You have to consent."

I shake my head. But I put my hand out anyway. Our three hands touch, making a pyramid. "Okay, I consent."

Sharrow grabs my hand and drags me into the middle of the dancing mob. I look back at Flyx behind me. He smiles, and I go all warm in the middle. I'm seriously glad we're not alone.

Sharrow turns to me, her eyes bright. "Dance," she shouts over the music. She bounces on the balls of her feet and bobs her head.

Flyx is bouncing too, face tipped toward the ceiling—he's not looking at me, and neither is Sharrow. I can do this.

I feel the music vibrate through me. I bend my knees. Just a little. And I don't die.

I do it again.

Still here.

I bounce a few times and have to admit—it feels *amazing*.

No one is watching me. No one cares, so why should I?

But I still feel a bit self-conscious, so I shut my eyes and focus on what the music *feels* like, letting my body go with it. It's like when I was dancing inside my mind back in Med when I was drugged.

Before long, I'm bopping around, eyes wide open.

Three songs later and we're all laughing while we flail like Animal on *The Muppets*.

Dancing, where have you been my whole life?

Sharrow motions for me to come closer and says in my ear, "I have to go to the lav. Stay with Flyx."

Before I can object, she's gone.

I look at Flyx. He's staring at me. My confidence evaporates, and I'm all awkward and self-conscious. I feel like I'm moving like a robot now, and not in a good way. I should have gone to the bathroom with Sharrow.

Flyx quirks his mouth in a smile, and it makes me tingle. Or maybe it's a cramp. Or maybe I'm going to barf. I don't think this could be any worse.

Then it gets worse.

The song changes.

It's a slow song.

All around us, people are coupling up.

I don't want to look at Flyx, but I have to. He's not smiling anymore. His eyes look all dreamy. He steps closer.

"Consent?" he says, touching my right hand gently with his.

I gulp. Nod. Then remember I have to say it out loud. "Y-yeah, I consent."

His arms encircle my waist. I slip mine around his shoulders. I expected it to feel strange, but the strange thing is, it doesn't feel strange at all. It's comfortable, even.

Then he snugs me in tight, our bodies touching. And it's not comfortable, in the best way.

Which is the worst. Sharrow is going to come back and see us. I can't do that to her. I won't.

I push back to say I need to go. But our eyes lock. Then his mouth is on mine. Warm and soft.

And I don't want to say no.

I kiss him back.

After a moment, he pulls away and looks at me. He smiles, then goes in for another kiss. This one makes me all warm and buzzy.

The song ends way too soon. Then I remember —*Sharrow*. She should have been back by now. Did she see us kissing?

"You hear that?" Flyx stretches up on his toes, craning his neck to see over the crowd. "Come on." He grabs my hand and whisks me toward our table.

The minute I see Sharrow, I know what Flyx heard. *Bel.*

Bel is shouting at Sharrow. "I told you—"

"*There she is.*" Sharrow points at me. "See? It's fine."

Bel swivels her rage to me. "We're going. *Now.*"

I check the time on my personal. It's barely after eleven. But the look on Sharrow's face begs me not to argue. So I don't. Even though the look on Bel's face begs me to push her buttons.

Flyx leans close. "Good luck tomorrow," he says in my ear, so close his breath tickles. He gives my hand a squeeze then lets go. "See you soon."

I nod, then look over at Sharrow. Crap. She's staring right at us.

I'M in a bed in "my room" adjacent to Bel's, staring at the dark ceiling, stewing in guilt. I need to figure out how to win Bel over so I can save my family, but I can't think with all these *feelings*.

This is ridiculous. I need to focus.

I'll tell Flyx I can't kiss him anymore. That we can't do that to Sharrow.

Or to Jake.

God, how long has it been since I even thought about Jake?

I'm a terrible person.

I should message Flyx right now and tell him we're done.

I try to make myself. But I can't.

Instead, I get up and pace, forcing myself to focus on the plan. Even if it takes all night, I'm damn well going to figure out how to bring Bel in on the con.

CHAPTER THIRTY-TWO

FLYX

S leep's impossible. My mind keeps replaying tonight.
When Allie and I kissed, the rest of the uni disappeared.

But the song ended. And Bel happened. That's when I saw it in Allie's eyes—the guilt. The regret.

I felt it, too. I still do. But I can't help that I don't know Sharrow. Her reality, her memories, her feelings, are not mine.

The logical side of my brain says I don't know Allie either. Not really.

So why do I feel like I've known her forever? Like there's been an empty place inside me my entire life waiting to be filled by her?

I think...I think I love her.

My wrist buzzes. I want it to be Allie. I need to tell her—

It's Dietrich.

I climb out of bed. Duty calls.

"THE PRESIDENT ARRIVES IN THE MORNING,"
Dietrich says. "I need to know what Allie's planning—that's
why I orchestrated your little meet-up tonight."

I should have realized she'd facilitated it.

Dietrich leans forward, eyes hungry. "Tell me."

The betrayal's putrid in my gut. "She's planning to go
back to 1906 to change things back to the way they used to
be. She wants me to rig one of the wormhole machines,
either the main one in Detention, or the one in the TIC."

"What did you tell her?"

"That I'd try."

"Good. Stall her until after the president's visit. Tell her
you're missing a part."

This confirms my assessment that she had a part
removed. "Affirm."

"Who else knows about Allie's plan? Bel?" She leans
over the desk, hands clasped, anxious for my answer.

"No, Bel's not part of it. She doesn't know anything."

"But Sharrow..." She sounds so disappointed.

"She knows." I don't want to get Sharrow in trouble, but
I need to build trust with Dietrich. Besides, it seems like
Dietrich already knows.

"Sharrow's not planning to *travel* with Allie, is she?"

"What? No. I mean, she's not a Jenny—wouldn't the
radiation be a problem?"

"No one's going to *actually* travel," Dietrich snaps. "I
need to know their intentions. Their plan. What else do you
know?"

"That's it. I told you everything."

CHAPTER THIRTY-THREE

When I wake up in "my" room, the first thing I think of is Flyx.

No! I can't have feelings for him.

Fine, it's too late for that. But I don't have to give in to them. No more kissing, or dancing, or thinking about him. No more Flyx.

Good luck with that, I hear in my head.

Yeah. I definitely need luck.

Bel flounces into the room dressed in her fancy diplomat clothes, hair and makeup already done. "What are you still doing in bed?"

"Chill out. I just woke up."

"What's wrong with you? We need to leave in five minutes."

"What?" I jump out of bed and run for the closet. Why am I always doing this to myself?

I'm yanking clothes off hangers like a maniac when Bel starts laughing.

"You're so easy!" She punctuates this with a little snort.

"You're not late. I couldn't sleep, so I got ready early and thought I'd mess with you."

"Very funny." I drop the clothes on the bed. "Now you owe me a coffee."

"No I don't."

"Yes you do. Rule number seventeen—when you punk someone first thing in the morning, you owe them a caffeinated beverage."

"There's no such rule."

I put my hands on my hips and stare her down.

She stares back. Then rolls her eyes. "Fine." She stomps dramatically to the kitchen.

"Cream and sugar," I call.

I hear clanking and can't believe she's actually getting me coffee. Maybe some part of her wants to be friends. I wish I had more time to let that play out naturally. But that's not in the cards.

I finally figured out last night what I have to do. And it makes me sick to my stomach.

Bel comes back and puts a coffee mug on the night-stand. "Why aren't you dressed yet?"

Here goes. "I don't like what I picked out last night." I hold up the yellow and brown checked dress. "Don't you think it's a bit...blah? Like something Sharrow would wear?" I'm careful to conceal how much I hate myself for this.

"Oh gods, completely. Let me find you something." She shoulders past me into the walk-in closet and pages through the hanging outfits. She pulls out a long hot pink shirt with black polka-dots. It reminds me of Good & Plenty candy from the movie theater.

"Nice. Really bold." I strip down and slide it on over my head.

Bel hands me black leggings and a short sweater with wide pink and black stripes. I slip those on, too.

"What shoes?" I ask, taking a swig of my coffee. It's weak and tepid, so I put it back down, but I don't give her crap about it.

"You definitely need boots." She looks at the row of shoes along the bottom of the closet and wrinkles her nose. "Come with me."

I follow her into her room. She rummages through her closet, and I can't believe how much progress I've already made—loaning me shoes is pretty much girl code for being friends.

She emerges with royal blue patent leather mid-calf boots. "Perfection."

Blue boots with a pink and black outfit? Maybe she's punking me again. But I put them on and look in the full length mirror, and have to admit the effect is fantastic.

She looks at my reflection, cocking her head. "Nice."

"Thank you," I say, meaning it.

"Now if only we could do something with your hair."

I comb my fingers through the long strands, pulling out tangles. "Sharrow said she was going to do it for me, but I think her taste is...questionable."

"Sit. I'll do it."

I sit on the stool in front of her dressing table, angling away from the mirror. I can't look at myself. I wish I knew a quicker way to get on the good side of a mean girl than by badmouthing another girl. Especially when that girl is Sharrow.

Bel takes the brush to my hair, not bothering to be gentle. When the knots are out, she parts my hair in three sections and braids each of them individually. Way beyond my skills.

Maybe now's a good time to bring up the crew. I need her to remember them and want them back.

"Did you ever do Vee's hair like this?" I ask.

"Not like *this*. But yeah, I did her hair." She sounds a bit wistful.

"It's funny how I thought you two were sisters, and now it turns out we all are."

"Looking back, I'm surprised I didn't suspect. Vee and I were so much alike, the most like actual sisters."

I let that hang in the air for a moment. "I bet you miss her."

"Done," she says.

I check out my hair in the mirror. "Wow," I say, equally wowed and horrified at the three braided buns on my head. One is front and center, the others on the sides like Princess Leia. I have to wonder if Bel is setting me up. "Thank you," I say for lack of anything else.

"Crowns are the new thing in all the fash-vids. Next time I'll try four or five."

Crowns? Okay, crowns. Hmm. I think she's being genuine. And she said "next time." Total progress. "Maybe I could try it on you sometime," I suggest.

She frowns, but then shrugs. "Sure, I guess. I mean, if you can't pull it off, we can take it down."

She doesn't have much confidence in my hair-styling ability. But honestly, neither do I.

"We need to go get our makeup done now," she says.

"Someone's doing our makeup for us?" That seems weird.

"Our *deformities*, remember?"

"Right!" I'd completely forgotten.

IN A ROOM OFF THE CLOTHING "STORE," two makeup artists create our fake deformities. I have one on my left forearm and another on my right shoulder. They're deep red and purple, and somehow the artist made them look gnarled and bumpy, though she warned it's just an illusion and I shouldn't let anyone touch them. She complimented my crowns which I could tell made Bel feel smug.

Bel's deformities are yellow-brown, and she's got three. She's wearing her hair down, so they put one on the back of her neck. She's also got one on each calf, which will be easy to show because her pant legs are loose, like she's wearing a long, blousy skirt that's been sewn up the middle. She swears it's the height of fashion, but they look like clown pants to me.

It's time. We head to Dietrich's office to meet the president's daughters. It feels like bees are swarming in my stomach.

This has to go well. If it doesn't, Bel will blame me and our bonding will go down the toilet. No time travel. No saving my family. No escaping recycling.

If I don't nail this con, it will be my last.

No pressure.

When we get to the reception desk, I spot two girls down the hall at Dietrich's door, and I'm stunned. "That's them?" I whisper to Bel. "They're younger than I expected and...not white."

The older one is pre-teen with black wavy hair and brown skin. The younger one can't be more than six or seven. She's got long blond ringlets and lighter brown skin. They both look mixed race.

"So what?" Bel says.

"Uh, since when are Nazis okay with that?"

She gives me a look that would dry out a raindrop. "Did you not watch the vids?"

"I *did*." Sorta.

"Nazis were racist. ASPs aren't."

This doesn't compute. "What about all that racial purity stuff?"

"They say they're *perfecting* the human race, not purifying."

Perfecting. Okay, maybe they've evolved *a little* for the better, but they're still Nazis.

"Tell me the girls' names again," I say.

I sense Bel rolling her eyes. "The older's Liddy. The little's Maisie. You get *her*—I can't stand kids."

"Wait, are we splitting up?"

"No, nafe, we're tag-teaming."

I glance around the lobby. "I don't see Weasel."

"*Weasel*—that's good," Bel says, and I think maybe she means it as a genuine compliment.

"Isn't she coming to supervise or whatever?" I ask.

"She was, but my mom convinced the president it would put the girls more at ease—and show the world there's nothing here to be afraid of—if it was only the four of us."

"But isn't your mom trying to show the exact opposite— that it *is* dangerous?"

"Duh. She got rid of the chaperone to make it easier for us to convince the girls. Plus she was worried about when you slip up."

"*If* I slip up, you mean."

She shrugs. "Even without a chaperone, it's still not going to be cake. You'd better not blow it."

"Relax. I'll be fine." *I hope.*

I DON'T KNOW what Bel was so worried about. We did a photoshoot with the girls, then the tour, and it all went great. The girls were super easy. After we showed them around, we had cookies and played with a kitten Dietrich had her receptionist bring in. The kitten was a smart move —definitely the highlight.

During the tour, we also made sure to privately show them our "deformities" which seemed to sufficiently appall them. Mission accomplished.

But there's still an entire forty minutes before we drop the girls off, and we're out of things to do. The girls are bored and getting more bored by the second.

I know what I'd show them if we were in the private sector.

"Bel, we're dying here," I whisper. "We have to do something fun, like the slides."

Her mouth makes an "O" and she nods. "Girls, would you like to go on a slide?"

"Yes!" Liddy says.

What? I give Bel a wide-eyed, what-the-hell look.

She gives me a look that says *ease out, nafe.*

At the top of the slide, which I really hope is in the public sector, the girls are balls of nervous energy even though this slide's not very steep or long—from the top I can clearly see the pads at the bottom. Seems like it was made for little kids, though I haven't seen a single kid other than our guests the entire time I've been here.

"Why can't we go together?" Liddy asks.

"Not safe," Bel says.

"This is dangerous?" Maisie's eyes are wide.

"That's not what I meant," Bel says, clearly frustrated. Kids are even less her thing than mine.

"What she means," I explain, "is you don't want to go at the same time because you could bump together and get hurt." I have no idea if it's true, but the girls seem to buy it.

"I'm scared," Maisie says.

"If you want to change your mind..." Bel suggests.

"Noooo," Liddy says.

"How about if we show you?" I ask. "Bel, you go first."

"Okay," she says. "You sit on the edge, feet in front, arms to the sides." She demonstrates. "If you tip, put your hand down for balance. It's easy. Watch." She pushes off and slides down on her rear end.

The girls watch with rapt attention, the little one covering her mouth with her hands.

Bel reaches the bottom, gets to her feet and holds her arms in the air. "Ta da!" Her voice carries up to us.

The girls erupt with laughter and clapping.

"Now your turn, Liddy," I say.

She sits and looks up at me. "Is this right?"

"Perfect. Go whenever you're ready."

I see her gather her courage. After a moment, she pushes off. Her arms fly out to her sides and she lets out a piercing squeal.

Maisie, beside me, grabs my hand and grips it like a banshee.

"It's okay," I tell her. "She's having fun."

Maisie doesn't take her gaze from her sister.

When Liddy reaches the bottom, she tumbles and rolls. Maisie gasps and squeezes my hand harder.

Liddy bounces to her feet, laughing. "That was gail!"

"See?" I say to Maisie. "She's fine. She liked it."

Maisie shakes her head, still gripping my hand. "I don't know."

"Come on, Maize," Liddy shouts. "It's a bluster!"

"You're going to like it, too. I promise." I ease into a sitting position, gently pulling Maisie with me. Once she's seated, I extricate my hand from her grasp. "You're doing great," I say, my voice soothing. "Now push off with your hands."

"I don't know how." Her voice is quavering.

"Like this." I put my hands by my sides, and I don't mean to push, but suddenly I'm sliding. Crap!

I wrench around onto my stomach so I can see Maisie. "Come on," I call to her, reaching my hands out. "I'll catch you!"

She shakes her head and backs out of sight.

"Maisie!" Liddy cries. "Come back."

"Stop! Stop right there!" Bel calls.

I'm still looking backward when I reach the bottom, and I crumble into a pile like a rag doll. I scramble to my feet, craning to see Maisie. "Where is she? Where'd she go?"

"She's gone, genius," Bel says.

"Oh no, oh no," Liddy says. "We have to find her."

"We will," I say, praying it's true because it has to be. "How do we get back up there?"

"Utility stairs." Bel runs around to the side of the slide and opens a door to a dark, narrow hallway. I can't see more than a foot inside.

"No way," Liddy says, backing away. "I'm not going in there."

"You stay with her," I tell Bel as I take off running. I have to find Maisie or—

I can't even think about what will happen if I don't.

CHAPTER THIRTY-FOUR

FLYX

I was dreading today's lockdown when Dietrich assigned me to hang with Sharrow and get info about Allie's plans. I couldn't exactly tell her I don't need to spend time alone with Sharrow for that.

I cogged it would be awk and uncomfortable with Sharrow, esp given how I feel about Allie. But it's actually been phee. Turns out we like same-same—manga, Free-bop, soft pretzels, ska music. And she seems excited about one of my faves—swimming in the cistern.

"We have it to ourselves, entire?" she asks, her voice low, and I realize it's not swimming she's thinking about.

I feel guilty, like I'm misleading her, but it's not like I have a choice.

I crack a glow stick and drop it through the hole. It hits the water far below and floats, lighting the surface and the brick dome of the cistern in a blue glow. I crack three more sticks, dropping them in.

"Ready?" I ask.

"More than." She lets her towel slide to the ground.

I can't help eye her body—the singlet is practically see-through. She's not looking at me as she grabs the ladder and climbs down, but I can tell she cogs I'm scoping.

"It's cold," she calls as her feet reach the water.

"You'll get used to it once you start moving."

"Or you could warm me." She looks up, bathed in the blue echoing off the water and walls.

Any doubts about her intentions evaporate. How in the uni am I going to nav her feelings without hurting them?

I leave my towel with hers. "Move out. I'm coming in."

She submerges, bubbles bursting at the surface as she sinks into the depths.

I quick-climb halfway down the ladder, then drop. My chest constricts as I go under, bracing against the chill. I descend all the way to the bottom, then push for the surface, breaking through near the curved wall. My eyes are drawn to Sharrow, floating on her back in the center of the pool. It's surreal with the blue light bouncing, the total silence.

"This is so phee," she says. "I can't believe you got my mom to agree to this."

When Dietrich gave me the assignment, coming here popped into my head. I asked on a whim. I didn't expect her to agree.

I shiver, then dip below the surface again and swim hard for the other side to get warm. It feels good to push my muscles—this is the only cistern sally enough that I can.

After several times back and forth, I pop up to see Sharrow by the ladder, eyeing me. She motions me over. I feel a dull dread, but I don't cog how I can refuse.

I swim to the opposite side of the ladder so we're facing each other, the rungs between us.

"Why haven't you ever brought me here before?" She shoves me playfully. We had to leave our personals behind, so she's being bold.

"No idea." It's bizarre that a version of me had a relationship with her that I can't remember.

She moves to my side of the ladder and trails her hand down my chest.

"I'm sorry I don't remember...us," I say.

"We can make new memories." She tilts her face up. "You could kiss me."

I'm tempted—who wouldn't be? She's pretty and smart and nice.

But it wouldn't be fair to her. I'm not in love with her. I'm in love with Allie. "I...I can't. I'm sorry."

She pushes away from me, grabbing the ladder. "Why did you do this?"

"What do you mean?"

"If you're not interested, why are we here?"

I'm sure it's the wrong thing to say, but I tell her the truth. "Your mom."

"Oh gods, could this be any more embarrassing?" She turns away so I can't see her face.

"I *am* interested in you as a friend—"

"Stop, okay? You're making it worse. I want to go back now."

I look at the old-fashioned watch on my wrist. "We can't for another hour."

"Rot it all!" She swims away. I think she's crying.

"Sharrow—"

"Leave me alone." She goes as far away from me as she can get.

Seeing her hurting tweaks something in me. I have to make it right.

I swim over. She turns her back to me, treading water. I float there, the silence aching with things unsaid.

Then finally I take a resp and start talking.

"Since you're stuck here for a while, I have an idea. How about I tell you about my life, so you can get to know me, the me I am now. Then maybe you'll decide to tell me about you. And if you want, you can tell me about us. That way, we'll both cog samewise, even if our memories don't match."

I wait a few beats for her to object. She doesn't, so I continue.

"Okay, I'm a gen-fab, given to a woman who agreed to have me, not *chose* to. Turns out, that's more of a distinction than you'd guess...."

CHAPTER THIRTY-FIVE

"Maisie, where are you?" I shout as I head down the dark passage.

I can't see two inches ahead. I'm going to have to risk my flashlight.

I activate it and stare ahead at a dead end.

That can't be right. No way Bel would be punking me now—there's too much at stake. There's got to be a hidden ladder or door.

I shine the light across the cement walls, coming to a stop on metal rungs embedded to form a ladder. I grab hold and start climbing, heart slamming against my ribs.

"Maisie!" I shout upward. I quiet my breathing and listen, but there's no response.

Near the ceiling, there's an opening in the wall. I climb up and shine my light into a short tunnel with a door on the other end. That should lead to the slide. I hope.

I heave myself into the tunnel. It's too low to stand, so I crawl. When I reach the end, I turn off the flashlight and push open the door. Yes! It's the platform at the top of the slide.

But no Maisie.

I see Bel and Liddy below. "Which way?"

"Try back the way we came," Bel says.

I cross to the access tunnel. Yellow bulbs hanging from the ceiling glow with fake cheer. Maisie is nowhere in sight. "I'll be back as soon as I find her," I shout as I dash down the tunnel.

At the end is the main hallway, lit with normal office-y overhead panels. There are closed doors on either side, none of which we opened on our way through. Maisie wouldn't have opened one, would she? Surely she'd have gone back the way we came, maybe tried to find the lobby and the kitten.

I hurry past the closed doors—there are like ten of them —and with each one, my doubt increases. She could be behind any one of these doors. She could be *anywhere*. There's too much to search. I have to narrow it down. But how am I supposed to know what a lost, scared kid would do?

Wait. I *do* know.

I got lost at the zoo once when I was little. It was free admission day for San Francisco residents, and my mom was so excited to take me. While I was looking at the lions, a group came in, and somehow I got separated from my mom. I thought she left me, and I was terrified. I don't know why, but I didn't look for her. For some reason, I *hid*.

Maybe Maisie is hiding.

Now I'm looking with a different eye. Where would she hide? Where's the *first* place she *could* hide?

I retrace my steps and open the very first door. It's a long-abandoned office. Desk and empty bookshelves heavy with dust and cobwebs. No sign anyone's been in here in the last decade. But I know what I would have done as a scared kid.

I circle behind the desk where the chair has been pulled away just enough for a small child to shimmy into the footwell. I crouch down and there she is, her eyes wide, lower lip quivering. I sit down cross-legged, not fully blocking her exit, but enough that I can grab her if she bolts.

"Hi," I say, my voice soft, not a hint of anger.

I'm silent, waiting to see if she'll engage. She makes eye contact but doesn't say anything.

"You were scared, huh?" I venture.

She nods.

"That's okay," I say. "I remember one time I was scared at the zoo when I was about your age."

"The zoo?"

"Yeah, there were all kinds of animals, but I loved the lions the most. I could watch them forever. I was watching them when a whole bunch of people all came to see the lions. Suddenly I couldn't find my mom. And I was really scared."

"What did you do?" she asks, eyes full of curiosity now.

"I did what you did. I ran and hid. That's how I was able to find you. Because I remembered what it was like to be scared and alone."

She nods. "My mom went away. Like your mom."

I haven't heard a thing about the girls' mom. Only the dad. "Oh?" I'm afraid to say the wrong thing.

"I miss her. Especially at night. My dad says I have to sleep by myself. But I miss my mom and sometimes I get scared and sneak into my sister's room. She doesn't tell Dad."

"It's good to have a sister, huh?" And I think maybe it

actually could be, even if that sister is Bel. "Do you want to go see your sister now?"

Maisie nods.

"We have to go back to the slide, but don't worry—we won't go down it," I tell her. "After we tell Bel and Liddy I found you, we'll leave the way we came in. Does that sound okay?"

Maisie nods again.

"Good. When we see your sister, and my sister Bel, we all need to have a talk about keeping this our secret. We're not going to tell your dad you ran away, okay?"

"Are you sure?" Maisie asks. "We're not supposed to keep secrets."

"Sometimes it's okay to keep a secret," I say. "Like when you sneak into your sister's room at night."

She nods. I hope she means it.

SAYING goodbye at Dietrich's office, Maisie throws her arms around me.

"Remember to keep our secret," I whisper.

She pulls back, all serious. "I promise."

Dietrich leaves with the girls, and Bel and I go back to her chambers. We don't say it, but I know we're wondering the same thing—what are the odds the girls won't blab?

I give it eighty-twenty in favor of keeping the secret, which isn't great. But honestly, how big of a deal is it if they tell? It's not like it gives away anything about time travel or the Resistance.

We make peanut butter and jelly sandwiches, and it feels weirdly normal being in the kitchen together.

Bel grabs two cans of diet soda and hands me one. "Perks of the public sector."

"Cool." I hate diet soda, but it's worth it for the bonding points.

We deposit our PB&Js and drinks on the coffee table and plop down in the armchairs. I notice we're sitting the *exact* same way—legs stretched, feet splayed, arms hanging off the sides—I let out a guffaw. She laughs, too, though more daintily.

I think our mutual secret has served to bond us more than anything I've orchestrated. I wouldn't exactly say I *like* her, but I have less hate, which I wasn't expecting. It feels like a betrayal of my dad, but it's worth it if my plan works.

I lick the ooze of raspberry jam from the edge of my sandwich while I steel myself for the next round of Sharrow-bashing. I hate it so much.

Should I go for her hair this time? Her job?

The door opens and Dietrich enters, saving me.

"Hello, girls."

"Hi," we reply in chorus.

"Great job this morning," she says.

"Thanks," I say, feeling all proud. But I stop myself. This isn't my real life. I shouldn't care if Dietrich approves of me. All that matters is saving my real family.

"The colonel wanted me to bring you to the city this afternoon, but I declined."

"The city?" I ask.

"New Francisco," Dietrich says. "I have meetings, then a formal dinner-dance in honor of the president."

I'm curious about New Francisco, but not enough to get dressed up and make chitchat with a bunch of Nazis. Plus, I'd bet good money the dancing won't be anything like at the club.

"What are you going to wear?" Bel asks.

"I can't decide. I'd love your opinion," Dietrich says, motioning Bel to come with her.

Bel hops up and follows. I take a bite of my sandwich and slump back in the chair.

"Allie, come on," Bel says from the hallway.

"What?"

"Help us pick her dress."

Color me surprised.

I've never seen Dietrich's bedroom. I don't know what I expected, but it isn't this. There's pink everywhere. Dusty pink wallpaper littered with puffy roses. A pink-dressed vintage doll posed in a pink wingback chair. A four-poster bed overflowing with pink floral bedding. I didn't peg Dietrich for a girly-girl.

"Model for us," Bel says, climbing onto the bed and nestling into the mountain of pillows.

Dietrich disappears around a corner.

Bel looks at me and pats the bed.

This is an opportunity to suck up to Bel without having to bash Sharrow. I put my con-face on, slip off the blue boots, and climb up.

Dietrich comes out in a gold dress, form-fitting from neck to feet. It glitters as she walks, reflecting the light like it's made from a million tiny mirrors.

"Wow," I say, without meaning to.

"Hmm," Dietrich says. "I wonder if it's *too* too."

I lean toward Bel and whisper, "I have no idea what that means."

"It definitely says 'look at me,'" Bel tells her mom, at the same time instructing me. "Show us what else you have."

Dietrich disappears again, and I give Bel another opening to "teach" me.

"What are we looking for?"

"Well," Bel says, sitting up straighter. "The event calls for elegant and sophisticated, but not flashy. She should go for beautiful in a reserved way, rather than sexy-hot."

"Gotcha. Then that gold dress was definitely 'too too.'"

Dietrich comes out in a black tank dress that goes to her knees. It follows her curves without being skin-tight.

"What do you think, Allie?" Dietrich asks.

I didn't expect to be up so soon. Here goes. "It's pretty, but...boring?"

"Totally boring," Bel says, *agreeing* with me.

"I think so, too." Dietrich disappears again.

"That dress was a classic cut and style," Bel instructs. "But more appropriate for a cocktail hour. It lacked the presence for a dinner-dance with the president."

"Are you sorry you're not going?"

"Not really. Dressing up's phee, but the event will be dulldrudge."

"Think we could find something phee to do while she's gone?" I say, conspiratorially.

Bel groans. "There's nothing to do in here."

I lean closer. "I didn't mean *here*."

A sly smile curves Bel's lips. "I'll see what I can do."

Dietrich emerges again, this time in a light gray, almost silver, dress. It's sleeveless, floor length, and body-hugging, with cuff-like folds over the hips that make her waist look small.

Bel looks at me. I'm up again. I search my brain for the right vocabulary.

"Elegant," I say. "The bodice is modest but not uptight. The cut accentuates your figure. It's subtly sexy. It makes an impact. The right kind of impact."

"Exactly what I was thinking," Bel says.

Nailed it.

"I agree, this is the one," Dietrich says. "Thanks, girls. I'll get this packed up for tonight."

"When are you leaving?" Bel asks.

"As soon as I change back into my work clothes. I won't be home until late, but there's plenty of food here, and you girls can watch vids and get to bed early."

"Rot," Bel says. "I've got the craves for a veggie burger from the Donut Shoppe."

"The lockdown is still in effect," Dietrich says.

"Does it have to be?" Bel asks. "We really wanted to spend time with Sharrow. Please, Mom?"

Dietrich's expression changed immediately at the mention of Sharrow's name. "Well, the ASPs have all left, so there's no real reason not to lift it."

I gotta give it to Bel. She knows how to work her.

"Thanks, Mom." Bel hops off the bed.

"But be back before midnight," Dietrich says, heading out of the room again.

Bel and I share a grin.

"I mean it—don't be late," Dietrich calls. "We have lots to address in the morning."

Fear zings through my nervous system. On tomorrow's agenda: deciding if I get recycled.

CHAPTER THIRTY-SIX

At the Donut Shoppe, Bel and I are sharing nachos loaded with jalapeños and "real dairy soured cream" when I see Calix and almost inhale a chip.

"What?" Bel says.

"It's Calix." I point to him over by the machines with an older man I've never seen before.

Bel turns to look. "Yeah, so?"

"He was *recycled*." He looks normal, for him—same anatomy book face tattoo, same wavy hair. And very much alive.

"Looks like he's getting the newbie tour." Bel flicks a jalapeño off a chip before putting it in her mouth.

I watch as the older man shows Calix the machines. Calix is nodding, smiling, like nothing's wrong.

"I don't get it," I say. "He's a *doctor*. It makes no sense to erase all that knowledge and have him start over."

"Correct, that would be stupid," Bel says, shielding her full mouth with her hand. "They only erase memories of being here. Nothing earlier."

"They can do that?"

"Eh. More or less." Bel crunches for a moment while we watch Calix fill a bottle with liquid nutrition.

This is my fault. I feel so guilty. And sorry. So sorry. I wish I could—*why can't I?*

I leap to my feet and rush over to Calix. He glances up, looking puzzled.

"I know you don't remember me." My words come out in a rush. "But I want to say—"

"Step *back*," the older man commands in a threatening tone.

"But I—"

The man comes toward me menacingly, and I back up, bumping into someone—Bel.

"She's leaving," Bel says.

"This is a violation—"

"She's new. She didn't know." Bel turns to me and says through her teeth, "Back to the table, *now*."

Calix looks troubled. "Wait. Don't I know you?"

"Allie, *go*," Bel says, looking like she's about to pop a vein in her forehead.

I start back to the table, watching Calix over my shoulder. His bottle is on the ground, leaking brown goo on the floor. The other man is gripping his arm—what about consent?—forcing him to the door.

"Wait," Calix says. "I think I...I need to..."

"Allie," Bel says, getting my attention. "Sit. Don't look."

"*No*," I hear Calix protest. "I need to find out—"

Then they're gone.

"I *knew* you didn't watch all the safety protos," Bel blurts. "Didn't you see that red arm band he was wearing? That means he's newly recycled and you're not supposed to interact with him."

"Why?"

"Isn't that obv? You made him try to remember. If he does remember, they have to give him the drugs a second time. That rarely goes well."

"Oh." I didn't think I could feel guiltier. I was wrong.

I look at the doorway, remembering him there with a look on his face that will haunt me forever.

I put my head down on the table, trying to pull myself together. I've got to regroup. I have to talk to Bel about the plan.

"Oh," Bel says. "It's *her*."

I lift my head and see Sharrow heading for us.

"How phee," Bel says sarcastically.

It's game on. I'm not ready, but I don't have time to be picky.

Sharrow arrives at our table with a smile. "Hey," she says, all upbeat and friendly.

"Yeah?" Bel says. The subtext is *Why are you bothering me?*

I want to say something to soften Bel's response, but I can't—Sharrow has to be the shared enemy.

"What's up?" I say without inflection or eye contact, like I don't care at all.

"Uh, just wondering how your tour went," Sharrow says, clearly deflated.

"Perfect." Bel flips her hair and looks around the room, like everyone there is more important than Sharrow.

"Yeah, it went great," I say, looking at my nails. I toss a glance at her. "Anything else?" My self-hatred roils in my stomach, threatening to erupt and destroy the world.

"I...I guess not." She seems so hurt.

"Good. We have things we need to talk about. *Privately*," Bel says. "Right, Allie?"

"Yeah, *privately*." I'm a monster.

I try to convey with my eyes that I'm sorry, but I can tell Sharrow doesn't get the message. I need to get her alone so I can explain.

She hangs her head and turns away.

Out of the corner of my eye, I see Bel watching me. It's a test to see if I'll kick Sharrow when she's down. I don't think I can.

But this is a test I have to pass.

"Sorry, Sharrow, but we're making delicate decisions here, and your man-hands are too clumsy," I say, loud enough that everyone can hear.

Bel and I laugh, and there's tittering from several people around us.

Sharrow dashes for the exit.

First Calix, now this. I want to melt into the floor and disappear forever.

"Can you believe her?" Bel says, taking a chip from the nacho plate, looking at it, then putting it back.

"Right?" I make myself say.

I glance at the exit. Sharrow's standing in the doorway. *With Flyx.* My heart leaps into my throat. Was he there the whole time?

He turns and meets my gaze.

Oh no. He saw everything.

I need to explain, to him and to Sharrow. They'll understand I had no choice, that it's part of the con.

Flyx and Sharrow leave, together. I stare after them, sick to my stomach.

"Hello?" Bel waves her hand in front of my face. "What's wrong with you?"

"Nothing, I'm fine." I have to look past the fact that I'm a complete and total asshat and get my head back in the game, or all this will have been for nothing. I fall back on a universal excuse. "Just tired, I guess."

"What's the story with you and that Flyx character? If you ask me, you could do a whole lot better."

"Yeah, no. I'm not interested in him."

"Good, because *ew*."

"Seriously *ew*," I force myself to say.

Bel pushes away the plate of nachos. "I need to go for a run."

That's the last thing I want to do, but the clock is ticking. "I could go for a run."

Bel looks at me knowingly. "Right."

"Unless you'd rather do a movie binge," I suggest. It would be much more conducive to bringing her in on the plan. Plus, popcorn.

"A vid? Negative. I need to work off these k-cals." She pushes the nachos further away. "I'll take you to Middies so you can take a nap."

Crap, she's getting rid of me. I can't let that happen.

"No, I want to hang out. I'll go for a run," I say, hating the edge of desperation in my voice. So uncool.

"Ease out," Bel says. "I'll only be an hour or so. *Then* we can watch some vids."

Phew. She's not trying to get rid of me. "Sounds good."

If I'm lucky, I can use this hour to make things right with Sharrow.

I CURL up on Bed 13 looking sleepy while Bel changes into a jumper at her locker.

"Better be here when I get back," Bel calls from the door. "No slipping out when someone opens the door."

Good—she still has no idea I have a personal.

"I'm not going anywhere." I yawn and snuggle my pillow. When I hear the door shut, I peek to make sure she's gone, then push up my sleeve. My first instinct is to message Flyx, but I catch myself.

"Message Sharrow." The window displays a blinking cursor. "I'm sorry about before. It was just part of the con— getting Bel on board. I didn't mean it."

The words appear on the screen, then send.

I get up and pace in the aisle between rows of beds, waiting for her reply. Five minutes pass like five hours. I can't stand this! Should I message Flyx?

No, I definitely shouldn't message Flyx.

Why hasn't Sharrow messaged back? I told her it's just part of the con.

But maybe she's never pulled a con. Maybe I blindsided her. Maybe she's hurt and crying. *Maybe Flyx is comforting her.*

Ugh! I hate that that idea hurts so much.

The walls are closing in. I need to get out of here, go somewhere, anywhere but inside my own head.

I check the time. I have plenty of time before Bel's back.

I bank my personal to the door and it slides open. The coast is clear—but where should I go?

I need air, sun, sky. *The roof.*

Immediately I think of Flyx—his piercing eyes, that grin, those lips...

But I'm not going to message him. I'll go alone and clear my head. I'll look out in the daylight and see what's become of my city.

When I get to the roof, the sky blazes orange with sunset, and I drink it in, only now truly feeling how much I've missed daylight.

I stand there, staring. Stalling.

I need to see my city. But I don't want to.

Enough. Time to get it over with.

I pull back my shoulders, then march to the wall.

I gasp.

I'd tried to prepare myself, but how can you really prepare for something like this?

It's so much worse than the 1906 quake. It looks like something heavy came down and smashed everything. The buildings are crushed and crumbling, the roads are rubble. It's barely recognizable as my city at all—no bridges, no Transamerica building, no Coit Tower. The only thing familiar is the clock on the Ferry Building. Cracked and broken as it is, I would know it anywhere.

I can't change this.

I can—hopefully—go back and save the crew and my parents. I could even stop myself from killing Beck. But just like I can never un-know that I once killed him, I can never un-see this devastation. I'll always know that this is coming, and that nothing I do can stop it.

My shoulders slump as I look out at the ruins. I feel deflated, defeated.

But...maybe knowing this destruction is coming will make me appreciate my city even more when I have it back. I hope so. Because the alternative is living in a world shadowed by ghosts of the future. Or worse, living in that future, not ever getting back to my own time.

The sun's down now, and still nothing from Sharrow. The wind gusts and I hug my arms to my chest, feeling cold inside and out. There's that sleeping bag in Flyx's shelter. I'll wrap up in it and then...I'll message him.

I crawl inside and sling the sleeping bag around my

shoulders. I'm about to message Flyx when I hear something outside.

Voices—one male, one female.

Is it Flyx? Did he bring Sharrow here?

I can't even think about the trouble I'm in if it's *not* Flyx. I lean back into the shadows. Hopefully whoever it is won't look in here.

The voices get louder.

"So how do you know about this place?" That's definitely Flyx.

"You showed me." *Sharrow.* "We used to come here. It was our special hideaway from the world." The pain in her voice couldn't be more obvious if she were sobbing.

"I'm sorry," Flyx says, and he does sound sorry. "I wish I could remember."

"Me, too."

They go silent. I imagine them standing at the wall, looking out over the darkening city. In my mind's eye, there's a tear sliding down Sharrow's cheek, and Flyx wipes it away. Does he draw her to him, hugging her to comfort her? Or something more? Are they looking into each other's eyes? Does he kiss her?

My chest aches.

Stop it. It's not like Flyx and I belong together. If anything, he belongs with Sharrow. And if they're drawn together because of how I hurt Sharrow, then I have only myself to blame.

Sharrow breaks the silence. "I came up here tonight to remember how it used to be."

"How it used to be with us?" I hear the pain in Flyx's voice as clearly as Sharrow's.

"Yes and no." Sharrow sounds shy. Embarrassed. "Before this morning—before we spent lockdown together—

I still hoped I could win you back, that we could be like before."

They spent the morning together? I have no right to be jealous, but I am.

"But now," Sharrow continues, "I realize it can't ever be that way again. I know you like Allie. I accept that. I mean, I'm trying."

"How can you say that after how Allie treated you?" Flyx says.

Oh God, I really am a monster.

"She messaged me that she didn't mean it," Sharrow says. "It's part of her plan to get Bel on our side."

This should make me feel better, but it doesn't.

"I came up here," Sharrow says, "to remember who *I* was before. To try to be that person again."

"How do you mean?"

"I was different before. Happy."

"And you're not now...because of me." Flyx sounds so wounded.

"Not *just* because of you. It's my mom...she's different. Even though she shouldn't have changed. With Bel here, it's...my mom's not the same."

"I'm sorry," Flyx says.

But *I'm* the one who's sorry. If it weren't for Bel and me changing the past and coming here, Sharrow would still be her mother's only child and Flyx's girlfriend.

Hopefully after I leave, Flyx can fall in love with her again. It won't change how I've hurt her, but it might make amends, at least a little.

"I wish I knew what to do, how to make it better," Flyx tells her. I imagine him taking her hand, giving it a little squeeze. My heart squeezes a little too, despite my resolve.

"I rationed coming here would help," Sharrow says. "I

always felt like I could think better up here. Then I saw you, and for a second it was like old times."

"Sharrow, I'm sor—"

"*Don't*. Don't apologize again. It's not your fault. It's no one's fault. It just is."

It's my fault, I want to scream.

"I don't know what to say, if not 'I'm sorry.' I *am* sorry," Flyx says.

"I know." Sharrow sighs, her grief palpable. "Let's agree to keep the past in the past and go forward as friends, okay?"

I feel tears on my face. This is so unfair.

"Rot!" Sharrow exclaims.

"What is it?"

"Tag from Bel. Allie's not where she's supposed to be."

I check the time—it hasn't been an hour yet. Why would Bel be looking for me?

"Did she check her tracker?" Flyx asks.

Tracker? My hand goes to my neck where the bump is. I totally forgot about it—I'm such an idiot!

"No access—my mom's off-site. Can you hack it?" Sharrow asks.

"Affirm. Tell Bel to stand down—she can't tell your mom about this. I'll find Allie and bring her to the Donut Shoppe."

"Okay, please hurry."

I hear gravel crunching as Sharrow leaves.

Then Flyx sticks his head in the lean-to.

I grimace. "Busted."

He shakes his head. He's not smiling.

"I'm sorry," I say. "I didn't mean to eavesdrop."

He looks away, then back again. "You shouldn't have come up here without telling me first. I could have covered your tracks in the system."

"I didn't think. I forgot about the tracker." My cheeks are burning.

"We'd better go."

FLYX SENDS me into the Donut Shoppe without him. Since Bel hates him, he figures going in would make a bad situation worse.

I see Bel and Sharrow—Sharrow's sitting, Bel's pacing.

"Where have you been?" Bel says.

"I wasn't feeling well. I was in the bathroom."

"I *looked* in the bathroom."

"I thought a walk would help, but it made it worse." I wrap my arms around my stomach. "Too many jalapeños, I guess."

"I told you not to leave Middies. Now we have no time to get ready."

"Ready for what?"

"We have to go to that dinner thing after all," Bel says.

"Can't you tell your mom I'm sick?"

"I could go instead," Sharrow offers.

I don't deserve her kindness.

"The colonel asked for Allie *personally*," Bel says.

"Me? As in *only* me?"

"Affirm. But I'm coming, too. The colonel won't dare turn me away."

"What does he want with me? Is he a creeper?"

"He's definitely a creep," Sharrow says.

Bel dismisses her comment with a huff. "My mom and I suspect he's gotten a whiff of something that made him suspicious."

"Like...?" I prompt.

"Most likely it's merely a few things that don't add up," she says. "If he knew anything for *sure* he'd be storming with his troops. So we think he's info-questing. And we —*you*—have to make sure he doesn't find out anything."

This is serious. "Can't your mom get me out of this?"

"Negative. If she tries any harder, it will fuel his suspicions. You have to go."

"I can help with your hair and stuff," Sharrow says.

"We can manage," Bel snaps.

Sharrow looks crushed.

"Thank you, though," I tell her before I can stop myself.

Sharrow hangs her head as Bel ushers me out the door.

CHAPTER THIRTY-SEVEN

B el strides across the Atrium in her slinky iridescent pink gown, having zero trouble in her orange platform shoes. Meanwhile, I'm struggling to keep up without breaking an ankle in the strappy bronze wedges she made me wear. They match the patent leather corset Bel laced over my white dress. I vehemently objected to both the shoes and the corset, but I did it silently. It was more important to let Bel win. Thank goodness this corset is more comfortable than ones in 1906, or I'd have had to rethink that decision.

We enter an office building and hurry across the lobby to an outer door. As soon as Bel opens it, I'm hit by a gust of wind and a loud whirring—a helicopter.

"Get in," Bel says, motioning me forward.

My hair whips in my face as I crouch-jog to the helicopter. A man drops out of the open doorway. I'm about to ask him how I climb up, when he grips my waist and lifts me. Another man grabs me under the armpits and hoists me in. They do the same to Bel.

She sits in one of the passenger seats, crossing her legs

artfully. Her hair is still perfect in a sleek bun, her makeup pristine like she's ready for a photoshoot. Meanwhile, I sit beside her with hair stuck to my lip gloss.

We buckle in as the men close the door and take their seats in the cockpit. Without warning, the helicopter lifts straight up, leaving my stomach behind. I watch out the window as we rise above the ruined buildings of downtown until the buildings are swallowed by darkness, then I sit back feeling queasy and completely out of my comfort zone.

"How long till we get there?" I shout at Bel.

She points to her ear and shakes her head.

I go back to looking out the window. After a few minutes, I see lights in the distance. As we get closer, they take the shapes of buildings, including a pointy one that looks like the Transamerica Pyramid. But of course it can't be. Then I see the unmistakable silhouette of the Golden Gate Bridge. Is New Francisco an exact replica of San Francisco?

I turn to ask Bel but she's staring out the other window. She wouldn't be able to hear me anyway.

The sound of the motor changes, then there's a jolt. I think we landed.

One of the men comes back and motions for us to unbuckle, then opens the door and jumps out. A second later, he reaches back inside and lifts us each down.

We're on a roof overlooking dozens of rooftops all around us, like we're on the top of the world.

The man shoos us away. I crouch after Bel, across the helipad and down a few steps to the main part of the roof where there's a man in a black suit, his dark hair flapping. He motions us inside, then ushers us into an elevator, and pushes the "1" button.

I have that weird stomach-floating feeling as we descend, the digital display counting down from sixty.

I expect the man to say something, but he stares at the countdown. Bel's doing the same. I run my fingers through my tangled hair and wipe the makeup from under my eyes, trying to salvage my appearance.

When the doors open, we follow the man into a lobby that looks like the set of a futuristic movie. The walls are polished metal and extend up three stories to a ceiling lit with zig-zagging white lights. The floor glows blue, like we're walking on glass over neon water. There are no other people in sight, and our footfalls echo in the vast space.

"This place is *crazy*," I whisper to Bel.

She shoots me a *shut up* look.

We approach a set of double doors that look like they're for giraffes. The man pushes one open and steps aside for us to enter.

Inside's a dome with purple lights that snake up the sides and come together in a swirl pattern above. Half the room is empty, the other has a dozen round tables filled with people staring at us. It's completely silent, like all conversation stopped when we entered.

Dietrich walks elegantly over to us, presenting a toothy, fake smile. "You're late," she says through her teeth.

Bel smiles back and doesn't say anything.

"Follow me. Act natural." Dietrich makes a sweeping turn and leads us past people in fancy clothes.

No one takes a drink, no one says a word. They just stare at us. I force myself to smile like this is totally normal.

We arrive at a table with three empty chairs. Dietrich steps up to one of them. "Everyone, this is Bel and Allison."

Bel curtsies. "My apologies for our tardiness."

All faces turn to me, so I attempt a curtsy, too. "Hi," I say with an awkward wave.

"So glad you could make it, Allison," the colonel says. "Please, sit beside me."

Crap. "Of course." It's not like I can decline.

He stands and pulls out the chair for me. As I sit, I hear sounds returning to the room—talking and laughing and clanking of dishes—like everything had been paused until that moment.

Bel sits in the chair beside mine, with Dietrich on her other side.

"Allison, this is Robert Lawrence, Minister of Finance." The colonel gestures to the middle-aged man seated on his left. "Beside him, his lovely wife Colleen. Then Vice President Tuolome and her husband Pierre."

I nod at each, processing the fact that the VP is female.

"Pleased to meet you," the VP says. "I'm afraid we've already eaten, but I can have plates brought for you."

"That's kind but not necessary," Dietrich replies on our behalf.

I haven't eaten since the nachos, but I don't say anything.

"Bel and Allison took the first daughters on a tour of their facilities today," the colonel announces to the table. "Allison, why don't you tell us about it?"

He pins me with his beady eyes, and my gut says this is a trap.

I look to Bel for help.

"The girls were lovely, weren't they, Allie?" Bel says, coming to the rescue. "We showed them the facilities, and they were so gracious—I'd expect nothing less—but in all honesty, they were most impressed by the kitten the receptionist brought in."

Everyone laughs politely.

"Allison," the colonel says, bringing the attention back to me. "What was your favorite part of the visit?"

He's definitely putting me on the spot for a reason. Without knowing what it is, I could accidentally play into his hands.

"My favorite was the kitten, too," I say, choosing the only answer that doesn't seem dangerous.

There's more polite laughter.

"Yes, of course," the colonel says. "But in all seriousness, tell us about showing the first daughters the facility."

He won't let it go! I nudge Bel under the table.

"I enjoyed showing them the science labs," Bel says. "Maybe one of them will grow up to be a groundbreaking scientist, like you, Monsieur Tuolome."

"You flatter me," the VP's husband says with a very French accent.

"*Sil vous plait, monsieur*," Bel continues, "tell us what you're working on currently."

"Surely you are not interested in atmospheric physics," he replies.

"We absolutely are," I say enthusiastically.

He launches into a description of a project that has something to do with the rain forest and the ozone layer. It's way over my head and so boring it hurts, but I lean forward, listening intently, so I don't have to look at the colonel.

My body tenses in case he tries to grope me under the table. But I don't get the creeper vibe. He wants information.

The scientist talks on and on until he's interrupted by a man's voice coming over a microphone.

"Ladies and gentlemen, may I have your attention.

We're pleased to present...Vanilla Jasmine and the Static Syndicate."

A portion of the wall raises like a garage door and the crowd applauds as a stage extends into the room. On stage is a slender woman in black whose skin looks lavender in the strange light. Behind her, there's a man at a piano and a string quartet. The musicians start playing, and the woman begins to sing.

"Allison," the colonel says. "Would you care to dance?"

"Dance? No one's danc—" I look out to see people streaming into the open space in front of the stage. "I mean, I don't dance."

"Nonsense." He stands and extends his hand to me.

I look to Bel, wide-eyed.

"She's shy," Bel says. "But I'll dance with you."

He stares down at me. "Allison, I insist."

"I guess he's not taking no for an answer," Bel says, shrugging.

There's a lump in my throat the size of a baseball, and sweat breaks out along my hairline as he leads me onto the dance floor.

Ballroom dancing looks the same here as in my time, at least from my limited experience seeing it on TV. But that doesn't mean I have the first clue how to do it.

The colonel steps in front of me and takes my right hand in his left. I put my free hand on his shoulder like the other women are doing, and he places his other hand on my waist. *Ew.*

He takes a step backward, pulling me forward, then reverses, pushing me back. I stumble and he grips me tighter.

"I'm a terrible dancer," I say. "We really should sit this out."

"Follow my lead," he says sternly, continuing to move back and forth.

I try to follow, but I keep stepping on his shoes. "Can't we please go back to the table?"

"So you can ignore me again?"

"I was being polite to the other guests," I say, trying to deflect. But I can tell it's not going to work. He wants something from me, and he's not going to stop until he gets it.

"Tell me about your life, Allison."

"My life?" Wait, he's not asking about the visit with the girls. This changes things. I shift my thinking—what can I say that won't give me away as an outsider? "I'm pretty good at academics—both math and English. And not terrible at science."

I pause, but he doesn't say anything, so I keep going.

"Never been great at athletics. Like dancing." I laugh.

He gives a perfunctory laugh. "What about in your leisure time? What do you like to do?"

"Read," I say without hesitation. "I spend a lot of time in the library. It's like home." Oh crap. Do they have libraries?

"Mmmm," he says, noncommittally. "And you like animals—you mentioned the kitten."

Phew. It's okay—he moved on. "Yes, I love puppies and kittens. Who doesn't? Bunnies are cool, too. Turtles. Parrots. All kinds of pets, though I've never had one myself." I half-consider mentioning the synth pets, but it's too risky. Besides, he seems to be buying everything, so no need to try harder.

"What about larger animals?" he asks. "Apes, elephants...*lions*."

The bottom drops out from my stomach. "Excuse me?"

"Wondering what your favorite *zoo* creature is."

He can't be making casual conversation. *He knows.*

"I'm not feeling well," I say. "I need to use the ladies' room."

He jerks me closer. "What's wrong," he says directly in my ear, his breath hot. "You don't want to tell me a story about the zoo?"

"I'm going to throw up," I say, my voice high.

He backs up and I yank myself free, hurrying toward our table as fast as I can without causing a scene. I feel him right behind me.

Bel sees me coming and stands. I go straight over and put my arms around her, as if in a hug. "Bathroom, *now.*"

She laughs like I said something funny, then turns to the table at large. "Please excuse us for a moment." Then she takes my elbow and leads me away.

I glance back and the colonel is pissed, but not pursuing.

At the giraffe doors Bel whispers, "Do you really need the lav?"

"We need to talk."

She steers me into the hallway to our right. There are doors that say "men's" and "women's," but I beeline for the one that says "storage." It's unlocked.

"Seriously?" She follows me in, flips on a light, and pulls the door shut. "What is going on?"

"The colonel. He knows something."

"Like what? What did he say?"

"He asked me about my favorite animals."

"*That's* what got you buggy? You've got to toughen up."

"He brought up *lions.* I think Maisie must have talked, and he knows about her getting lost."

"What? What do lions have to do with anything?" she asks.

"When I found Maisie, I told her a story about when I was little and I got lost at the *lion* exhibit at the zoo."

"A *zoo?*" Bel grips my arms. "Do *not* tell me you said you were at a zoo."

"I...is that bad?"

"*We don't have zoos.*"

Oh God. "So this is way worse than him finding out we lost Maisie. He'll know I'm not from here. And if he already has suspicions about time travel..."

"Wait, back up," Bel says. "Maybe it's not that bad. Did you say anything *to the colonel* about a zoo? Anything at all? This is important."

I close my eyes, replaying the conversation in my mind. "No. I didn't talk about any zoo animals or say the word *zoo.* I'm positive."

"Then we might be okay. We could say you talked to Maisie about a zoo from a storybook and she misunderstood."

"You think that will work?"

"Don't underestimate my mom. She'll handle it. This will bring more scrutiny, and she won't be happy with you, but it does not mean we're blown. Actually, it's goo, if you think about it. It explains why the colonel is suspicious."

I meet her gaze. "But your mom still won't be happy with me. You know what that means. What she'll do to me."

Bel looks away and the silence stretches.

Of course she doesn't care if I'm recycled. She didn't care before, and nothing's changed. I was a fool to think any of the bonding was real for her, just because it was—a little —for me.

"Fine, I'm out of here." I reach for the door.

"Wait," Bel says. "I won't let her recycle you."

I turn back. "You can stop her?"

"I have to tell her *something* so she can deal with the colonel," she says. "But I won't tell her it was you."

I can hardly believe what I'm hearing. "You're going to say it was you?"

She laughs. "Of course not." She shakes her head like it's the most ridiculous thing ever—typical Bel. "I'll bring it up in casual conversation that, after seeing that kitten, we were pretending to be kitties. And then it evolved into a game of lion tamer at the zoo. She'll absolutely believe it because I used to pretend to be a kitty *a lot* when I was little."

"But...she doesn't remember when you were little."

She waves me off. "I'll go through old vid-pics with her and bring it up nat-like. It'll be fine."

"Thank you," I say genuinely. I'm relieved but also encouraged. The bonding efforts *are* working. "What do you say we leave now. I don't want to face the colonel again."

"Suck it up because we have to to back in there."

"Why?"

"When you were dancing, my mom told me the first daughters were asking for us."

"They're here? I didn't see them."

"In the presidential box."

"The what?"

"Come on. If we're gone any longer, it will be suspicious."

"But what if the colonel corners me again?"

"Ease out. I won't leave your side. And I'll tell mom we're leaving after we see the president."

"We're going to see the president?"

"Duh."

CHAPTER THIRTY-EIGHT

Back in the ballroom, Bel and I head straight for Dietrich. I stay glued to Bel's side and keep my gaze down.

Bel whispers in Dietrich's ear. Immediately, Dietrich stands.

"It was so lovely to dine with you," she says to the others at the table, without a hint of unease on her face. "We're going to pay our respects to the president, then we must be getting back. Good night."

The colonel stands. "I'll accompany you."

"No, thank you," Dietrich says. "The president wishes to see the girls alone."

I don't know if this is true, but the colonel sits back down.

"Very well." He doesn't look happy. "I'll speak with you again. *Soon.*"

A shiver runs up my spine. I hope soon never comes.

I stay close to Bel as we follow Dietrich toward the front of the room.

When we're out of earshot, I whisper to Bel, "What did you tell her?"

"That he was being nosy." She whispers so loudly I cringe, but Dietrich doesn't look back.

"Does she think he's a threat?"

"Being cautious. She doesn't trust anyone."

As we approach the front of the ballroom, I see a window in the wall. I don't know how I didn't see it before. Beyond the glass a man is sitting at a table with Maisie and Liddy.

"What the heck?" I ask Bel.

"Security. Act like it's norm. Act like *everything* is norm."

On our side of the glass are two large men in suits. Dietrich goes up to them.

"Allison and Bel to see the president," she says.

"Yes, ma'am, we're expecting them," one of the men replies, opening a door.

The other man goes through the door into a chamber that has nothing but another door on the other end.

"I'll wait here," Dietrich says.

Bel steps in without hesitation. I follow with my heart in my throat, and the door closes behind me.

Inside the chamber there's a humming sound, then a bright flash, blinding me. Surprised, I gasp. Bel squeezes my arm—a warning. *Right.* Act like it's normal.

"You're clear." The man opens the other door. "Proceed."

I guess it's a good thing I hid my personal device before we came.

Bel nudges me through the door ahead of her.

"Allie!" Maisie cries, leaping up and running into my arms.

"Hi," Liddy says. It looks like she wants to jump up, too, but she stays seated, glancing to her father for approval.

"Ladies, I've heard so much about you," the president says, standing. He's tall and skinny, and younger than I expected—maybe forty—with a dark beard and close-trimmed black hair. His smile is easy.

Maisie pulls me to the table. "This is Allie."

"Pleased to meet you, Mr. President," I say, shaking his hand.

His grip is firm, but he doesn't try to crush me.

"Nice to meet you, Bel," he says, extending his hand to her.

"It's an honor to meet you, sir," she says.

"I wanted to thank you for escorting my daughters today," he says, still standing. "You made quite the impression."

"It was our pleasure, sir," Bel says.

Maisie tugs on my skirt. She's staring at me with an odd expression, like she needs to tell me something—probably that she blabbed about getting lost. I hug her to my side, silently reassuring her it's okay, even though it might not be.

"We had a really fun time," Liddy says. "Especially with the kitten."

"You and that kitten are all they've talked about," the president says. "I believe a kitten is in our future."

"And you guys, too," Maisie says to me.

"Us?" *In their future? How?*

"What she means," the president says with a chuckle, "is they'd like to see you again."

"Soon," Liddy says.

"We'd love that," Bel says, giving Liddy a genuine smile.

"We'll be in touch," the president says.

"*Soon*," Liddy says again.

"John will see you out." The president gestures to the man who brought us in.

"Thank you, Mr. President," Bel says. She does a little nod-curtsy thing, then walks toward the door.

Maisie throws her arms around me again, and I hug her back.

"'Bye girls," I say. "Nice to meet you, sir." I nod, but I don't try the curtsy with Maisie still attached.

"Come here, dolly," the president says. "You need to let your friend go." He pulls Maisie into his lap and nuzzles her with his beard until she giggles and squirms.

He seems like such a nice man.

I CHANGE INTO PAJAMAS IN "MY" room, trying to psych myself up. I'm out of time. I have to talk to Bel *now*.

"Allie, come in here," Bel calls from her room. "I've got some clothes for you."

Perfect—another of those girlfriend milestones. I head into her room. Her bed is piled with clothes a foot deep.

"What the...?" I say. "You've been here like *three days*—how can you have this much stuff?"

"Fine, okay? I kinda went haywire-house when my mom realized I was her daughter and told me to fill up my closet. But then this afternoon during my run, I realized, since you're sticking around...." She quirks a grin. "You're going to need more stuff. Good stuff. For when we hang out."

Bam. This is what I've been trying to accomplish.

But something's off. Her words have a tinge of desperation....

Then I remember: without me, she's alone. Despite

being in her real time, despite her mother acknowledging her, she didn't really come *home*. Now no one knows her. And you can't be Queen Bee by yourself.

This feeds perfectly into my plan—her using me, *choosing* me, to prop herself up.

But even though I know this in my head, my heart's not in on the con. It remembers all those times I ever wished I fit in, wanted to be popular, to belong. All the times I was desperate to be chosen, but wasn't.

Now, in this moment, I am chosen. And I feel myself being caught in Bel's gravitational pull.

"Isn't it phee," she says, gesturing to the pile of clothes. "You don't ever have to wear those horr-awful jumpers again. I mean, the thought of Sharrow in that mint green atrocity makes me want to retch."

And she's back. The spell is broken and I'm in my right mind again. The con is on.

"Right?" I say. "Those jumpers are beyond lame."

"Don't just stand there. I need my bed back."

"Thanks, Bel." I smile.

She smiles back. "No prob. I'll help haul this stuff to your closet."

Time's running out, and it's not going to get better than this.

"Cool, but first, there's something I need to talk to you about."

She holds up a finger for me to wait. "Oh, I love this song!" she says loudly. Then she does something on her personal and the music that's been playing in the background gets a lot louder. I can't see any speakers, but they must be built into the room because it sounds like the music is all around us.

Bel pushes some clothes out of the way and sits on the bed. I sit beside her and she leans in close.

"You can't be too careful," she says in a low voice. "What's up?"

I'd been planning to appeal to her about saving the crew, but I realize that nothing is more important to Bel than Bel. It has to be about her.

"I can tell that things are not as good for you here as they were before history changed." I see on her face that my words hit home. "You've been so good to me, and I want to return the favor and help you get your old life back."

"I'm listening."

"If I go back to 1906 and—"

"You can't—"

"Hear me out. If I stop you from shooting Maxen, then you'll be born like normal. Time will roll forward the way it was meant to, and you'll have your life back."

Bel's cultivated eyebrows bunch in a scowl. "Interesting, but nothing's changed—my mom's not going to let us go. Besides, even if she did, we can't get involved in 1906 without seeing our other selves."

I'm about to tell her that seeing ourselves is not actually a problem, but I bite my tongue. If she knows the truth about that, it will call into question why Beck couldn't show himself at the wormhole. And there's no way I can tell her the real reason.

"First of all, there's no 'we,'" I say. "*I'm* going back to stop you. And it won't be hard to avoid seeing myself—you and I didn't see each other on the morning of the quake before we met at the wormhole. So I go back before that, and make sure you don't shoot Maxen."

I hold my breath, my stomach in knots. *Please, please, please.*

Finally she says, "What's in it for you?"

"I get my life back, too."

"Oh. So you want to do more than just stopping me from shooting Maxen," she says in an accusing tone. "How many times do I have to say it—you can't change history. It only gets worse.

"I don't want to change history. I want to change it *back*. You know as well as I do that my mom and the crew aren't supposed to die there any more than Maxen. Plus, for you to get your life back, Maxen's life has to go forward exactly like it did before. That means he has to get in the wormhole with my mom. I get my life back, you get yours. And the crew doesn't die either. *Come on,* Bel. *Please.* I know I can do this."

She stares at me, biting her upper lip. I watch her expressions closely, but have no idea which way she's going to go.

Finally she nods. "Okay."

"Okay what?"

"Okay I agree that to get our lives back, the crew— ourselves included—can't show up at the wormhole during the quake. Then no one gets killed, your mom and our dad go forward with their lives like they did before, and we get our lives back."

I let out a long breath.

"But," she says.

Damnit, why'd there have to be a but? "But what?"

"I still don't see how you think you're going to change my mom's mind about time travel. She never changes her mind."

I swallow, hoping I've played this right. "But she did change her mind. About you being her daughter because of that report."

"Yeah..."

"The report she gets tomorrow will say her plan all along has been for me to travel back to 1906. She doesn't remember that plan because there's been a change in the timeline, but she'll trust the report because she thinks it came from herself."

"Lemme guess—your pal Flyx is in on this."

"He's the one giving her the report."

Bel nods. "And you want for me to what? Stay out of the way?"

"Pretty much. For this to work, you can't tell her your memory is different from what the report says."

Bel nods again.

"Then I'll go back to 1906 and make everything right," I say. "I promise. I'll get your old life back. You have my word."

"Your word? That's sweet. But I don't need it. I'm coming with you."

Shit.

AS SOON AS I CAN, I say goodnight to Bel, close my door, and dive under the covers to message Flyx.

"Are you there? I have good news and bad news."

It's really late, and I tell myself not to expect a message back, but he answers immediately.

FLYX: tell me

"Bel agreed to the plan!"

FLYX: how'd you manage that?

"All that pretending to be her bestie and bagging on Sharrow—I'm not proud of it, but it paid off."

FLYX: so that's the good news or the bad?

"What I did to Sharrow is awful. But the bad news is that Bel is coming to 1906 with me."

FLYX: so? I'm sure you can pretend to be her friend a little longer

"It's not that." I hesitate. What I did to Sharrow pales compared with what I did in 1906. Flyx already thinks I'm a horrible person. I can't tell him what I did, but I have to tell him something. "The problem is, I lied. About something really big. If Bel comes to 1906, she's going to find out."

FLYX: we'll figure out something

He doesn't ask me what I lied about. That's good, I guess, but I don't feel good about it. He's probably imagining the worst. Or he just doesn't care.

"I hope you're right."

A whole minute passes, and Flyx doesn't respond, so I continue. "So you'll fix the report to say Bel and I are both going?"

FLYX: done

"Cool."

If I'm being honest with myself, I want him to ask to meet up. I need to know he doesn't hate me.

I tell myself it doesn't matter what he thinks of me. I'll be gone soon. Back to my real life—Jake, Bibi, the Main, pulling cons on tourists.

But it does matter.

"Okay, goodnight," I say.

I deactivate the personal without waiting for a response, then bury my face in my pillow and sob.

CHAPTER THIRTY-NINE

"Are you going to sleep all day?"

I pull my head out from under my pillow. *Bel.* "I'm not falling for that again." I roll over and pull the covers to my chin.

"I'm not joking. *Look.*"

She holds out her arm, displaying the time. "Shit!" I bolt up and shove back the covers. "Why didn't you wake me sooner?"

She shrugs. "Splash some water on your face—you look like a corpse."

"Thanks a lot." I'm sure she's right, but it's not exactly BFF-like to say so, especially not before caffeine. "Coffee?"

"No time."

Ten minutes later, we walk into Dietrich's office, and Flyx is standing with her behind the desk. I should have been expecting him, but seeing him puts me off balance. Or maybe it's the lack of caffeine. Yeah, I'll go with that.

"Hi Mom," Bel says, all innocence and light.

Dietrich looks from Bel to me. "You'd both better sit down."

I lower myself into a chair. I should be excited since I know what's coming. But all I feel is dread.

"Apparently there's been a history-change," Dietrich says, sounding grim. "A significant one."

"Don't worry, Mom," Bel says. "Whatever it is, I'm sure I can help."

Nice.

"It won't be news to you since you're Jennys," Dietrich says. "But I don't have any memory of it. According to my report, we have an operative in 1906 who has information vital to stopping the ASPs. He's injured and unable to travel, so I need a team to go back and retrieve the information."

"That's not exactly correct," Bel says.

What the... Is she improvising? Flyx and I look at each other. He gives a slight shrug.

"That operative is my father," Bel says. "And the mission is not just about retrieving information. The mission is to bring *him* back."

Dietrich picks up a tablet and scowls at it. "I don't see where..."

"*Mom.*" Bel leans forward. "Dad is the only one who can stop the ASPs. That's why you sent *him* back, and why we need *him* to return. That's the mission. It's always been the mission. Trust me. Trust in our plan—the plan you and I made together. Trust *us.*"

Slowly Dietrich sets the tablet down. She nods. "I do trust you, Bel."

I'm impressed at Bel's skill, but she *changed the plan.* We were never supposed to retrieve Beck. To do that, we have to go back to before I killed him, several days prior to the quake. How am I going to explain that?

Dietrich straightens in her chair. "The information

repository is in place for a reason. I trust it, and I trust you three." She looks from Bel, to me, to Flyx. "We're on a one-week countdown—better get to work."

"A whole week?" I blurt.

Dietrich frowns at me. "It will take that long for Flyx's tattoo to be removed."

What? Flyx coming was not part of the plan. I look at Bel and her face is a blank. Did she know?

"Hopefully less than a week," Flyx says, shooting me a glance that says *shut up.*

"We need to leave as soon as possible," I say. "We should go without him. We should leave now."

"But my notes clearly say he's essential to the plan," Dietrich says, narrowing her eyes. "What's going on here?"

"Nothing. Allie's just anxious." Bel turns to me with a look of warning. "Allie, we talked about this, remember? It doesn't matter when we leave—we can always go back to the same point in history."

"That's good," Flyx pipes in. "Because even without the tattoo removal, I don't know how much time I'll need to refit the wormhole machine."

Bel and Flyx are both looking at me, silently screaming to keep my mouth shut.

"Right. Sorry," I say, backing down. If I'm not careful I'm going to blow this. "Bel's right—I'm anxious."

"Then it's settled," Bel says. "I'll take Allie to the mall and get started on our clothing."

Flyx nods. "I'll meet you after I scope the wormhole repair. I can talk to Tryda about my tattoo—maybe there's a way I can be ready to leave sooner." He looks at me apologetically.

I look away. I'm still pissed. They both changed the plan without talking to me.

Bel and I exit into Dietrich's chambers, and I wheel on Bel. "What the—"

"*Later.*" She banks her personal to the yellow wall.

As we walk to the mall, I try to wrap my brain around this new scenario. Flyx has never traveled before. Even though he monitors history for his job, I doubt he knows enough about 1906 to fit in. With a week to prep, he might squeak by, but the mere fact of him being in 1906 could change things in ways we can't predict.

And an even bigger problem: how am I going to keep Bel from finding out I killed her dad?

I'm finally going back to 1906—I should be *excited*. But with Bel and Flyx coming, I don't see how it can go well.

I try Bel again. "We need to talk."

"You have the patience of a gnat. Can't you ease out for one more minute?"

I press my lips together.

We head down a flight of stairs and through a steel door. Now I can hear the mall in the distance.

"Okay," Bel says close to my ear. "*What?*"

"Did you know?"

"Of course not."

"What the hell's he thinking? Why's he suddenly coming with us?"

"Isn't that obvious?"

"Uh, no."

"He's in love with you. Or he thinks he is. Gods, you really are obtuse."

"But...no. I mean he did like me, but then stuff happened. He, he saw things, he learned things about me, and now he thinks I'm horrible."

"Thinking and feeling are two different things," she says, as if this explains everything.

"What are you talking about?"

She shakes her head like I'm hopeless. "Haven't you ever had a thing for someone you don't even like?"

"Wait, what?"

"You really are a nafe, and not only about time travel."

Could Flyx be in love with me, even after everything that happened? I remember the way he looked at me, remember how it felt when we kissed... Could it be that way again? I'm thinking of the kiss, and Bel looks over and laughs at me.

"Shut up!"

"Fine. But get your head out of the clouds. We've got heaps to do, starting with getting our clothes made."

"What happened to the stuff we arrived in?"

"Incinerated," Bel says. "I already pulled pics and patterns from the archives for our outfits. I'll have to do that for Flyx now, too, since he won't have a clue. You know he doesn't have a clue about any of this, right?"

"How is this even going to work?"

"It won't. It can't. You need to talk him out of coming."

IN THE PAST TWO HOURS, Bel and I got measured, picked fabrics for our dresses, and selected a pattern and fabric for Flyx. One week's not enough time to have shoes made, so we chose from existing stock. I'd have loved to wear the blue boots Bel gave me, but there's no way that would fly, so I picked some practical brown boots that aren't nearly as cute. To my surprise, Bel went practical, too. At least for her. There's no way *I* could wear cream-colored boots with three-inch heels—I'd fall in a mud puddle in the first five minutes.

Now Bel's off looking for containers for medicines and toiletries that won't look out of place in 1906, and I'm trying to find a passable travel bag.

I can't stop thinking about what Bel said—*Flyx is in love with me*. It makes me feel all woogly, but I wish it didn't. If I'm going to fix the past, I have to be over him. And I have to convince him to stay in 2053.

For the thousandth time, I glance around looking for him, and this time I spot him. My stomach does a flip. I wave and he jogs over.

"Hey." His voice is low and smooth, like a caress.

My palms are suddenly sweaty, my mouth dry. "Hi," I croak.

"I'm sorry. About before," he says. "I should have told you, but I didn't want you to tell me not to."

"About that...."

"Hey, Bel," he says, looking over my shoulder.

"What are you doing?" Bel says. "We don't have time for standing around."

"Ease out, I just got here," Flyx says. "*And...*" He looks mischievous. "I fixed the wormhole machine."

"Already?" I exclaim. "That's fantastic!"

"Good," Bel says. "Now *we,*" she gestures from herself to me, "can be on our way."

I give her a sharp look, trying to convey that I haven't had time to talk to him yet.

"You're not getting rid of me that easy," Flyx says.

"You're not coming if you don't get that tattoo taken care of," Bel says. "Better see to that."

"Done." Flyx opens his hand and shows her a tube. "Semi-perm makeup. Won't come off with a hose."

"Fine," Bel says with a huff. "Go do your measurements

and meet us in Orange in ten. You have a lot of history to learn."

"You forget, history's my job," Flyx says.

"Seriously, nafe?" Bel cocks her hands on her hips. "You think being a loggie has prepped you for this?" She chuckles without humor. "You have no idea."

She flips her hair and marches off.

Flyx and I look at each other.

"She's right, you know," I say softly.

"Allie, come on," Bel shouts.

I jog to catch up with her.

CHAPTER FORTY

FLYX

Roleplay was a disaster. Bel said I was nox, the worst she'd ever seen, that I'd def jeopardize the mission and I should back out. Allie didn't defend me. She *nodded.*

But there's no way I'm quitting, so I'm going hard at the tutorial modules while Allie and Bel build a cover story.

Now it's well past midnight, I have a screen-headache, I'm wiped, and I'm starving. But I'm not stopping, at least not until they do.

Allie looks exhausted, too. It makes me want to go to her. But I force my focus back to the language tutorial. I didn't cog how different they talked in 1906. It'll be near impossible for me to speak without vanking our cover. Maybe I can pretend to be mute.

"I'm going home to sleep for a few hours," Bel says.

Finally.

"You coming?" she asks Allie.

"Not yet."

"Samewise," I say. If Allie's not leaving, I'm not.

"*You* should stay all night," Bel tells me. "But Allie

doesn't have a personal, so take her to Middies when she's done. In the morning, I'll tag up when to meet back."

She gathers her things and leaves without a goodbye.

When the door shuts, I turn to Allie. "Does she really have to come with us to 1906?"

"It's late. Maybe we should head to Middies now after all."

"I was hoping we could talk..."

"No," she says, rising and coming toward me. "Tomorrow will be a long day." She pins me with her gaze and mouths *roof*, then puts her finger to her lips.

"Affirm. We'd better get some rest," I say for whoever might be listening.

ALLIE LOOKS stunning in the moonlight, and I want to kiss her more than I've ever wanted anything. I step as close as I dare. "Consent?"

"I...that's not why I wanted to come up here. There's something I need to tell you." She looks so serious.

I realize there's something I need to say—I don't want any secrets between us. "I need to tell you something, too."

"Okay," she says. "You first."

I go to the wall and look out at the dark ruins, getting my thoughts together. For a moment I question—do I really need to confess? She'll probably never find out.

But I realize that doesn't matter. I need to come clean for my own sake.

She steps beside me and I turn to her. "Okay, please cog there's nothing to worry about—I'm only telling you because I don't want to keep anything from you." I look into her eyes, willing her to understand. "Dietrich asked me to spy on you."

"*What*? When?"

"When she caught me giving priv info about Kaitlin. I let her cog that what she had on me was enough to make me her spy. But I never was. Not for a minute."

"That's how you got yourself out of trouble?"

"I never told her anything that would compromise you, I swear."

"What *did* you tell her?"

"Only things that wouldn't hurt you or bollix the plan. And I used it to our advantage, getting access—"

"How do I know you're not playing both sides?"

"If I were, why would I tell you? I promise, Allie, I'm on your side, one hundred. I always have been. Even when I was saving my hind, I never betrayed you, not actual. If I was against you, why would I have gone along with the report that's allowing us to travel?"

"But now you're coming, too. So you can keep spying?"

"No, I swear, I—" I see the turmoil behind her eyes. I think she wants to believe me, but is afraid to trust me, to trust that my intentions are pure. Instead of pleading my case harder, I need tell her what's in my heart.

"Allison, my odd-clothed girl. I promise you that everything I've done, I've done for you. I want to be with you, wherever you are, *when*ever you are. I want to be there for you, always. Please, *please* believe me. And if you can find it in your heart...forgive me."

CHAPTER FORTY-ONE

I look into Flyx's eyes.

I believe him.

He didn't betray me. I know he'd never betray me.

But that doesn't change what I have to do.

"Allie?" he says, his voice choked with emotion. "Say something?"

I should go for the jugular, tell him I don't forgive him, that I hate him and I never want to speak to him again.

I open my mouth, but I can't bring myself to do it. Not like that. "I forgive you."

He smiles as a tear spills over and runs down his tattoo. He extends his hand to me. "Consent?" he whispers.

I should say no. But I tell myself I can have one last kiss before I break his heart. And mine. This is goodbye. "I consent."

He touches his nose to mine, tentative, gentle. I slide my arms around his neck and press my lips to his. He grips my waist, pulling me close, kissing me hard and fierce and urgent.

I don't want to stop. But if I don't stop now... I press my hands to his chest, making space between us. Space that I need, but don't want.

"We can't do this anymore," I whisper.

"What do you mean?"

"This. *Us*. We can't anymore. It's over."

"But you said you forgive me."

"It's not that." I back away, out of his arms.

"You know how much I care about you, right? And you care about me. I know you do."

"I mean it. We're done."

"But, but why?" He looks devastated, confused.

I harden my heart as best I can and proceed with my plan. "Don't you feel like this isn't right? Like this isn't how things are supposed to be?"

"No, I don't feel that way at all. We belong together."

"You belong here. I don't. It's as simple as that."

"I belong with you, wherever—whenever—you are."

I shake my head, hating myself. "I should have told you this before.... When I go back to 2018, there's someone..." I take a breath. "Someone I care about. His name is Jake."

"Oh." He recoils like he's been punched. "I thought you felt samewise..."

"It's complicated."

"Not for me."

"It is if you're being honest." I look into his eyes, making sure I have his attention. "You don't know me. Not really. You were in a *relationship* with Sharrow."

"But I don't remember it!"

"Still, she cares about you. A lot. And if I weren't here..."

"But you are!"

"I'm leaving."

"And I'm going with you," he insists.

"You shouldn't be. After I fix things in 1906, I'm going back to my life, to my real time. To Jake." It hurts, but I forge ahead. "You should stay here. With Sharrow. That's how it's supposed to be."

"It wouldn't change anything. I wouldn't forget you. Or how I feel. How would that be fair to Sharrow when I want *you?* When I love you...."

My breath catches and I ache to tell him I love him, too. But sometimes you have to do what's right, even if it hurts. And this is going to hurt.

"I don't love you," I say. "I don't want you to come with me. I don't want you at all."

I search his face for the pain I know I've caused. But I don't see pain. I see determination.

"You can't stop me from coming with you," he says, his voice low and confident. "Unless you're willing to sabotage your own travel. So we're both going or both staying. You choose."

Is this what he thinks love is? Forcing me to be with him?

I can't look at him.

I turn my back and walk away.

The fact that I thought I loved him makes it worse.

Climbing down the ladder, I know one thing: I'm not staying in this time. I'm going back to 1906 to save my family. So I guess that means he's coming with me.

Or does it?

The inkling of an idea flashes through my mind. I grab it before it can slip away. I examine it, turning it around, viewing it from every angle.

I climb faster. *I think this could work.*

When I arrive at Dietrich's chambers, I'm winded, but I have a plan.

I should knock—I'm not supposed to have a personal— but I'm not ready to wake Dietrich. So I bank my device, praying it works.

The door slides open. No alarms beep, no one calls out.

Silently, I creep forward to Bel's room, slip inside, and close the door.

"Bel," I whisper, crossing to her bed.

I turn on the flashlight and she bolts to a sitting position. "*What?*"

"Shhh. Don't wake your mom," I whisper.

"What are you doing here?" she says in that ungodly loud whisper of hers.

I sit on the edge of her bed and say in a low voice. "Flyx won't budge. He said that either he comes with us or he blows it so we can't go at all."

"Rot," she says. "All right, we'll make another plan in the morning. Now go away." She adjusts the wide headband holding back her mass of hair, then tucks herself under the covers.

"I *have* a plan," I say. "And it can't wait until morning. We need to travel now."

She sits up and faces me. "Now? Like *now?*"

I nod. "Before he wakes up."

"When he wakes up and we're gone, he'll tell my mom everything."

"Maybe, but so what? She can't stop us—we'll already be gone."

"*Some people* want to come back to this time."

"No, not *this* time. Once we put things right, this timeline won't exist. You'll come back to your old mom, the way things used to be."

"*Before my life got vanked...*"

"Exactly."

Bel purses her lips, then nods. "Okay, I like this. But you've forgotten one thing—the wormhole machine."

"Flyx already fixed it."

"I know. That doesn't mean we can access it. Not without Flyx."

"What about that backdoor into the system? You can give yourself access."

"No, I checked when we first got here. It wasn't there."

I'd anticipated this. "Then we need your mom."

"That's going to be easy, *not*."

"I have an idea. It's a little crazy, but I think it will work." I dive in. "We tell her the truth about Maisie, the zoo, and the colonel. But we exaggerate a bit about the colonel being onto us. We tell her we just found out—somehow—that's the colonel poses an immediate threat and we have to leave right away."

Bel's mouth forms an "O".

"Can you think of a way to explain how we found out?" I ask, crossing all my fingers.

Her face draws into a smile. "What do you take me for? You're not the only Jenny."

"I was hoping you'd say that. Let's go wake her."

"Now? But our Victorian clothes aren't ready yet."

"We'll get them on the way. I've got it all figured out. Come on."

We cross the hall and open Dietrich's door. Immediately, a light comes on and Dietrich sits up in bed. "What is it, girls?" she asks, like she's perfectly awake.

"There's a problem, Mom," Bel says, crossing the room and climbing onto the foot of the bed. "It's bad."

I stand near Bel, but I keep my mouth shut. Bel's got this part.

"What happened?" her mom asks.

"I have a spy embedded with the ASPs, and she sent word—"

"*Why don't I know about this?*" Dietrich bolts upright.

"You do. You did. You helped set it up, but you forgot with the history change. Either you didn't write it down, or you haven't seen that report yet—it doesn't matter. What matters is what she said."

"Tell me.'"

"Colonel Marek is onto us."

"The Resistance?" Dietrich asks.

"Worse. Time travel."

Dietrich gasps, but regains her composure quickly. "How?"

I decide to slip in here and claim responsibility—it'll make Bel's solution look stronger. "It's my fault. I didn't know there weren't zoos in this time, and when Maisie ran away—"

"The details don't matter now," Bel says. "What matters is they may be readying for a surprise visit."

"*May* be?" Dietrich says.

"Isn't that enough?" Bel says.

"Enough for what? Do you propose we evacuate the entire populace and scuttle everything in the Zone based on a *maybe?*"

"Of course not," Bel says, indignant. "I can travel back to 1906 right now and fix everything."

"*We* can," I say. "By putting the timeline back the way it was, making it so I never come here, and thus never tip off the colonel."

"Yes, but it's bigger than that," Bel says, her tone a bit

more scolding than it needs to be. "I'll bring back my dad. He knows how to make sure we never have to deal with the ASPs again."

"But we have to leave *now*," I stress. "Before the ability to time-travel is taken away forever."

Dietrich's brow furrows. Bel bites her lip. I hold my breath.

Finally, Dietrich nods. "Okay."

There's a loud click outside the room.

I gasp. "What was that?"

Dietrich looks at her personal. "It must be Sharrow leaving for early shift."

I dash out, clicking on the hall light as I run to the living room. "Sharrow?"

There's no answer. I check everywhere. She's not here.

I return to Dietrich's room, where she's now dressed in a black suit.

"She was already gone," I say. "I wanted to say goodbye."

"Do you think she heard what we were saying?" Bel asks.

"She could have," Dietrich says. "Is that a problem?"

Bel and I exchange a glance.

"That depends," Bel says. "How cozy is she with Flyx these days? We don't want him to find out we're leaving."

"But he's going with you," Dietrich says.

"Actually, we have concerns about that," Bel says.

"*I* have concerns about you changing the plan—he's supposed to go," Dietrich says.

"He doesn't have the skills, Mom. And he can't acquire them in an hour, a day, or even a month. Allie and I can do this mission, but not if we have to worry about him vanking everything. We need to cut him loose. Now."

Dietrich looks like she's about to object again, so I jump in. "I know he was spying for you."

"He *what?*" Bel says.

"But you don't need him," I continue. "Bel's going with me. You trust her, right?"

Dietrich looks at Bel. "I do."

"Then it's settled," Bel says.

CHAPTER FORTY-TWO

FLYX

In my dream, Allie whispers in my ear that she loves me. Then the words transform. *"Wake up."* I feel breath on my ear, the voice no longer Allie's.

"Flyx, wake up."

I open my eyes to Sharrow leaning over my cot.

"What is it?" I ask. "What's wrong?"

She smiles, her eyes sad. "I came to say goodbye, since we might not see each other again."

I rub my eyes and sit up. "Wait, what?"

She sits, perching on the edge of my cot. "I understand. And I want you to know I don't blame you."

"Understand what? Blame me for what?"

"For whatever happens. Like, if I'm not here when you get back."

"Oh!" I feel like an idiot. "You're worried you might not remember me? Because if that happens, I'll take you to our spot on the roof and I'll tell you everything. I promise."

"I appreciate that." She nods, but I can tell I missed the mark.

"What is it you're not saying? You can tell me, Sharrow. I'm your friend. I'll always be your friend."

She meets my gaze. "I know what this trip is really about. I know Bel and Allie are going to get their old lives back."

"Yeah..."

"Bel and I were born the same month of the same year to the same mom. In different timelines. There's this timeline, when I'm born. And the timeline Bel wants to get back...when I'm not."

The bottom falls out of my stomach. "*No...*"

"So I'm saying goodbye." She brushes my shoulder with her hand, ignoring proto.

To hell with proto. I pull her into a hug and hold her tight.

I backflash on the report I saw in the TIC—the timeline when Allie and Bel and the crew are born. There is no Sharrow. How did I not remember that?

She pulls back and wipes away tears. "Enough of this sappy stuff," she says with a forced laugh. "You'd better hurry. You don't want them to leave without you."

"What do you mean?"

She frowns. "They're getting ready to go now."

"*What?*"

"I overheard them talking to my mom when I got up for shift. I don't think they're even going to say goodbye to me."

They're leaving now. Without me.

I throw back the coverlet and leap to my feet. "We have to stop them."

I wake Daum, and the three of us double-time for Detention.

CHAPTER FORTY-THREE

It's eerie as Bel, Dietrich, and I make the long trek from Dietrich's chambers to Detention, our footsteps the only sound in the deserted wee hours of the morning.

Please work, please work, please work, I repeat like a prayer with each step.

We're so close to making things right.

We pause at the top of the long staircase while Dietrich releases the door to Detention. Bel looks at me and nods. I try to smile.

Dietrich opens the door and strides into the room, every bit in command. Two guards scramble to get out of the easy chairs and come to attention. The holding cell is vacant.

"You're dismissed," Dietrich barks.

"Yes ma'am," they both say, grabbing their packs and scurrying out without question.

Dietrich makes sure the outer door closes, then enters the wormhole room. Bel and I follow, my heart hammering in my ears.

Dietrich crosses to one of the blank cement walls and

banks her personal to an invisible sensor. A control panel appears on the wall.

This is it. It's really happening.

Dietrich turns to me. "Bel told me you'll get period clothing en route?"

I nod.

"Give me your personal devices," Dietrich says.

Bel hands hers over. I open my mouth to protest, but Dietrich cocks her head and extends her hand.

"You don't think I know?" she says.

I hand mine over. I guess I wasn't as sneaky as I thought I was. She probably knew the entire time and allowed it so I could communicate more easily with her spy. *Which I did.*

My cheeks heat. With anger at Flyx, but more at myself.

Dietrich turns to the panel and presses a sequence of buttons. "Take your positions."

I follow Bel to the center of the room. Then suddenly she bolts over to Dietrich and hugs her. Without a word, she rejoins me and slips her hand into mine.

This is really happening. My chest tightens, my entire body wound tight.

"Good luck and gods speed," Dietrich says. She flips open a cover on the panel revealing a lever. "Engaging now."

"Stop!" Flyx shouts, running into the chamber with Daum and Sharrow on his heels.

Dietrich turns, her hand poised over on the lever. "*Sharrow?* What are you doing here?"

"*Damnit,*" Bel says as Sharrow rushes into Dietrich's arms.

Flyx slides between Dietrich and the panel, and closes the cover over the lever, exhaling audibly.

Dietrich extracts herself from Sharrow's grasp. "Someone tell me what's going on."

"You can't let them go," Flyx says.

"Stand down," Dietrich tells him. "You've been removed from this mission."

"We had a *deal*," he says to her.

"She doesn't need your *services* anymore," Bel says.

"I told her everything," I tell him. "It's for the good of the mission."

"They're lying to you," Flyx says to Dietrich. "They faked the report to get you to let them travel. The whole thing's a scam."

"What are you—"

"Don't listen to him, Mom," Bel says. "You know who you can trust."

"You can't trust *her*," Flyx insists. "She lied about everything. There's no operative in 1906 with information that will take down the ASPs. This is a personal mission for Bel and Allie to change history so they can get their old lives back."

"Shut up, liar," Bel says. "Mom, it's not true."

"It *is* true," Sharrow says. "They've been planning this all along."

"You can't let them go through with it," Flyx shouts. "Because if they get their old timeline back, this one is erased forever, and Sharrow along with it."

I gasp. "Oh no. *Sharrow*. I didn't—"

"Shut up!" Bel says.

"Bel, is this true?" Dietrich says.

"Mom, I—

"What about the ASPs being onto us?" Dietrich strides toward us. "There is no spy in the ASPs ranks, is there? You lied. About all of it."

"Not all—" I cut off my excuse at a look from Dietrich.

"Do you know how close I was to pulling that lever?" Dietrich says in a low voice. "How close I came to losing Sharrow forever?"

"It's not like you'd have remembered," Bel says.

"You selfish bitch!" Flyx shouts, coming toward Bel.

"*Flyx*," Dietrich says, stopping him in his tracks. "I'm in your debt. Now please leave, and take Daum with you. Say nothing of this to anyone."

Flyx draws a breath to speak, then an alarm blares. He looks at his wrist and I can *see* his personal. It's flashing, emitting the sound—all the personals are doing it.

"*Gods*," Bel says.

"What's happening?" I say, completely in the dark about what this means.

"The ASPs breeched the perimeter," Bel says. "They're *in* the private sector."

I've never heard terror in her voice before.

"Bel?" Dietrich asks.

"I don't know, Mom. I was lying about the spy."

"But it's true about the zoo and the colonel being suspicious," I say. "He must have put it together."

The alarms are still blaring, panic on each face in the room, including Dietrich's.

"What do we do?" Sharrow says.

The alarming ceases. The overhead lights shut off, plunging us into complete darkness, except for the lights on the control panel—*the machine still has power*.

Yellow emergency lights come on, illuminating grim expressions on everyone's faces.

"Get in the other room—I need you all clear," Dietrich commands. "I'm destroying the machine."

"Wait!" I rush to Dietrich, grabbing her arm. "Stop—you don't have to. Send me back—I can fix this."

"There's no time."

"Allie's right," Bel says. "She's the one who caused this. If she never comes here, this won't ever happen. We've got to change back the timeline."

"But *Sharrow*," Dietrich says.

"It's okay," Sharrow says. "We can't let the ASPs take the Zone."

"Sharrow, come with us!" I say. "You'll be a time orphan, but you'll be alive."

"She's not a Jenny," Dietrich says. "She won't survive it."

"You don't know that. My mom did, *twice*," I say. "We won't take her all the way to 1906. We can drop her some-place close. Please, what do we have to lose?"

Dietrich looks at Sharrow, then back at me. "Okay."

"Okay?" I say, not believing my ears.

"Mom, you can come, too," Bel says.

"We can all go," Flyx says. "There's a timer setting on the trigger."

"Can you set the auto-destruct if you use the timer?" Dietrich asks him.

By the look on Flyx's face, the answer is apparent.

"I'm staying behind," Dietrich says. "Everyone else get into place."

"What about the TIC?" Daum says.

I'd forgotten he was here. We all look at him.

"Rot," Flyx says. "We need to make sure Remo destroys it." He taps on the face of his personal but nothing happens.

"Comms are down throughout the complex," Dietrich says. "The only way to reach him is on foot."

"I'll go," Flyx says.

"No," Dietrich says. "You'll tolerate travel almost as well as a Jenny. I need you to stay with Sharrow. I'll trigger the destruct here, then head to the TIC."

"What if you don't make it in time?" Flyx says. "Let me go—I'll blow the TIC."

"*I'm* going," Daum says, already at the door. "Fix the timeline so I'm not dead." Then he's gone.

Flyx pulls Sharrow to the center of the room. "Come on. We can't let his sacrifice be for nothing."

"Hold on tight," Bel says, extending her hand to me again.

I take her hand, then grab Sharrow's free hand with my other.

"Ready to engage," Dietrich shouts. "In *three...*"

There's a frantic pounding on the outer door.

"*Two...*"

"Is it Daum?" I ask.

"*One!*"

A vibration starts in the floor, and I hear a low grumble, like the beginning of a quake. Then there's an explosion— the outer door disappears in a blast and ASPs flood in, pointing guns. The room shakes violently, the floor bucking. I struggle to keep my balance.

The wormhole appears, a tiny floating silver bubble.

But it's too small. It's too late.

CHAPTER FORTY-FOUR

The wormhole is growing, but not fast enough.

The colonel steps forward and we lock eyes across the chaos. He *smiles*.

"Go now!" Dietrich shouts.

She's going to destroy the machine.

The wormhole is scarcely a foot across. We'll never make it.

But then I remember—I pulled Bel through a wormhole that size before. Can I do it with four of us? I've got exactly nothing to lose.

I run at it, pulling the others with me as gunshots erupt and muzzle flashes light up the room. Bullets pass through the wormhole. It wavers and distorts, then begins to buckle.

I push off hard, leaping, diving headfirst into the wormhole as it's collapsing in on itself.

There's silence as my head enters the wormhole, but I feel my body still in the room, hands gripping tightly to Sharrow's and Bel's, holding on with everything I've got. I concentrate, willing my body to continue forward, pulling the others in with me.

But it's too slow.

I can sense bullets flying, the wormhole collapsing. I yank hard on Bel and Sharrow, screaming with the effort, the sound bouncing along the tunnel of mirrors. Then their voices join mine, echoing into the past. Finally, Flyx enters howling in agony, a trail of red flowing behind him. He lets go of Sharrow and grabs his leg, which starts him tumbling.

"He's shot!" I let go of Bel and Sharrow, and struggle to reach Flyx, getting nowhere.

"Put pressure on it," Sharrow tells him.

"Bel, help me," I shout.

Suddenly everything stops. It's like she *made* it stop. Like when we were in the wormhole before.

Bel swims to Sharrow in a graceful dolphin motion. "She's the medic." She grabs Sharrow's shoulders, and propels her to Flyx.

"I need something to make a bandage," Sharrow says, pressing her hand to the wound on Flyx's calf.

"On it," I say, grabbing the sleeve of my shirt at the shoulder and yanking, trying to rip it at the seam.

"Here, try this," Bel says. She pulls off her headband, handing it to Sharrow.

"Rot everything," Flyx says, grimacing.

"I think the bullet just grazed you," Sharrow says, examining the wound. "You'll be fine if we can get the bleeding to stop."

She binds his leg with the headband. Flyx groans as she pulls tight on the bandage, securing it. Sharrow wipes her hands on her jumper, then grabs Flyx's wrist to take his pulse.

In the silence I hear *her* breathing hard, not him.

"Try to relax," she tells him.

"Sharrow, are *you* okay?" I ask.

"Fine," she says, focusing on Flyx.

But she doesn't look okay. She's pale, trembling.

"Bel?" I ask.

"It's the radiation," she says. "She's been here too long already. We need to get her out. Tell me where we're going?"

"2018. We'll get them to Sink. Flyx's tattoo shouldn't stand out too much in that time."

"That's what you're concerned about? The tattoo?" Bel says, wide-eyed.

"No, it just made sense—Sink helped my mom with radiation sickness—he'll know what to do. Plus we can sneak into Beck's house and get Victorian clothes when no one's there. Then catch the quake to 1906."

"*That's* your plan?" Bel looks at me, incredulous. "What makes you think the house will even be there, much less the clothes? We're not coming back to how it was in our time-line. Maxen *died*. The crew was *never born*. It's possible Sink doesn't even exist."

"He's there," Flyx says through clenched teeth. "He might not be alive now, but in this timeline, 2018 is the last place he was."

"How do you know that?" I ask.

"Doesn't matter," he says. "Sharrow's bad off. We have to do something now."

Sharrow moans and slumps against him. There's no time to think it through.

"Do it," I tell Bel.

"You'd better be right." The wormhole starts moving again. Or *we* do—it's hard to tell.

"How are you doing that?" I ask her.

"My tat." She touches behind her ear.

"The implant?"

"Can you go faster?" Flyx asks. "She's unconscious."

"Almost there," Bel says, scanning the images zipping by.

"Stop as close to the quake as you can," I say. "We should only need a couple of hours."

The images are whipping by so fast, it's hard to tell for sure, but something doesn't look right.

"We're close," Bel says, as we slow.

"Are you sure we're in the right time?" I ask, peering at the buildings. "I don't see the Main."

"This is right," Bel says. "*See?*"

The buildings rock and shake with a quake, then go still. Bel stops the wormhole. It's nighttime, the buildings dotted with lit windows.

But it's the wrong buildings.

"This can't be the right year," I say.

"It doesn't matter," Flyx says. "If we don't get her out of here now, I don't know if she'll make it."

Sharrow barely looks alive.

Bel loops her arm through the crook of Sharrow's elbow. "Allie, take her other arm and grab Flyx's hand. We're going now."

Bel reaches for the side of the wormhole with her free hand, and we string out in a line behind her like kids playing train. Her hand breaks the plane, then we're tumbling through cold, dark air.

We land hard, piling on top of each other. Flyx yelps in pain. Sharrow's silence is worse.

Bright lights flash on, blinding me. Bells ring, like recess at elementary school, but loud and unceasing. I blink at the stars in my vision and cover my ears.

The room is vast and white with sparse office furniture.

Not a single bookcase. I don't know what this is, but it's not a library.

The alarm bells stop and a door opens at the far end of the room. A man rushes in pointing a handgun. "Hands up! Don't move!"

"Which is it?" Bel says in a snotty tone. "Hands up or don't move?"

"I wouldn't test him," a familiar voice calls from behind me. "We don't get many visitors, and he's a bit jumpy."

"*Sink!*" I scramble upright.

"Get down!" the guard shouts.

"It's okay—he knows me," I say, turning to look at Sink. Only it's not Sink...not exactly.

Standing there is a slender man in blue pajamas. From amidst a cloud of silver dreadlocks, Sink's lined face stares out at me. As in *staring*, with *eyes*.

"Sorry, I don't know you," Sink says. "Billy, put her in lockup. The ginger, too."

Billy. Is that *Cowboy* Billy? Oh my God, it *is*. What the heck is going on?

Billy points with his pistol toward what looks like a glassed-in conference room.

"Sink," I say, feeling desperate. "It's me, Allie. The last time I saw you was in 1906. In jail. I told you not to gouge out your eyes, and you obviously *didn't*, so you've got to remember."

"I've never seen you before," Sink says.

"*Please.* I know you. You're Oscar Sinclair. You were partners with my dad, Maxen, on a mission in 1906."

"Your friends don't look too good," Sink says. "The sooner you get in lockup, the sooner I get them to Med."

"Sharrow's hardly breathing," Flyx says.

"Come *on*." Bel drags me into the glass room.

Billy shuts the door. I hear it click, then click again as he locks it.

Sink scoops Sharrow into his arms—he's strong, far from the frail, crazy homeless man I knew.

I watch as Flyx rises and hobbles after Sink, with Cowboy Billy bringing up the rear, gun pointed.

Flyx looks back, meeting my gaze for a moment before he disappears through the door.

"Great plan." Bel rolls her eyes.

"You're blaming *me*? You're the one who brought us to the wrong time."

"I'm not the one who effed up," Bel says, pointing at a calendar on the wall.

It's 2018. I made it back to 2018. But it's some crazy messed-up version of 2018.

And somehow I managed to land back in jail with Bel. Where, once again, no one knows us. And once again, Bel's blaming me. And rolling her eyes.

The difference this time is I know a quake is coming soon. I can still get back to 1906. I can still make this right.

ACKNOWLEDGMENTS

I owe thanks to so many for assisting with this novel.

I have enormous gratitude and appreciation for my family who is a constant source of love, support, and assistance. Always first and foremost, my husband Jody: you make this—and everything—possible. Huge thanks also to my sons Kit, Jack, and Duncan, and to my parents and sisters, for the encouragement, ideas, and unflagging confidence.

I am very fortunate to have an incredible writing community that aids and assists me in this and all my writing endeavors. In particular for *Shake*, I owe a debt of gratitude to:

Todd Fahnestock, coworker, compatriot, and constant companion: you make my writing life joyful, my stories richer, and my days infinitely more productive and fun.

Mandy Houk, critiquer, editor, proofreader extraordinaire: this book is so much better because of your enthusiasm, sharp wit, and eagle eye.

Barb Nickless, voice coach and critiquer: Allie and I owe you so much.

Marie Whittaker, Queen Bee (who is nothing like Bel): your friendship, encouragement, and assistance are like sunshine.

Kevin Ikenberry, story structure guru: you have opened my eyes to patterns and techniques that improved this story and will impact everything I write from now on.

My life as an author is enriched by my phee Reader's Group—thank you one and all for your time, support, and enthusiasm. In particular I'd like to thank Nathan Dodge who submitted the idea for the "personal devices" used in this story.

I couldn't be happier with my cover artist, Rashed AlAkroka (www.artstation.com/artwork/lWnX5) whose artistry, technique, and professionalism are unmatched. Thank you, Rashed, for sharing your talent and friendship.

And finally, this book literally would not exist without my fantastic publisher, Parker Hayden Media. Pam McCutcheon and Laura Hayden, your hard work, insight, and wisdom make my books better and make me a better writer. Plus you're awesome friends and incredible humans I can always count on.

While it has taken a village to produce the story-world for the In Real Time series, any errors, inaccuracies, or artistic license are mine alone.

ABOUT THE AUTHOR

 Chris Mandeville grew up in California, spending lots of time in Allie's stomping grounds, San Francisco. She now lives in Colorado with her family and her service dog, Finn.

Chris can write anywhere, but her usual spot is a comfy chair at home in the Rocky Mountains where the only sound is the wind in the trees, her coffee cup is in reach, and Finn is snoozing by her feet. She's not a morning person by any stretch of the imagination, but she wakes up with help from lots of coffee and a little yoga, then writes for the rest of the day. Most evenings, she and her husband take walks in the woods, with Finn frolicking alongside.

Chris writes science fiction and fantasy novels and short stories, as well as nonfiction books for writers, and is the author of five published works. She and Finn can often be found at events for writers and readers along Colorado's Front Range. To learn more about Chris and her works-in-progress, and to join her Reader's Group, visit ChrisMandeville.com.

ALSO BY CHRIS MANDEVILLE

In Real Time Series

Quake

Shake

Break (coming soon)

Other books by Chris:

Seeds: a post-apocalyptic adventure

Undercurrents: an Anthology of What Lies Beneath

52 Ways to Get Unstuck: Exercises to Break Through Writer's Block

Made in the USA
Lexington, KY
24 October 2019

56022120R00197